CITY OF ANGELS

If you like THE A-LIST, you may also enjoy:

The **Poseur** series by Rachel Maude
The **Secrets of My Hollywood Life** series by Jen Calonita
Betwixt by Tara Bray Smith
Haters by Alisa Valdes-Rodriguez
Footfree and Fancyloose by Elizabeth Craft and Sarah Fain

CITY OF ANGELS

THE A-LIST
HOLLYWOOD ROYALTY

ZOEY DEAN

SAN DIEGO PUBLIC LIBRARY
TEEN SPACE

3 1336 08556 6843

poppy

LITTLE, BROWN AND COMPANY
New York   Boston

Copyright © 2010 by Alloy Entertainment

All rights reserved. Except as permitted under the U.S. Copyright Act of 1976, no part of this publication may be reproduced, distributed, or transmitted in any form or by any means, or stored in a database or retrieval system, without the prior written permission of the publisher.

Poppy
Hachette Book Group
237 Park Avenue, New York, NY 10017
For more of your favorite series, go to www.pickapoppy.com

First Edition: March 2010
Poppy is an imprint of Little, Brown and Company.
The Poppy name and logo are trademarks of Hachette Book Group, Inc.

The characters and events in this book are fictitious. Any similarity to real persons, living or dead, is coincidental and not intended by the author.

alloyentertainment
Produced by Alloy Entertainment
151 West 26th Street, New York, NY 10001

Cover design by Andrea C. Uva
Cover model photography by Roger Moenks
Cover background photography © iStockphoto.com / Ann Marie Kurtz

Library of Congress Cataloging-in-Publication Data
Dean, Zoey.
  City of Angels / Zoey Dean. — 1st ed.
     p. cm. — (The A-list, Hollywood royalty)
  "Poppy."
  Summary: Jojo Milford has been cast as the lead in Beverly Hills High's musical, even though teen star Amelie Adams also tried out, and the competition between the two of them, as well as the other wealthy and well-connected students, keeps everyone on edge.
  ISBN 978-0-316-07393-6
  [1. Interpersonal relations—Fiction. 2. Dating (Social customs)—Fiction. 3. Theater—Fiction. 4. High schools—Fiction. 5. Schools—Fiction. 6. Beverly Hills (Calif.)—Fiction.] I. Title.
  PZ7.D3473Ci 2010
  [Fic]—dc22
                                                                              2009045628

10 9 8 7 6 5 4 3 2 1

CWO
Printed in the United States of America

For my Grandma Iva, with all my love.

If you obey all the rules, you miss all the fun.

—Katharine Hepburn

DRAMA QUEEN

Amelie Adams crammed the last of her textbooks into her narrow locker, managing at last to wedge her world history textbook in between *Charles Dickens: A Biography* and *Jane Austen: A Life*. (Her English lit teacher had been so delighted that someone had actually bought the supplementary reading for the first time in all her years at Beverly Hills High, she'd given Amelie extra credit.) All in all, Amelie Adams, a.k.a. Fairy Princess, the Kidz Network sensation, a.k.a. the only teen at BHH with squealing preteen fans, could say her first day as a regular high-school student at Beverly Hills High had been a success. She was posting solid numbers on her "normal girl" scorecard:

REMEMBERING THE COMBINATION TO YOUR LOCKER AND FILLING IT TO BURSTING
  +2 NORMAL-GIRL POINTS

GETTING EXTRA-CREDIT POINTS
  +1 NORMAL-GIRL POINT

EATING CAFETERIA FOOD INSTEAD OF CRAFT SERVICES
  +5 NORMAL-GIRL POINTS

CHECKING YOUR AGENT'S TEXT DURING CONSUMER
ECONOMICS
    −2 NORMAL-GIRL POINTS

BELIEVING THAT BUYING RECOMMENDED READING IS
IMPORTANT, NOT JUST A TEACHER'S PET THING
    −1 NORMAL-GIRL POINT

Even with a few Hollyweird moments, her first day had gone almost scarily well. So scarily well that Amelie hoped she didn't owe her firstborn child to the gods of high school happiness in return. It wasn't like there'd been any standout moment. It definitely wasn't like some teen movie where the new girl instantly rises to new heights of popularity.

She shut her locker, slinging her slouchy blueberry-colored Kooba tote over her shoulder. Play tryouts were starting soon, with the potential to add at least five normal-girl points to her tally. She was covertly consulting her map to figure out where to find the auditorium when she heard a trio of squeals.

"Oh my God, you're really her!" said a petite girl who came up to roughly Amelie's shoulder. She was clearly the leader of the group, even though she was a head shorter than her two friends—matching languid, brunette bookends to the speaking girl's pert blond centerpiece. "Don't tell anyone, but we totally had a slumber party to watch *Fairy Princess Charms the Big Apple* this summer. Before we became high schoolers. I'm Yvette. That's Sasha, and she's Palmer." She pointed at the other two girls, who nodded in unison.

"Oh, thanks," Amelie said, looking up and down

the hallway and praying there were no witnesses. She had gone all day without a situation like this. The trio gazed at her, their eyes flicking over her face, her blue-and-brown plaid shirtdress, her yellow-gold Tiffany key necklace, and her fresh-from-the-box, distressed-leather cognac ankle boots. She smiled broadly, against her better instincts. It was all straight from the Kidz Network Handbook, under the "Greeting Fans in Unofficial Settings" chapter. The tally raged on in Amelie's head.

BEING APPROACHED BY FANS AT YOUR LOCKER
 −1 NORMAL-GIRL POINT

CONSIDERING KIDZ NETWORK GUIDELINES
 −2 NORMAL-GIRL POINTS

Yvette whacked Sasha lightly on her thin arm. "Where's the thing? Amelie Adams doesn't have time to wait around on us."

Sasha jumped to attention, producing a glossy magazine. *Everything Fairy Princess*, it screamed in lipstick-pink type across the cover, which was emblazoned with a dozen different shots of Amelie. Amelie in a tiara, Amelie holding an official Fairy Princess doll, Amelie at a premiere, Amelie on the set. It was an older magazine, the kind filled with pages to pull out and hang on your wall. Even though *Fairy Princess* was still superprofitable, all the covers Amelie had seen on her last Barnes & Noble visit were dedicated to Reese Rubello, the spunky new star of *Lights, Camera, High School*, a show about a regular high-school girl who secretly heads a hot TV show on her father's television network by night, using her classmates' antics as story fodder. Young girls didn't care about magical ponies or sparkly dresses anymore; they wanted stories about being a superstar in Hollywood. *If only they knew that the reality is so much lamer than they realize,* Amelie thought, grimacing at a bad open-mouthed photo of her singing the national anthem at a Dodgers game.

"Can you sign a picture for each of us?" Yvette asked, thrusting the magazine and a Sharpie at Amelie. "I flagged them."

Pink glittery Post-it flags stuck off the top of three pages, each one marked with a different girl's name. "Sure," Amelie said sunnily, brandishing the marker and quickly autographing the designated pages. Without even realizing it, she flicked her forearm in the signature Fairy Princess wand wave. *Elbow left, wrist swish, elbow right, wrist swish.*

Minus two more points. Or maybe ten.

"Here you go," she said when she finished, handing the magazine back to Yvette. Amelie tried her hardest to beam brightly, even though these freshmen were ruining her daily tally.

"You. Are. So. Awwwwe-some," Yvette said, as Sasha and Palmer flashed their first smiles of the whole exchange. "Thanks!" She tinkled away on her floral-print flats, clutching her signed photo of Amelie and Ryan Seacrest to her chest. Amelie prayed silently that Yvette wouldn't hang it in her locker.

She closed her own locker and made for play tryouts. Drama Club sounded like a lame thing for a professional actress to do, but wouldn't it prove that she wasn't some egotistical Hollywood star if she was willing to try out for a high school production? Her normal-girl points would be through the roof.

Her boots clicked across the crisp white tile, and Amelie found herself fizzing with excitement, imagining a day when she wouldn't have to tally points. She'd just *be* normal, with her days as Fairy Princess a rosy memory. She turned a corner, her eyes raking over the details of a poster for Homecoming next month, and crashed head-first into a chest. One that smelled of cotton and Downy and, inexplicably, toast.

Amelie looked up. "Jake," she said, too breathlessly for someone who hadn't been running. "What are you doing here?" It came out like an accusation. She cringed. She'd been fantasizing about her first run-in with Jake Porter-Goldsmith, her former tutor and current crush—the real reason she'd come to BHH. But this was *so* not the spotting-each-other-across-a-crowded-cafeteria moment she'd been hoping for.

Jake grinned. "Um, I go here," he said. "Remember?"

Amelie beamed up at him, praying the power of her GO SMiLE–whitened teeth would erase her awkward opening. "Of course, silly," she chided, giving him a big hug. She had to remind herself they weren't dating—yet—and pulled away from his solid chest with a little regret. "I go here now, too."

Jake smiled, more loosely now. Amelie tried to get a read on his face. Was he happy to see her? "I heard," he said. "So I guess your mom finally got where you were coming from."

Amelie's heart did a backflip on her internal trampoline.

He *remembered*. "She finally got it," she said, nodding. It definitely hadn't been professional momager Helen Adams' idea to send her budding-starlet daughter to high school. In fact, it had been Jake who'd first suggested it.

When Amelie's most recent teen movie, *Class Angel,* had been filming at BHH, the producers had decided to cast a regular high-school student to fill the down-to-earth male lead. Jake had shown up one day to take Amelie to tutoring and had left with the part. Over the course of filming, he'd started dating their co-star, Kady Parker, and suddenly Amelie was seeing him not as Jacob Porter-Goldsmith, math tutor, but as Jake, boyfriend material. But it wasn't just her feelings for Jake that were changing. Showing up to BHH every day during filming, Amelie had found herself longing for that kind of nor-malcy. Pulling into a high school parking lot instead of a movie studio. Eating lunch in the school cafeteria. Maybe even—*gasp!*—being walked to her locker by a real, live boyfriend. A heart-to-heart with Jake one night after a long day on set had led her to the simple solution: Take some time off from Fairy Princess, and enroll at BHH.

And now, here she was. And here was Jake, suddenly single after Kady had left to film a movie in Prague and dumped him. "I'm glad we ran into each other. Maybe you can walk me to tryouts? If it's not out of your way. . . ."

Jake nodded, one of his brown curls flopping ador-ably onto his forehead. "Sounds better than Mathletes practice," he said. He took a few steps down the hall and waited for her to catch up. "Consider me your personal welcome wagon."

FLIRTING WITH A CUTE GUY WHO ISN'T YOUR CO-STAR
   +3 NORMAL-GIRL POINTS

WALKING DOWN THE HALL OF YOUR HIGH SCHOOL WITH
SAID CUTE GUY
   +5 NORMAL-GIRL POINTS

BELIEVING THAT CUTE GUY INTERACTION IN FRONT OF
HOMECOMING POSTER IS A SURE SIGN THAT YOU WILL BE
GOING TO HOMECOMING DANCE TOGETHER
   +10 NORMAL-GIRL POINTS

I am glad you are no relation of mine.
You've always been cruel, never learned kind.
Memories of how you treated me live on in my head,
And I'll never forget, even once you are dead . . .

Still flying high on her meet-cute with Jake, Amelie
was almost surprised by her enthusiasm as she belted out
the folk rock–inspired "Song to Mrs. Reed." Making eye
contact for the briefest of moments with the director
before raking her gaze over the freshman girl asked to
stand in for Mrs. Reed, Jane Eyre's mean aunt, Amelie
fought the corner of her lip as it threatened to turn into
a satisfied smirk.

She had reason to be confident. She'd risen through
the ranks of Kidz Network's in-house talent program.
You had to prove yourself to be a worthy backup singer
and dancer before moving to tier two, "featured sec-
ondary." Tier three meant graduating to being a "name
performer," and once you did that, you got your own
franchise. (Provided, of course, you had high enough
ratings and a face fit for a twelve-inch doll.) When she'd

taken on the role of Fairy Princess at the tender age of eight, she'd become the youngest franchise in Kidz Network history. If she could handle the cutthroat world of Hollywood, she could handle the rigors of a high school drama club tryout.

Amelie wrapped up her song and let her body loosen up. She belonged on this stage, under the warm glow of a spotlight, with the faces of the director and a smattering of fellow auditioners a little hazy through the glare. Or maybe they were hazy because she was still in a dreamlike trance from being so close to Jake. "Is there anything else you want to see?" she asked, looking at the director in anticipation of another directive.

"That was very nice," Mr. Potter, the director, said. He nodded approvingly, his pale face a moonish orb floating above his black turtleneck. He was very into the musical, probably because he'd written it. Amelie remembered reading in the trades about a *Jane Eyre* musical a few years ago. Apparently, Mr. Potter's script had been to development hell and never emerged. So now it was a high school production. "Lovely voice. Now, we just want to see you alongside our Mr. Rochester."

Amelie nodded amicably, working out the kinks in her neck and exhaling for a count of six, just as her mom's yogi chiropractor had taught her. She refastened the bottom button of her pink Lela Rose cardigan, which had come undone while she sang, and flicked a strand of strawberry-colored hair out of her eyes. A group of stage crew boys watched her from the wings.

A tall guy emerged from behind a background painted to look like the inside of the Thornfield parlor. It was as nice as any of Amelie's movie sets. From what she had heard, the original director of this semester's play had defected to head the student film production, a short movie called *Student Body,* about a student serial killer who targeted corrupt class presidents. The original play had been scrapped, and now they were supposed to put on *Jane Eyre: The Musical* with just a few weeks' rehearsal. The short rehearsal time gave Amelie an even bigger confidence boost: They'd need a pro like her if they wanted to get this show off the ground in a hurry.

"Hi," the tall guy said, wiping paint on his Levi's as he unbuckled a tool belt. His eyes were a deep green. "I'm Nick Hautman." A strand of dark hair fell across his forehead. He had a slightly nervous bearing, and his shoulders seemed tense. Almost as if he were afraid the athlete he'd stolen his 6'3" height and broad shoulders from was coming back to claim his body. His presence was all drama geek, and Amelie found herself wishing Jake would be playing the Rochester to her Jane. This guy was just a little too nerdy.

After a pause, she remembered to say, "I'm Amelie Adams," feeling a little jerky for just figuring the guy would know who she was. *Minus two normal-girl points.* She stretched out a hand, and Nick clasped it firmly.

"I know," he said, looking down at his shoes as he blushed. "You probably don't remember me, but we starred in a Kidz Network TV movie together when we were six. *Juice Sleuths?*"

Amelie clasped a hand to her mouth, bangles jangling loudly. "Oh my God! Nicky!" They'd played the younger siblings of two friends who operated a kid detective agency out of their lemonade stand. She hugged him. "So, what have you done recently?" Instantly, she cringed at the question. It was such a business thing to ask, and not very normal-high-school-girl of her. Her numbers were plummeting.

Nick gestured wide with his arms, as if to say, *This.* He leaned in and whispered, "I sort of retired after that. Told my mom I just wanted to go to school with my friends. So far, it's worked out okay. You've done a bit better, though." He grinned sheepishly, his green eyes only half meeting hers.

Exhibit A, Amelie thought, beaming at Nick. He was her proof: It was possible to transform from childhood star to above-average high-schooler.

"Flip to page eighty in your scripts, the scene between Jane and Mr. Rochester on the eve of their wedding." The director flipped eagerly through his pages, as if he couldn't wait to reread what he'd written. Amelie found the mark and quickly skimmed the page.

"Do you really think this is a good scene to audition with?" she blurted, before she knew what she was saying. "At this point in the book, Jane is overcome with emotion. And she's normally such a reticent character. It's not really illustrative of the bulk of the role." Amelie smushed her lips before she could go on.

"I think this scene will be fine, Miss Adams," Mr. Potter sniped. "Please begin."

Nick took her hands in his and gave her a little wink before they began. His palms were warm and dry. "Are you nervous, Jane? Hungry? Does the thought of our London trip take away your appetite?" Nick let his hands linger in hers before letting go. He crossed to an ornately carved red sofa, folding his tall frame into it.

"I can barely see my prospects ahead of me, sir," Amelie said, passing before him, staring out over the mostly empty auditorium. Unlike Jane, *she* could see her prospects. Playing out in her mind's eye was a fantasy of her and Jake as BHH's reigning couple. She could practically see the yearbook layouts now: CUTEST COUPLE, with a heart-shaped photo of her and Jake looking into each other's eyes. And DRAMA QUEEN, with Amelie wearing her Fairy Princess tiara while holding a playbill from *Jane Eyre: The Musical*. Hmm, yearbook. That was another possibility. . . .

"I hardly know what thoughts I have in my head. Everything seems unreal," Amelie continued, crossing the stage and sitting at Nick's feet. This line, she could get behind. She was performing not on a soundstage, but on a high school stage. Along the far ceiling were banners celebrating the award-winning mock trial team. In cases next to the rows of seats were trophies and framed photographs of past Drama Club stars.

"*I'm* real. *I* have substance. Go ahead, touch and see if I'm real," Nick said, stretching an arm in front of her face. Amelie patted his bicep daintily. It was impressively chiseled and made her think of Jake's arms around her when they'd shared an onscreen kiss. Amelie forced her thoughts back to the audition as Nick came to his next line. "Now tell me, how do you feel, on this eve of your life changing?"

"I just wish this hour would never end. It's perfect, and I fear what comes tomorrow," Amelie said breathlessly.

"That was lovely, and full of emotion," the director said, cutting her off. "Now you see why I wanted you to do that scene."

"You're right," Amelie agreed. She flashed him her most agreeable smile, and Mr. Potter beamed back. Perfect. Five normal-girl points for knowing when to be a kiss-up.

Amelie followed Nick offstage. "You were great," he said, picking up his tool belt and refastening it.

Amelie smiled, grateful. "I probably shouldn't have questioned him like that, though," she said. The director probably thought she was annoying, and her classmates probably thought she was a show-off.

"If he knows what's good for him, he'll be glad to have a professional in the lead," Nick said. "You should stick around. You'll see you don't have much competition."

"Maybe I will," she said, grinning. "Thanks for the pep talk." She hopped down the stage steps and took a seat a few rows behind the director. Nick was watching her and gave a little wave. She waved back and settled into her chair as a high-voiced freshman tried out for the part of Adèle. It couldn't hurt to get the good news in person. Besides, nothing said *school spirit* like rooting on your fellow thespians.

BECOMING THE DRAMA CLUB'S STAR MEMBER
BONUS NORMAL-GIRL POINTS

SEE JANE ACT

"Jojo Milford, reading for the part of Diana Rivers?"

Mr. Potter flicked back the shock of black hair that hung jaggedly over his forehead. Jojo stifled a giggle before crossing to the front of the stage. Her evil stepsister, Myla, referred to the English teacher-slash-drama-coach-slash-wannabe-screenwriter as Harry-Gone-to-Potter. *He really does look like a pudgy adult Boy-Who-Lived,* Jojo thought, trying to suppress a smile. Myla was a horrendous bitch, but she called them like she saw them.

Jojo looked out over the small crowd of student crew members watching the tryouts, her eyes landing on Amelie Adams. She'd auditioned just before Jojo, and now she sat confident and poised, a few rows behind Mr. Potter. It was obvious why Jacob Porter-Goldsmith used to have a crush on her. With her full red curls and creamy skin, Amelie had only been a BHH student for one day, and already the most desirable guys in school were debating who would land her. Jojo, on the other hand, was a nobody, mostly thanks to her popular step-sister's well-documented dislike of her. And if Myla didn't like you, nobody did. Apart from an all-too-brief period of friendship, Myla had been consistently evil to Jojo since Jojo had arrived in September. Jojo was now suffering through an extended bout of PMS—Pissed Myla Syndrome.

But she wasn't wasting any more time worrying about Myla's opinion of her. She had colleges to impress, according to her guidance counselor, who'd had a conniption that morning when Jojo admitted she didn't have any extracurriculars here at BHH. She'd played soccer at her old school, in Sacramento, but tryouts for BHH's team were long over. Even though Jojo's parents, celebrity super-couple Lailah Barton and Barkley Everhart, could have called in a favor, Jojo was trying to just be Jojo Milford again. And that meant settling for any old extracurricular activity, not diva-ing her way into the one she really wanted. That was Myla's territory.

She'd opted to try out for the school play because she figured she actually had a shot. Jojo would have preferred a straight play to a musical, but she was no stranger to singing and dancing. Her dads, Fred and Bradley, had raised her to be well-rounded. So although she'd played soccer and Little League every year, she'd also taken dance and voice lessons. Her adoptive dads would have loved to see her go out for the play, but they'd gone on sabbatical in Greenland for a year, which was why she had moved to Beverly Hills—she was living with her real parents, "Barbar," who'd given her up for adoption sixteen years ago to preserve their fledgling movie star careers.

Jojo walked to the center of the stage, her Frye boots echoing loudly in the auditorium. She turned and faced Mr. Potter, not knowing what to do with her arms, which felt pointless hanging at her sides. How had Amelie made this look so easy? Jojo shoved her hands in the pockets of her jeans—plain, boot-cut Levi's from her pre-BHH days—and gave Mr. Potter a tight-lipped grin.

"Actually, can you sing Jane's song when she's considering John Rivers's offer of marriage?" Mr. Potter requested, pulling his unfortunate round glasses down off the perch of his nose. He was loving his moment, even if putting on his play had been BHH's last resort. *Jane Eyre: The Musical* had been optioned and dropped by Nora Ephron a few years back, and rumor had it that Mr. Potter had been trying to get BHH to put it on ever since.

"But I'm trying for Diana Rivers," Jojo insisted. She'd thought about going for the lead, but since this was her first play, she didn't want to risk trying for the biggest part and then getting no part at all, or getting a lowly part in the chorus. She needed meat for her college applications, even if it was lean meat. Besides, Amelie Adams had just auditioned for Jane. Her casting was inevitable, so why was Mr. Potter wasting time?

"Please indulge me, Miss Milford." Mr. Potter tapped his pen against his clipboard just as insistently.

A freshman stage assistant scurried up to her, thrusting a page of song lyrics into her hands and plucking from them the pages for the scene she wanted to audition with.

"Think Amy Winehouse or Daisy Morton when you're singing this one," Mr. Potter said, his watery blue eyes wide. "I wrote it in a bluesy-pop vein."

Jojo tried hard not to laugh. In Sacramento, drama teachers considered it hip to switch the annual play from *Our Town* to *Grease,* and here teachers took inspiration from cracked-out pop stars? "Sure thing," Jojo said perkily. She reminded herself she wasn't *that* nervous. There weren't that many students even trying out, so she was bound to get something. This being Beverly Hills High, students didn't exactly care about the stage—actor-hopefuls preferred the more professional (and Steven Spielberg–funded) Cinema Club, where her classmates were making *Student Body*, a high-school political thriller written expressly for them by Ang Lee.

By comparison, only about two dozen kids had shown up for today's play tryouts. Most of BHH's actors had been involved in the original play, David Mamet's *Speed-the-Plow*, and had followed the director when he'd defected to work on the student movie. The remaining drama students were either theater purists, a rarity in L.A., or students who'd never acted before and saw the advantage in all the good actors being occupied elsewhere. Jojo knew however meager her game might be, she would do better than the trembling freshmen girls who'd auditioned just to be in the same room with Amelie Adams. As long as Jojo had a few lines, she really didn't care what part she got.

Miss Daly played the opening chords on the piano, and Jojo studied her sheet music. She looked out over the small crowd, reminded herself that this wasn't life-or-death, and sang.

> *You want me to play the wife,*
> *To live your version of a life,*
> *You, I should honor and obey,*
> *Save true love for another day.*
> *And damn, what have I gotten myself into?*

Jojo sang her heart out, fighting the smile that pulled at her lips when she imagined Mr. Potter hanging out in coffee shops, working on his "hip" musical and wearing his trademark black turtleneck even in summer. When she and Myla were on good terms, Myla had found his dating profile on Nerve.com, in which he bragged about being "a beatnik with a heart that beats for the Brontë sisters." They'd laughed till they cried, and then Myla had started a Twitter account called Mr.Potter'sTurtleneck that detailed his fictional dating travails. It was fun having a wicked stepsister—when you were getting along.

As she came to the end of the song, Jojo surprised herself by taking a little half-bow. She didn't mean it in a *This is theater!* way; it had just happened. Dorky. Across the auditorium, she caught Amelie's eye and smiled. Amelie seemed distracted, which Jojo understood. BHH was a lot to take in all at once. As a quasi-veteran, Jojo felt like maybe she should extend an offer of friendship. Of course, this would be a great gesture of magnanimity on Jojo's part. Her BHH crush Jake Porter-Goldsmith had once had a crush on Amelie. But so what? That was in the past. Ever since Jake had stopped dating Kady Parker, he'd been flirting with Jojo. She knew she didn't always read boys right, but Jake didn't seem like someone who'd play her. Soon enough, Jake and Jojo would be dating and they could all three hang out.

"That's all I need to see," Mr. Potter finally said, steepling his fingers as he examined her. "I had a feeling about you."

Jojo clutched her script pages so tightly she thought they'd turn back to pulp. All she'd wanted was a part in the supporting cast, and now she was going to get nothing because he'd made her try for the lead?

"Josephine Milford, you'll play Jane Eyre," Mr. Potter said, looking as delighted as was possible for him.

The room was silent as Jojo looked out over the empty rows of seats. Seats that would be full when the cast performed in three weeks. Before she could utter a thank-you—or more appropriately, express disbelief— three muttered words echoed through the auditorium.

"What the fuck?"

The words had escaped Amelie's lips before she had a chance to consider them. She could practically count on one hand all the times she'd uttered the *f*-word, and yet there it was, on her first day of school. She couldn't have felt trashier if she were wearing a pair of Lindsay Lohan's leggings. That had to cost her all the day's normal-girl points, not to mention some of her dignity.

As faces turned to stare at her, she felt a full blush coming on. Smiling sheepishly, she held up her new BlackBerry. "Sorry. I just heard one of the Olsen twins is up for a part in the new Coppola movie. Can you believe that?" *And why not believe it,* she thought, *if you believe a complete nobody would play Jane Eyre instead of me.*

Mr. Potter looked at her with something resembling disdain—or perhaps it was constipation. "Yes, very interesting, Miss Adams," he said. "By the by, you'll be playing Blanche Ingram." Amelie strained to smile with gritted teeth. She wanted to kick a hole through a set and knock over every candelabra in the Thornfield parlor, preferably while they were on fire. She wanted to pull Mr. Potter's turtleneck up over his sallow face. But instead, she calmly rose from her seat and feigned happiness, pretending she had to go tell someone about her amazing part as Blanche Ingram right this instant. She swept down the aisle of the theater, plastering a fake smile on her face, but no one was paying any attention to her anyway. All eyes were on the new Jane Eyre.

Jojo concentrated on her toes flexing inside her boots. She might as well have been accepting an Oscar, she was in so much shock. "Miss Milford, please stay so we can get your measurements for the costumes," Mr. Potter said, shooing his wardrobe assistant, a sophomore named Lola Esperanza, to the stage. The girl was cute, like a slightly chubby version of Amanda Bynes, with a tape measure circling her neck.

"Congratulations," she said to Jojo, expertly measuring her bust. "Thirty-five! I think B!" She shouted to a wiry boy with a clipboard. Normally, Jojo would have been embarrassed to have the world learn her boobage, but she was so happy right now, she didn't care.

Jojo smiled down at Lola, who was now gaining an intimate knowledge of Jojo's butt. So this was for real. She was the *lead*! She'd been telling herself she didn't care, but the vote of confidence—being chosen over a real, paid-millions actress—actually felt great. She tried to pep-talk herself: *This is right. You are the daughter of two of America's finest actors. This makes sense.*

But as Amelie breezed past, collecting her script from a freshman production assistant without making even a nanosecond of eye contact, Jojo suddenly realized that everyone might not think so.

WHAT A DISC!

Jacob Porter-Goldsmith and his friend Miles Abelson trudged disappointedly to the parking lot after their Mathletes practice had been canceled. Miles was disappointed because things were looking up for him and Molly Marcheesi, a fellow Mathlete who had an obvious fetish for any guy who could tell a parallelogram from a hexagon. Jacob, who went by Jake now (at least most of the time), was disappointed in himself because he was actually relieved Mathletes was canceled.

It was supposed to be Jake's first practice back on the team after spending the last month as a star of the movie *Class Angel.* Not having a movie career was one thing, but being the team's quadratic equation leader? The mighty hadn't just fallen; he'd been drop-kicked from an impressive height. And Jake, who could probably determine the fall's velocity and trajectory, felt it in full force.

"Couldn't Mr. Clark's wife have had her baby on a *Wednesday*? Then we could have at least gone to Meltdown Comics for new comic book day," Miles sighed, dragging his lanky frame dejectedly across the pavement. He pushed up his glasses, one finger on the plastic bridge, and rubbed a hand over his pointy chin. Miles had decided to make facial hair his new thing, but the weird wisps of hair on his baby-smooth face could hardly be called a beard. "Do you think he'll name the baby Kent if it's a boy? Kent Clark. It would be awesome."

Jake tried to muster a laugh, but he was a little depressed, frankly. It was really settling in that he was going to be regular old Jacob again. No more teen star. Goodbye, top of the popularity food chain. Ta-ta, famous hottie horror-star girlfriend. Just as quickly as it had all come together, everything had fallen apart. Kady had dumped him and left for Prague, and his mom had forbidden any further movie roles. He'd just bumped into Amelie, who was a student at BHH now, but after hearing the way the school's male contingent was talking about her, she wasn't going to stay single for long. Even with his recently buffed physique and his brush with fame, he didn't have a chance against the rest of the BHH guys. It was probably for the best, though—after Kady, Jake had decided to give up on girls for a long, long time. They were bad for him. The occasional lunch table chat with Jojo Milford, no matter how cute she was, was all he'd allow himself.

"So what should we do, dude? Paintball? Arcade? That Brazilian buffet with the endless parade of meats?" Miles's voice rose an octave, and Jake could see right through his casual suggestion. Miles was suggesting every manly thing he could think of, to support Jake's girl ban. But the more macho the things Miles proposed, the less thrilled Jake became with his girlfriendless state. That was the thing with giving something up: It made that thing suddenly seem really enticing. Jake must have had his mom's gene for deprivation—every month, she'd declare a new high-calorie food forbidden, like ice cream, and two days later the freezer would be stuffed with Chubby Hubby.

Jake shrugged noncommittally. "We could see the new Sam Raimi movie at the Landmark," he suggested. He could handle sitting in the dark for a few hours, alone with his thoughts. He reached in his backpack to extract the keys to his ancient Corolla, but just as his hands fumbled with the Albert Einstein key chain, a red Frisbee clocked him upside the head and fell to the ground with a dull, plastic clatter.

Jake put a hand to his throbbing head. *WTF?*

"Dude, I'm sorry!" Tucker Swanson jogged up beside Jake, swiping the Frisbee from the ground in one continuous movement. "We don't have enough Ultimate players to keep this thing in check, you know?"

Jake shook his head. "No big deal," he said. "It's not a discus or anything. I think any head injuries will be minimal." He cringed at his nerdy overtalking. Past Tucker, he saw Geoff Schaffer, Mark Bauman, and his neighbor Ash Gilmour standing in a circle on BHH's plush-green front lawn, laughing. Jake felt self-conscious for a second—were they laughing at him? But then Ash looked up from the group and waved casually. Jake and Ash had been best friends back in the day, before drifting apart in middle school. But just over a week ago, their mutual girl troubles had reunited them. Ash's girl problems had eventually worked out: He was back with Daisy Morton, a completely insane but fairly hot English rock star who'd just been signed with Ash's father's record label. And Jake's problems? Well, he didn't expect a loving postcard from Prague anytime soon.

"You and Abelson want to play?" Tucker asked, slapping the disc lightly against his thigh. He ran a hand through his hair, mussing it. Tucker was known for his one-haircut-a-year rule. He shaved his head at the start of every school year, letting it grow out through the following August. Right now, it was short and preppy, despite the fact that Tucker was militantly anti-khaki, and currently wearing jeans so torn that a wardrobe malfunction seemed imminent. "Would help even out the teams. You're supposed to have, like, seven each, but some of the guys bailed on us. Pussy-whipped, you know?"

Before Jake had a chance to respond, Miles raised his arm for a high five, which Tucker delivered with bravado. "Yeah, bro," Miles said. Jake rolled his eyes as his friend pushed his glasses up his long nose again, wriggling his thick black eyebrows like a Marx brother. They seemed to be the only facial hair he could really grow. "We're totally in. No one's pussy-whipping this guy right here."

Jake's stomach turned, and not at Miles's overenthusiasm. They'd never played Ultimate Frisbee before. He could already picture Miles leaving the game with broken glasses and, possibly, a broken nose. His sad attempt at a beard would look much worse with blood dripping from it.

They followed Tucker across the lawn, a few steps behind him. Jake grabbed Miles's skinny upper arm. "What are you doing? We've never played Ultimate before."

Miles looked at Jake aghast, like he'd just asked him to go see the new *Twilight* movie. "Jake, it's *Frisbee*. How difficult can it be? And this could be good for us. This is just the man stuff you need to forget your lady problems."

Jake's eyes widened in panic as Tucker and Geoff tested out headlocks on each other. "Yeah, but a concussion isn't how I like to take my mind off things."

Miles chuckled, giving Jake a little punch on the arm. "How about you trust me for a change, Jake? I got your back." He sidled off toward the game, nodding assuredly at the other guys. Jake trudged behind him, unhappily noting that at least fifty percent of the BHH student body was still hanging out on the front lawn, making their evening plans. And every athlete and club member would invariably walk past after their practices and meetings let out for the day. Jake was sweating and the game hadn't even started yet. Guys like him and Miles were the last players picked in gym class, and now they were volunteering to demonstrate their lack of skill in front of the entire school.

Ash explained the rules in his laid-back way. You could hold the Frisbee for only ten seconds, you couldn't run with the Frisbee, you had to pass within ten seconds, and you scored when you made a pass into the other team's end zone. BHH's resident rock star, Ash had sandy, floppy hair that always hung over one eye, and a lean, muscular build from daily surfing and guitar-playing sessions—he was the type of guy girls wanted and guys wanted to be. And of course, he excelled at Ultimate, even though he could care less about winning.

"Why don't you and Miles be on a team with me and Tucker? You're supposed to have seven on a team for regulation, but at least with you guys, we're a little closer."

Ash grinned, slapping Miles and Jake on their backs as they came to join him on the lawn. Miles pulled a strap for his glasses out of his backpack and attached them firmly to his face. Jake felt embarrassed, until he noticed Mark Bauman had done the same thing. With two well-known environmentalists for parents, Mark had headed the Ecology Club all of freshman and sophomore years and even got the BHH cafeteria to go organic, but since his sustainable T-shirts and pimped-out Prius had started over well with girls, he'd been hanging with Ash and his friends.

A half hour later, Jake was drenched with sweat and his team was down 9–10 in an 11-point game. Jake was defending dark-haired Geoff Schaffer, the other team's best player and a surprisingly fast runner for someone who took so many smoke breaks. Still, Jake was managing to keep him contained and was actually enjoying himself. Maybe a little too much. A few points in, he realized he really wanted to win this game and started to really go for it. He'd scored three of his team's points and knocked Geoff on his ass twice. He had more foul calls than anyone on the field, but he couldn't help it. He needed a way to release some of the pent-up frustration coursing through his veins, and Ultimate Frisbee was way better than Mathletes.

Geoff's team had possession again, and Mark Bauman sent the Frisbee soaring through the air toward Julius Grand. Julius leaped for the pass, but Miles successfully blocked him, and the disc landed a few feet away, just in bounds. Jake broke into a sprint to the loose Frisbee, and Geoff took off right on his heels. Reaching it first, Jake dove for the disc just as Geoff ran up behind him. From the ground, Jake urgently hurled the Frisbee toward Tucker, releasing it only to hear a loud *thwack*. His hand had hit something hard.

"Shit!" Geoff yelled, clutching his nose. Blood dripped from it onto Jake's jeans. Silence overcame the field. As Jake watched the blood droplets fall, each one sounded in his ears like a scolding. Drip, *you*. Drip, *are*. Drip, *an*. Drip, *asshole*.

Jake looked around, horrified. Taking out all his aggressions was one thing, but breaking a guy's nose equaled over-competitive jerk. Who drew blood during a Frisbee game?

The other guys, including Miles, folded into a huddle around Geoff. Jake backed a few steps out of the circle, desperately catching Miles's eyes over Tucker's short blond hair. Jake couldn't read Miles's expression, only glimpsing his own reflection in his friend's glasses.

"Um, I'm really sorry, Geoff," Jake finally said. He ran his hand through his curly hair so roughly, he yanked a strand out painfully. He probably deserved that. "That was totally uncalled for."

Every guy in the circle turned to face Jake. "Dude, are you kidding?" said Tucker, who had caught the offending Frisbee in the end zone. "That was an awesome take-down! And a point! Geoffy here just needs to work on his reflexes."

"What reflexes?" Ash chided, helping Geoff to his feet. "I think you lose them right around the time you fry your billionth brain cell."

Jake shifted his eyes toward Geoff, who was holding his Grizzly Bear concert T-shirt to his nose, the blood soaking through the cotton. When he let go, the band's logo, a hairy black bear, had a perfect bloodstain dripping off its ass.

With the back of one hand wiping his still-bleeding nose, Geoff clapped Jake on the back with the other. "No big, bro . . . seriously. Chicks dig scars, right? And broken noses. Owen Wilson's nose is fucking mangled, and that dude gets all kinds of play when he's not going all emo on his wrists."

Jake couldn't believe this guy was thanking him for taking a pint of his blood. The guys took their positions on the field and motioned for Jake to rejoin the game. Miles grinned at him from his position at forward. He didn't even try to hide the look of sheer delight on his face. Neither did Jake.

After a few plays, Jake's team had possession and were working on getting the winning point. Miles was flipping the Frisbee over in his hands. "I've never figured out the escape velocity on one of these things," he said. At Tucker's confused look, he added, "The minimum speed for an object to reach in order to escape the Earth's gravitational pull."

"Dude, you just blew my mind, and I'm not even high," Tucker said, awed.

Ash cleared his throat, bringing his team's attention back. "Okay, so Jake, you're going to fake left. They're all going to think I'm looking for you, since you're a scoring machine. But as soon as their guys are on you, I want Abelson to cut right. I'll make the toss, and Abelson should be able to score. Got it?" Jake and Miles nodded, exchanging a glance.

"Hi, Jake," said a familiar female voice. Jake looked up as the huddle broke to see Jojo sauntering by, a confident half-grin on her face. She pushed a silky piece of almond-colored hair from her amethyst eyes and winked at him. A girl was actually *winking*. At *him*. Jacob Porter-Goldsmith, comic book collector, mathematical master. He mentally slapped himself as his eyes raked over her tan shoulders on display in a black racerback tank top. He shouldn't care that she was winking at him. He was off girls!

"Hey, Jojo," he replied, trying to ignore the other guys' low whistles of approval. He wanted to catch up with her, but the other guys were waiting to finish the game.

He jogged to his space on the field, gazing at Jojo's retreating form with such interest, he nearly tripped over Miles, who slapped him on the back and said, "She totally digs you, dude."

"Yeah, nice work, Jake," Julius Grand said, nodding as he wiped his sweaty brow with his white J. Crew under-shirt. He watched Jojo appreciatively as she strolled to the parking lot in her red motorcycle boots.

"Yeah, man, good job," Tucker agreed. Jake felt himself blushing and was glad he could blame his redness on physical exertion. It was a little awkward to have Jojo flirting with him right in front of Tucker, whom she'd been dating—if only briefly—just a few weeks earlier. "Jojo's cool."

"That she is," Ash said, clapping his hands. "But are we gonna finish this game or what?"

Everyone fell into place, and Jake somehow managed to remember the play, faking down the field as the other team charged after him. Across from him, Miles stood wide open. Downfield, Ash launched the Frisbee in a perfect arc. The guys surrounding Jake took off toward Miles, who quickly ran in reverse, toward the goal, as if he knew where the Frisbee was going to land. Which, given his mastery of physics, he probably did.

Miles evaded his defenders and leaped in the air, every inch of his skinny, five-foot-nine frame stretching until he was several feet off the ground. Jake could feel his mouth open wide as he gaped at Miles's LeBron-esque jump. The Frisbee landed perfectly in Miles's outstretched hand, and as he came down to the ground, he tossed himself a few inches past the goal line. They'd won. And Miles had scored the winning point. Jake laughed as his friend looked around in shock, amazed at his own athleticism. Across BHH's wide expanse of lawn, students had risen to their feet, all watching Miles's stellar catch in suspense.

Jake followed Tucker and Ash to give Miles a victory high five. Even Julius and the rest of the opposing team congratulated him. The circle broke, and Jake looked around for Jojo, wondering if she'd stayed to watch. Instead, his eyes landed on Amelie, standing just outside the front doors of the school and looking both as gorgeous and as miserable as a beautiful girl could look. Her red curls were pulled back in a loose bun, framing eyes so downcast it was a wonder they stayed on her face. Jake inhaled sharply. Sad girls ranked first on Jake's list of things he couldn't resist. They were like the mistake-ridden sudoku puzzles his dad left lying around the house—he had to go fix them, as soon as possible.

He excused himself from the guys and jogged over to

Amelie. "Hey, everything all right?" His nostrils tingled as he smelled flowery perfume. Immediately, it summoned up the screen kiss he'd shared with her on the set of *Class Angel*. At the time, he'd pretended it was no big deal, because he'd been with Kady. But he'd thought about it every day since.

"Sure, everything's fine, except for the part where I'm a total failure on my first day," Amelie said cryptically, before bursting into tears.

Jake instinctively threw his arm around her. "I'm sure you're not a failure." If anyone had failed, it was him. Swearing off the fairer sex was going to be harder than he'd thought.

At the edge of the parking lot, Jojo turned. Her eyes scanned the BHH front lawn, where the Ultimate game had clearly wrapped up. The guys were fishing their hoodies and sweaters out of a pile. No sign of Jake, though. The Everhart SUV would be arriving for her any second. She turned around, expecting to see Jake coming her way, now that he wasn't in the middle of his game. It wasn't every day that she actually *winked* at a guy. And it wasn't every day that she made the lead in the school play. Today was her day.

Jojo frowned as her eyes landed on Jake's mop of curly dark hair, all the way across BHH's front lawn. He wasn't alone. He had his arm around . . . Amelie. Her red curls clung to his shirt like tentacles as she buried her head in his shoulder.

Jojo clenched her teeth. She may have won the lead, but Amelie seemed to have landed the bigger prize. Forget the play—her life had officially become a bad reality show.

FATHER KNOWS BEST?

A sh Gilmour hadn't been inside Kitson on Robertson Boulevard in years. His ex, Myla Everhart, had proclaimed it tacky back in the ninth grade: *If I wanted to do the whole Paris Hilton thing, wouldn't I be carrying a rat in a pink sweater around in my purse?*

But Ash's new girlfriend, pop singer Daisy Morton, would probably like the store. Loud and colorful, the shop had something to look at in every corner, like the cover of her favorite Beatles album, *Sgt. Pepper's Lonely Hearts Club Band*. Long tables of girls' jewelry glittered under the lights. Piles of Junk Food T-shirts formed a cottony rainbow atop a silver pedestal. The kids' section was divided from the rest of the store, with shelves of expensive stuffed animals, kids' books, and bibs with sayings like BOOB MAN. Ash tried on a pair of black-framed Bottega Veneta sunglasses with square lenses that reminded him of an old-fashioned wood TV set in his garage. He looked in the mirror: A flippy piece of his dirty blond hair fell into his eyes. His surfer tan, viewed through the glasses, had the orange glow of fake baking. And for some reason, his lips looked inflated. He took the glasses off. He looked normal again. He put them back on. Insta-douche. For five hundred eighty dollars.

He wandered aimlessly, trying to kill time before meeting his dad down the street for dinner. He just hoped his father wasn't late; he had an iChat planned with Daisy for later. Unlike Myla, who had gone on a third-world tour and abandoned him all summer, Daisy had already proved herself to be devoted since leaving for her concert tour a few days earlier, making their iChat dates every night. He could barely believe how functional this relationship felt, considering Daisy was a rock star with a bad reputation.

He also couldn't believe how much he missed her after just a few short weeks of dating. She'd left on Monday, and she had just texted him from Philadelphia to say she was going to order room service—mac and cheese—and think of him. The dinner choice was meaningful: Ash and Daisy had shared a plate of it the night Ash discovered there was more to Daisy Morton than the drugged-up, drunk, and deranged persona she presented to the media. In fact, she was none of those things. It was all an act to sell records. Even Ash's father, Gordon Gilmour, the big-shot record executive responsible for bringing Daisy to the States, didn't know her secret. Now Ash wanted to find a gift to send to Daisy on the road before he had to meet his dad at the Ivy.

Ash picked up a gold peace sign pendant hanging from rainbow string. Too "Froot Loopie"—Daisy's term for hippie types. He dismissed a shiny pink scarf as too frou-frou. And it was too soon for a pair of red mesh underwear with rhinestone cherries on the butt.

On a table full of assorted knickknacks and oddities, a tin coin bank with a picture of a little girl playing the triangle practically lit up before his eyes. The print above the girl's head said, I'M SAVING UP TO START A ROCK BAND! He chuckled. It was perfect. He grabbed it off the table and picked up several glittery Hello Kitty pens to go along with it. Daisy was always thinking of new lyrics and never had a pen with her.

Ash was about to go pay when his iPhone buzzed in his pocket. He checked the screen and saw Daisy's photo, a pretty one he'd taken of her last weekend at Sidewalk Cafe in Venice. She wasn't wearing her Crazy Daisy makeup, so she was unrecognizable to the paparazzi, and her dark hair looked so soft and shiny in the picture, he could almost feel it against his skin. She had her head propped up on one hand and a Mona Lisa smile on her face as she gazed directly into the camera, her gray eyes silvery in the sunlight.

"Hey, I was just thinking about you," he said as he picked up. "Mostly 'cause I'm hungry and you have mac and cheese."

"You mean crap and cheese. You would think a city known for cheesesteak would be able to do cheese noodles, but no," Daisy said in her British lilt. Ash could hear the sounds of *SpongeBob SquarePants* in the background and couldn't help but imagine Daisy in a tiny tank top and pajama bottoms, curled up with a hotel pillow she was pretending was him.

"You're so lost without me," Ash flirted. "Go get a cheesesteak. See a monument or something."

Daisy sighed. "That would mean, I dunno, putting a

new crack in the Liberty Bell or something. There's a lot of pressure to wreak havoc when you're me. And plus, I'm already all snuggly in my hotel. Well, more or less. Which brings me to an idea I had."

Intrigued by the sexy note in Daisy's voice, Ash looked around the store to see if anyone could hear him. Since it was dinnertime on a Wednesday, Kitson was pretty empty, save for a pair of preteen girls trying on sunglasses while their mom sorted through stacks of True Religion jeans. Ash moved a few steps into a corner filled with ironic greeting cards. "Does this idea involve telling me what you're wearing?"

Daisy laughed giddily, sending a thrill up Ash's spine. "No, you bloody perv. But trust me, I look hot. Actually, what I was thinking was, you could fly out to the East Coast and join me on tour. Who else will make sure I'm properly fed from here to Minneapolis?"

Ash felt a dumbfounded grin spread across his face as he imagined delivering the Rock Band Savings Bank in person. Better still was the image of himself and Daisy sprawled together in the back of her tour bus, whiling away the hours between stops, listening to music and making out. Of course he would go. What teenage guy in his right mind could refuse? He'd somehow have to get out of school for a few weeks, but he'd deal with that later. Right now, all he wanted was to get this father-son dinner over with and get on the next eastbound plane.

"I'm pretty sure I have a copy of *The Care and Feeding of Rock Stars* at home somewhere," Ash said, his mind having drifted to the idea of sharing a hotel room with Daisy. "Consider me your official groupie."

"Yippee!" Daisy shouted, her evident excitement making Ash even happier to be going. Myla had always been demanding, yet rarely outright appreciative when he went out of his way to please her. "I'll see you soon."

She hung up abruptly, and Ash stood dazedly staring at her picture on his iPhone. He was going on tour. With his dream girl.

His daydream was interrupted by a tap on his shoulder. Ash wheeled around and found himself staring into Gordon Gilmour's stern, dark brown eyes. Gordon loomed over him by a few inches, forcing Ash to straighten his own shoulders to be on more equal footing. But something felt off. Usually, Gordon seemed as sharp and ready to spring as a coiled snake, but his normally tense face was slack, and he seemed a little dazed, like he didn't know how he'd wound up there. Still, Gordon arched one eyebrow, his trademark power move, and Ash wondered how much of his conversation with Daisy his dad had overheard.

"Dad, what are you doing here? I thought we were meeting at eight," Ash said, trying to circumvent any chiding from his dad for being late. Ash and his father had been butting heads ever since Ash had turned thirteen. But they'd been getting along halfway decently lately, mostly because Ash had agreed to "babysit" Daisy when she first came to L.A., on Gordon's orders. Serving as Daisy's minder had been a chore at first, until Ash had fallen for her. Gordon hadn't even said anything when the tabloids had first started declaring Ash and Daisy an item—*US Weekly* had already named them "Dash." When it came to dating rock stars, Gordon couldn't say too much. He had befriended his share back in the day. At Christmas, Keith Richards even sent fruit baskets with a carton of Camel cigarettes and a fifth of Jack Daniels tucked between the Florida oranges. Clearly, Gordon used to be a party animal before he discovered the Zone Diet.

To Ash's surprise, his dad shrugged. Gordon Gilmour never shrugged unless it was to show you how little your opinion mattered. He always had an answer for everything. Ash's eyes flicked to his father's pinstriped sleeve, where several of the brightly colored scarves he'd passed on as Daisy gifts were looped around his dad's arm. "Just looking for a surprise for Moxie," his dad said, sounding hopeless. "I thought she might need a pick-me-up."

Moxie was Ash's stepmother, even though she wasn't much older than his sister, Tessa. She was a former model from Russia, but ever since she'd given birth to their twin boys, Julius and Caesar, Gordon had been acting like she was some kind of goddess.

"Really? What's wrong with her?" Ash asked. As far as Ash knew, if Moxie wanted a pick-me-up, she bought herself one. "She run out of vodka for her coffee?"

Gordon shook his head, ignoring the comment. Usually, he never let Ash get away with a Moxie diss. "A just-because thing," he said instead. He placed a manicured—emphasis on the *man*—hand on Ash's shoulder, pulling him farther into the corner. "So, I couldn't help but overhear your conversation. With Daisy, I'm guessing. Can I give you some advice?"

Ash shrugged—the Gilmour shrug, to make sure his dad knew how little the advice was going to matter. He could care less what his dad thought. He didn't particularly want any of his advice, but he knew Gordon would give it to him anyway. His father was king of the nonsensical platitude. His guidance was often worthless, but his baritone was impressive, especially to Gordon himself. Sometimes Ash wondered if his father used the sound booths at his label, More Records, to record his authoritative speeches. "Sure, whatever," Ash said.

"It's more a caution kind of thing," Gordon started, fiddling with the tasseled end of a yellow scarf. "I've been around musicians for a long time now. And, well, they live different lives from you and me. They don't always follow the same code. It could be like sending an antelope to hunt with the lions. If you can't fake being a lion, you might get eaten alive."

Ash suppressed a laugh. His dad sounded like some weird, whiny guidance counselor who watched too much Animal Planet. "Are you saying I can't go?" Not that it mattered. Even if Gordon wouldn't sign him out of school, Ash was sure his mom would. She was big on all that experience-life stuff, and she'd do anything if she knew it would get a rise out of her ex-husband.

Gordon pursed his lips and scratched the side of his neck—his thinking pose. He looked Ash over from head to toe, his eyes lingering on the tin bank and its silly vow, *I'm saving up to start a rock band*. Ash clutched it tightly, as defiance and anxiety mingled in his brain. Ten seconds probably went by, feeling like full minutes, as an annoying remix of Lady Gaga's "Poker Face" burbled behind them. But in those ten seconds, Gordon hadn't said no yet. He tossed the scarves back onto the table and sighed for what seemed like forever. Ash shifted uncomfortably. His dad hadn't looked at him like this, really *looked* at him, in years. He kept his own eyes focused right back on his dad, hoping Gordon would see his determination. Would see that, like the Gilmour he was, he wouldn't take no for an answer.

Gordon sighed again, a shorter one this time. "No, I guess it could be a good thing. She needs someone around to keep her out of trouble. I'll call your school tomorrow."

Ash smiled thinly. His dad was so predictable. If it was good for the business, it got the Gordon Gilmour seal of approval, weird speeches aside.

"But Ash," Gordon said, grabbing and clasping Ash's shoulder tightly. "Be careful out there. I meant what I said. Musicians are a whole new ball game. One without any rules. But I guess you'll have to learn for yourself."

Ash nodded somberly, trying to suppress a smile. He planned on learning for himself. And he'd never looked forward to getting an education more.

MANNY POPPINS

"Myla, this is so cute! I'm going to borrow it, okay?" Talia Montgomery said, holding Myla Everhart's new Temperly London minidress up to her petite but buxom frame. The dress was so new, the petal-trimmed hem still had alteration pins in it. "I need it for that UCLA party next Thursday." Before Myla could even answer, Talia had pulled on the dress over her tank top and jeans. Myla cringed, knowing that Talia's C-almost-D-cups were going to stretch out the chest. Talia bounced over to Myla's full-length mirror, spinning so her new hair extensions whipped around her. Her friend's attempt at a short haircut hadn't worked out and certainly hadn't been growing out fast enough, but really, waist-length brunette extensions? All she needed were some overlong acrylic nails and she'd be a shoo-in as a greeter at the Playboy Mansion.

"And I'm going to borrow these Valentinos," said Fortune Weathers, grabbing the emerald-green open-toe pumps each bedecked with a shimmery matching bow. Myla shot her a look that Fortune pretended not to see. Instead, she smiled angelically, a bitchy twinkle dancing in her pale blue eyes. The shoes were still warm from Myla's feet. She and her friends had just returned from their weekly Beverly Center trip.

Fortune slid into the shoes before flopping into Myla's new violet CB2 parlor chair. She leaned her head back over one arm, her shoulder-length, butter-colored hair so shiny it looked like Barbie hair. She draped her legs across the other plush barrel arm, admiring the shoes on her wide feet. Fortune liked anything with bows, because she thought she was a gift to the world. "Perfect," she uttered, to no one but herself.

"And I need your Paul and Joe gold minidress. The sequin one?" Billie Bollman said from across the room, where she was sitting at Myla's vanity and sweeping different colors of Tarte eye shadow across her lids. From a brand-new, never-touched palette. "My dad is putting those downtown condos he can't sell up for rent, and he's throwing an open house party. There will probably be hot USC guys there. I'm going to be the next Ivanka Trump."

Yeah, maybe if Ivanka had Donald's chin, Myla thought, shaking her head as Billie applied highlighter in a way that accentuated her long, horsey face. Between her overuse of Myla's Benefit Coralista and the mishmash of brightly colored eye shadows that did nothing for her pale complexion, Billie was looking more and more like a drunk toucan. Myla herself couldn't make for a stronger contrast to her overly made-up friends: her long black hair was sleek but product-free, her green eyes lined only with mascara.

"Whatever," Myla said, hating them all as she leaned

back on her bed, sort of wishing she smoked. It would give her something to do with her hands besides balling them into tight fists. Her friends were ostensibly still in ass-kissing mode after last month's defection to Fairy Princess—they'd spent weeks kissing Amelie Adams's ass during the shooting of *Class Angel*, in hopes of meeting her co-star Grant Isaacson. But even their desire to be back in Myla's good graces couldn't overpower their usual behavior when tempted by Myla's closet. It was like a bad horror movie—*Invasion of the Inconsiderate Clothing Snatchers*. Myla never used to mind her friends rooting through her closet. Their sartorial demands always felt like proof that she had better taste than they did. But ever since her girlfriends had strayed, she'd started to find it annoying.

While her friends stayed busy changing into her best clothes, Myla slipped into her stretchiest yoga pants. She was so over this day already. If only they would leave, she could put on one of her *Thin Man* DVDs and forget her problems. Nick and Nora Charles were everything she thought a couple should be: ultra-stylish, somewhat badass, and banter champions. There was nothing sexier than that kind of back-and-forth. One of the highlights of her relationship with Ash had been the quips they'd traded.

A muffled version of Cobra Starship's "Hot Mess" flowed out of Myla's cavernous closet. She smirked. Talia's ringtone matched her new look. Talia emerged, now wearing Myla's favorite high-collared Theory cardigan, a multi-toned mohair sweater that hit Myla's knee but was floating mid-thigh on Talia, thanks to her boobs.

"Did you know about this?" Talia shrieked, waving her T-Mobile G1 phone back and forth as she sank onto the bed next to Myla.

Myla grabbed Talia's waving arm, holding it and the phone steady. It was a text from Moira Lacey, the biggest gossip in their school, always ready with a steady feed of information even though she was filming her terrible CW show, *School for Scandal,* in Vancouver. Her co-star and twin, Deven Lacey, was Moira's opposite—sullen, mysterious, a little bitchy, and often the subject of Moira's juiciest offerings. The text read, *Did you hear Ash is going on tour with Crazy Daisy??? I guess it's serious. Heard he's going to launch his solo career with a song about what a bitch Myla was to him.*

Myla dropped Talia's hand unceremoniously. "Not officially, but any idiot could see it coming," she muttered. This was a lie. If her friends weren't there, she would have pulled up the covers and hid underneath them until the next day. She'd been sure that Daisy was nothing more than a rebound, but if Ash was going on tour with her, that *was* serious. The idea of him writing a song about Myla wasn't as worrisome, though. Moira always embellished. And if it was true, at least the song was about her and not Daisy. Besides, Ash never finished anything anyway.

"You should really go to the UCLA party with me," Talia said, continuing to click through her text messages.

"Yeah, it's kind of sad that Ash has moved on, and you're still sort of wallowing," Fortune called from the chair. She had flipped on Myla's TV and was watching an episode of *Mad Men* that Myla had been saving on the DVR to watch when she was alone. "You should really let us help you."

Billie spun in Myla's vanity stool. She'd adjusted it to accommodate her long legs, which meant it would be too high next time Myla sat down. "I'll totally take you to this condo party with me," she said. "You should wear that one-shoulder Alice and Olivia dress. The minty-colored one. It matches your eyes. And I read somewhere that green reminds men of money and then they think you're worth more."

Fortune's head shot up over the arm of the couch. "Yeah, maybe we need to take you for a post-boy make-over," she said, eyeing Myla's yoga pants. "You've been dressing a little low-rent since the Ash thing."

"Guys," Talia scolded. "Don't be so mean. Myla doesn't have to get dressed up to be beautiful. And any-way, none of the guys at BHH will go near her because she used to date Ash, and everyone loves Ash. No one will risk upsetting him by dating his ex. Except Lewis. Who Myla does *not* want to make out with again."

Myla's melancholy morphed to anger. She didn't know if she was madder at her friends for their insensitivity or for being right. She *had* been wallowing. And she didn't know what her next move should be. She didn't mind being single, but having no one to even *flirt* with just sucked. Plus, none of her usual distractions—shopping, beautifying, even plotting revenge—felt enticing. After blowouts with Ash and Jojo at the *Class Angel* wrap party, she'd really meant to be a whole new Myla. But she didn't know what that was. And sitting around thinking about her feelings while everyone else was having fun made her feel as left behind as a pair of last year's tights in a Forever 21 clearance bin. You couldn't do introspection when you really wanted distraction. She needed a fresh new challenge to sink her teeth into.

A knock came on her bedroom door. Myla flounced over and flung it open, coming face-to-face with her sister, Jojo Milford. Jojo, her arms crossed over her chest, stood proudly in the doorway. She was totally drama-geeked-out, actually wearing her black *Jane Eyre* cast member T-shirt with a tight black American Apparel mini.

It was a semi-big deal that Jojo had beaten out Amelie Adams for the lead in the play. Everyone, including Myla, had thought Amelie's arrival at Beverly Hills High meant she'd be anointed the school's official drama queen. The very idea that Amelie would automatically be top of the heap at something—even if drama at BHH was for amateurs and stoners—had pissed off Myla, who prided herself on ruling the school. She had thought nothing would be more annoying than Amelie walking proudly down the hall as if being the lead in a school musical was anything more than being a trained monkey. And then the part had gone to Jojo. Myla was still on the fence about whether Jojo's victory was more or less annoying that Amelie's would have been. Another thing to add to her Introspection Checklist.

"Mom wants us downstairs for dinner," Jojo said. "Your friends have to leave." Jojo's easy composure was enough to raise a snarl on Myla's lips. Jojo was supposed to be afraid of her, but ever since she'd won the lead in the school play, she'd been walking around like the heir to the Everhart throne. Which she kind of was. She was their parents' biological child, whereas Myla had been adopted from Thailand when she was four. But Myla had been their daughter for twelve years, whereas Jojo had been in the picture for only a few short weeks. The fact that she'd gotten the part had apparently proven to Lailah and Barkley that Jojo took after them, and they'd spent every second since they'd heard fawning over their real, live spawn.

Talia, Billie, and Fortune filed out, their arms laden with Myla's clothes. They waved and blew kisses back at her, each one making sure to sneer at Jojo as they walked past. As if Myla would give them Brownie points for it.

Fifteen minutes later, Myla was done with family time and ready to retreat to her room. "Jojo, do you know if Mr. Potter subscribes to the Meisner or the Strasberg method of acting?" Lailah intoned, tucking a strand of her Japanese-straightened dark hair behind her ear. Myla bit down harder than necessary into her hummus-stuffed chicken. Lailah loved talking shop, and now she got to do it with her naturally born daughter.

It was the fifth *Jane Eyre* question in as many minutes. Myla could have announced she'd cured cancer in her chemistry class, and their parents would still be more interested in how many solos Jojo got. Jojo, idiot that she was, shrugged. "I don't think he has a method. To be honest, he's kind of a dope." Myla sat between them, feeling invisible, as Jojo's violet eyes locked on Lailah's matching set. The joys of shared DNA.

"Thattagirl," Barkley said, winking one pool-blue eye. He smirked, showing off the dimple it was rumored he'd had insured for several million dollars. "Don't take crap from directors."

"You said *crap*!" Myla's eight-year-old brother Mahalo pointed a barbeque sauce–covered finger at his father.

The other kids, gathered around the massive dining table in their high chairs and booster seats, all pointed at Mahalo. "No, you said *crap*," they said in unison. The kids had been going through a cursing phase that the entire family found amusing. Lailah shot the kids a half-hearted scolding look before dissolving in laughter.

With a distraction available, Myla was about to push her chair from the table and ask to be excused when Barkley cleared his throat. "Hey, guys, listen up," he said, using the football coach rasp he'd cultivated for *99 Yards of Destiny*. "Your mother and I have an announcement to make." It was so funny to Myla when her dad pretended to be in charge, like now, with his arms folded and his serious commander nod as they all fell silent. Though the tiny crow's feet around his eyes did make him look a little older and wiser, Lailah had probably scripted this moment for him.

"As you might know, your mom and I have been trying to have a baby for some time now," Barkley said awkwardly, folding Lailah's delicate, long-fingered hand into his own callused palm. Myla could see tears forming at the corner of her mom's eyes, and she fought the urge to roll her own. Lailah could whip up tears the way other moms could whip up Pillsbury slice-and-bake cookies— no effort required, and almost as good as the real thing.

"Where do babies come from?" Nelson decided to ask at that moment, standing up on his booster seat to reveal that he'd somehow removed his pants during dinner and was wearing only his Transformers undies and his favorite baby Doc Martens. Ajani and Indigo followed his lead, standing up in their high chairs, and the instant chaos forced Barkley and Lailah from their seats.

Myla shrugged, rising from the table. She might as well go chill in her room if they were done. Annoyingly, Jojo got up at the same time and dutifully tried to help corral the other kids.

"Wait, Myla," Lailah said, wiping a smear of hummus from Ajani's temple. In return, the little girl dabbed a spot of hummus onto Lailah's high cheekbone. "We haven't finished." Myla stopped near the stairs, just far enough from the rest of the family to feel like she didn't have to share the big moment.

Barkley grinned, loving being in the thick of a crazed parent moment. "To answer Nelson's question, in this case, babies come from Malawi," he said. "Kids, you're going with us."

Myla wrinkled her brow, her eyes scanning the crowded dinner table. They were adopting *again*? Where would another kid even sit? She shook her head. The table had every family member's name carved into its baseboard, and Jojo's hadn't even been added yet. It had been, what, just over a month since she'd shown up? And they were already bored. Bouncing Indigo on her hip as the rest of the kids ran around the dinner table, Jojo was trying to hide her shock at the parental diss, Myla could tell. She was cooing into Indigo's chubby toddler face with insane determination. *Good,* Myla thought. It was about time Jojo learned that no kid, even a bio-kid, would satisfy their parents.

"The big girls are staying here," Lailah said, looking

meaningfully at her two oldest daughters. *Great,* Myla thought. *Of all the people to share a house with, I'm stuck with the most annoying possibility.* Seeing the sick look on Jojo's face made it clear she wasn't too excited about the solo sister time, either.

"Girls, this doesn't mean you've got a free house," Barkley said, distracted as he attempted to put pants back on Nelson, who kicked his chubby legs in protest. As Nelson's pants went back on, Bobby took his off. "My new fourth assistant will be keeping an eye on things, and he'll be around to help you two if you need anything while we're away."

The doorbell rang. Myla ignored it, stepping back into the dining room and glaring at her father. His *fourth assistant*? If there was anything worse than sharing the house with Jojo, it was sharing the house with some wannabe actor who would suck up to them and do nothing but talk about his blossoming career on basic cable. "You hired a manny to look after us?" She asked irritably, her hands on her hips.

Barkley sighed, clearly wishing to be doing anything but explaining this situation. "Think of Danny as a minder, not a . . . manny."

The doorbell rang again. Myla had never heard it ring twice in her life—usually their housekeeper or valet got it. But Lucy and Charlie were off for the night, and the family was short staffed. "Wait, you hired a manny named Danny?"

"Myla, get that please," Lailah ordered, shooting Myla a *shut up* look as she crouched under the table to find Ajani's dropped Fairy Princess tiara. Her Cartier bracelets all clinked against one another as she gestured to the door.

Myla wound through the living room and huge foyer,

clipping past Lailah's annoying antique fainting couch that didn't match any of Barkley's modern furniture. She steered around the huge and ugly African fertility mask that Angelina Jolie had sent over as a frenemies gift to her mom. It was propped next to the door, still homeless, and seemed to sneer at Myla. She stuck her tongue out at it. While Angie could seemingly get pregnant at the drop of Brad Pitt's fedora, Lailah was older, and she and Barkley hadn't been so lucky. They'd been seeking the help of one of Beverly Hills' best baby-making doctors. Now they had Malawi.

She flung open the door without looking to see who it was. "Danny the Manny," she called over her shoulder at her parents. "I'm sure he has no problem being taken seriously."

Sneering, Myla came face-to-face with the single hottest guy she'd ever laid eyes on. His hair was as dark as hers, thick, and combed back off his face casually. His eyes were the same delicious dark brown as the Nutella gelato she'd eaten today, flecked with tiny golden-green dots. Beneath his tight baby-blue T-shirt, she detected abs that would make Ryan Reynolds jealous.

"Actually, girls really go for the manny title," he said, his voice deep. "Danny Beck." His hand was held out for her to shake, and she took it, barely conscious of what she was doing as she stared at him for too long a moment.

"Nice to meet you, *manny*," Myla finally retorted, dropping his hand. She smirked back at Danny as she sauntered toward the stairs, hoping he was watching her.

Suddenly, she couldn't wait to be left under the care of a manny.

PLAINLY, JANE

Jojo placed a hand on Amelie's wrist, her wide violet eyes focused on Amelie's aquamarine ones. "Do you really think you're the right woman for Mr. Rochester?" Jojo said urgently. "Or that he'd be the right man for you? He's quite wild, isn't he?"

As she did with all unpleasant things, Amelie pretended Jojo's hand wasn't there. She even tried to pretend Jojo wasn't there. Beyond the obvious annoyance of dealing with her co-star, she was irritated that Mr. Potter had written scenes into the play that existed nowhere in the book. Her favorite book. He'd reduced Charlotte Brontë's genius to a bad episode of *As the World Turns*. "I daresay a wild man needs the right kind of woman to tame him," Amelie intoned, suppressing a gag. Tame him? What was this? Single, unattractive drama teacher wish fulfillment?

Amelie forced a sneer off her face as her co-star continued to implore Blanche Ingram. Apparently, Jojo's version of longing for Mr. Rochester just meant widening her eyes even more. Amelie would have liked to poke them out.

"Cut! Cut!" Mr. Potter sprang up from his seat in the first row of the theater, pulling his shrunken black turtleneck down over an exposed strip of his pasty white stomach. "Amelie, let me give you a few notes on this scene."

Amelie smiled with closed lips, her fists forming into tight balls of fury. Every time she had a scene—which was infrequent, considering her bit part—Mr. Potter singled her out for notes. Had *he* ever worked with Meryl Streep? No. Amelie had, at age twelve. Had *he* ever had to say no to a movie with Sam Mendes because he was already working on a Wes Anderson film? No. Amelie had. Age fourteen. Had *he* ever singlehandedly turned a children's character into a multimillion-dollar franchise property recognized by people around the world? No. Amelie had. Fairy Princess. Ages eight to present. So, fine, playing Blanche Ingram now and the immortal guidance counselor in *Class Angel* were the first instances she hadn't been cast as characters still in prepubescence. But even her past of playing characters half her age gave her more credibility than Mr. Potter, a never-produced screenwriter who'd turned *Jane Eyre* into a high school musical.

All Mr. Potter had ever done, beyond teaching a few English literature classes at BHH and writing a musical that no studio would touch, was serve as a script reader for a small production company in Marina del Rey. And somehow, writing up notes on the hundreds of bad screenplays that seemed to grow wild in L.A. qualified him to critique *her*?

Mr. Potter gave her his condescending "gentle" face, a tight smile and squinty eyes that made him look like a mole. "I don't know what you learned on the set of *Fairy Princess*," he said, punctuating the *p* sound in *princess* with a glimmering spray of spit, "but you've heard of jealousy, correct? Blanche is coming from a place of insecurity. Even someone as self-centered as she is can see that Mr. Rochester and Jane have a rapport. If you find it hard to get there, just imagine that Selena Gomez got a part in the next Kidz Network Christmas special instead of you. Really put yourself in Blanche's shoes. Though I'm sure your own shoes are better and more expensive, it's the job of a true actor to really go there. I hope you understand."

Amelie just nodded. She could barely speak. Well, she could, but if she did, she'd go ballistic on this idiot. For the last week of rehearsals, he'd had some ridiculous note to give her at every turn. How could the school have hired him to do this? Well, actually, Amelie knew the answer to that question: He was a last-minute fill-in for a production gone wrong. Mr. Potter acted as if the fact that BHH's Drama Club was well funded enough to have a very well-cared-for performance space—even bit players like Amelie got their own dressing tables, and a cleaning team polished the floors every night—meant he was *somebody*. Really, the only quality he shared with great directors was a massive ego.

Proof positive that the guy had no idea how to direct: He'd chosen *Jojo* as his Jane. But Amelie would show Mr. Potter. She could do jealous. It wasn't hard. She *was* jealous of Jojo. She trained her gaze on her co-star and tried the line again. "I daresay a wild man needs the right kind of woman to tame him," she practically spat, looking into Jojo's innocent hyacinth eyes. Jojo stared back, cloyingly doelike, as though she thought she was a natural for Jane Eyre, one of the most complex female characters of all time. *The closest she comes to being Jane Eyre is pulling off the whole completely-plain-to-look-at thing*, thought Amelie, knowing she was in denial about Jojo's cute athletic figure and glowing complexion. But when it came to her acting talent in the real world, Jojo would barely get a part as a backup member of *Fairy Princess*'s Unicorn Chorus.

Mr. Potter cleared his throat loudly. Jojo cocked her head attentively at the director, while Amelie steeled herself for whatever insult he'd hurl her way next.

"Amelie, I think it would be good if you retreat backstage for a while to really think about Blanche's motivations, 'kay?" Mr. Potter checked his clipboard. "Jojo, let's have you and Michael run through the exchange just before the John Rivers–Jane Eyre duet, and then we'll come back to your scene with Amelie. Take a few minutes, Amelie."

Amelie slunk off to the sidelines, where Nick was waiting in his Mr. Rochester costume, slouching nervously as always in spite of his athletic frame. The high collar looked tight and uncomfortable around his neck. He offered her a cup of water from the cooler. Amelie took the paper cup, gulping, as he watched. "I thought you were really good," he said predictably, as Amelie tossed her crushed cup into the wastebasket. Nick would be cute if he wasn't so much like the saddest dog at the shelter. He was just too nice, constantly bringing her drinks, snacks, and compliments. "Mr. Potter doesn't know what he's talking about. But what can you expect? The guy's a little nuts. And I think he's threatened by you."

Amelie dejectedly nodded, waves of anger rising beneath her skin as she heard Mr. Potter call Jojo a "natural" for the five hundredth time that day. Nick's sympathy just made her feel sorrier for herself, and his male presence reminded her of someone who had been noticeably absent from her life recently: Jake. She hadn't really talked to him since the week before, when she'd bawled uncontrollably on his shoulder. That was definitely not on *Seventeen*'s list of tips to make your crush fall madly in love with you—a list she was taking way too seriously for her own good. What use was the tip *Have your own satisfying life* if your lives never intersected?

Across the stage, Jojo swept across the stage as she sang, trying to stifle her giggles as she watched her co-star Michael Pelipito do his best attempt at St. John Rivers. Which meant crossing his arms sternly over his ever-present Ed Hardy tee and curling his upper lip pompously. Still, Jojo had to admit, this whole leading lady thing felt good. She could see how her mom loved doing this for a living. It helped that BHH's school play took place on a giant stage with polished wood floors and plush red curtains, and that her dressing room was replete with gorgeous costumes. In Sacramento, her best friend Willa Barnes worked on the plays. That usually meant duct-taping over tears in the ratty gray curtains and using Lysol to disguise the old-lady smell of the costumes, all Goodwill store finds.

Satisfied with her and Michael's rehearsal of their

duet, "Why Not Wed?" Mr. Potter gestured for Jojo to wait and summoned Amelie to the stage once more. "I'd like to skip ahead a few lines to the end of the cocktail party, when Jane is cleaning up and Blanche catches her alone."

Amelie strode purposefully to the center of the stage, her eyes trained on Jojo as she waited for her cue. Looking to the sidelines, Jojo could see Nick, her co-star, staring besottedly at Amelie. He was totally and utterly mesmerized by her. She couldn't blame him. After meeting Barbar, Jojo realized it was true what they said about some celebrities just having It. Her parents definitely had that certain something, that glimmer of being magnetic and amazing and worth watching. Myla had It, too, though her It side sometimes competed with her Total Bitch side. And Amelie had It. She practically glowed, even when surrounded by her average, everyday classmates—though not many of them were really "average." Almost everyone here was someone. Even the kids from the wrong side of Robertson (a.k.a. the middle class) had the patina of being a little dangerous. But Amelie had that sheen of being the girl to watch. Even Jojo couldn't help but stare for a little too long at Amelie's perfect skin and pink lips.

"And . . . action!" Mr. Potter shouted from his seat.

Jojo picked up a teapot from one of the ornate end tables, cleaning up after the party at Thornfield. Amelie as Blanche Ingram roamed the room, humming lightly to herself.

"Can I assist you with something, Miss Ingram?" Jojo asked, setting the teapot down again and crossing toward her co-star. "A biscuit, perhaps? To help you sleep?" Jojo knew Jane was supposed to be all business, even a little brisk, in the scene, but she couldn't stop herself from sounding nervous around Amelie. Every time she saw her co-star, she thought of that first day she'd met Jake, when he'd been looking up *Fairy Princess* information in the computer lab. He'd claimed it was just to learn more about his tutee, but was it really? Or did Jake have a thing for Amelie? He'd seemed distracted since Amelie came to BHH, his face in a book every day at lunch. Maybe he was just busy. Or maybe he was avoiding Jojo now that Amelie Adams was around.

"Oh, nothing, Jane," Amelie said, smoothing the delicate lace that trimmed her skirt as she sat down on a period divan. She flicked her eyes over Jojo's drab Jane Eyre gown meaningfully. "I so admire you, though."

Jojo tentatively returned a book to a shelf at the far end of the parlor. Looking over her shoulder, she said, "I don't think I understand what you're getting at, Miss Ingram."

Amelie stood up, sashaying over to Jojo. She blinked, her long lashes fluttering against her high cheekbones. "You're just so very strong, going through life knowing you'll likely never be paired with a mate," Amelie intoned sarcastically as Blanche. "What a tragedy."

Jojo looked up into Amelie's perturbed face, forgetting that they were practicing. *Shit. Shit. Shit.* She'd been so absorbed by the memory of Amelie's head on Jake's shoulder that she'd blanked on her line.

"Um . . . ," Jojo said, staring at a tiny bit of tangerine lip gloss outside Amelie's lipline. Sadly, the eensy flaw was the only thing wrong with Amelie, whose waist looked so small in her Blanche corset, it was hard to believe she could breathe normally. Jojo bit her lip.

"Better not be paired than be paired with the wrong partner." *Ah, that was the line*, thought Jojo, relieved until she realized who was saying it. Amelie stood with her arms crossed, a slight smirk on her lips. To Jojo's horror, Amelie didn't stop with one line. "Now *that* would be a tragedy."

The rest of the cast was watching the whole exchange, and Jojo thought she could hear their silent mockery. She felt like the elephant in the room or Jessica Simpson in mom jeans.

From the floor, Mr. Potter clapped his hands. "That was surprisingly good, Amelie," he said. Amelie beamed. "Maybe we can end rehearsals for today and give our Jane a chance to read up." He raised a thick eyebrow at Jojo.

"See you," Amelie said melodically, in the most pleasant tone Jojo had heard from her yet.

Jojo glared at her co-star's retreating back. A minute ago, they'd been adversaries only in Jojo's head. But Amelie had just made their rivalry official.

MANNY ALIVE!

Jojo felt like she was sleepwalking downstairs early on Wednesday. For the second night in a row, visions of Amelie and Jake had danced in her head, keeping her from sleeping. She'd planned on a late night of studying the *Jane Eyre* script, but every time she'd started to read, she heard Amelie's voice saying all the lines instead. Seriously not helpful.

She needed coffee. And food. Since her parents left for Malawi on Sunday, she hadn't exactly been eating square meals. Last night she'd had nothing but half a leftover chicken wrap. When she'd come home from rehearsal, Myla's friends had been bossing Lucy around as she made Cobb salads for them. Jojo would have liked a salad, too, but didn't want to join in on any activity that involved such spoiled, awful girls. To her credit, Myla had helped Lucy clean up the kitchen, but even a show of rare decency on her sister's part wasn't enough to make Jojo want to share her company.

At the foot of the stairs, her mouth started watering. The smell of simmering peppers, black beans, cheese, and eggs wafted into her nostrils, making her feel infinitely better. Lucy was making her amazing huevos rancheros. In her hunger-fueled hurry, she half ran, half tripped into the kitchen, skidding across the dark marble floor in her gray Jimmy Choo ankle boots.

"Whoa, slow down there," said Danny, who was sitting at the kitchen island over a heaping plate of eggs. "Your dad would so not be impressed with me if he came home to you all limbless."

Jojo blushed. She'd forgotten Danny was staying with them. He slept in the guest house, and this was the first time he'd come for breakfast all week. "I'd have probably snapped my neck, really," Jojo joked back, looking over his shoulder to see if he'd eaten all the eggs. To her utter delight, Lucy loaded up a second plate and set it next to Danny's spot. "But I still would have found a way to eat these eggs. Thanks, Lucy."

Lucy smiled at the compliment, pouring Jojo a cup of coffee. Normally, she didn't let Lucy do all this running around on her behalf, but she was truly starved. Danny slid the remainder of the *L.A. Times* over to her, smoothing out the Sports section he was reading. He smiled brightly. He was fully awake and dressed, so he must have gotten up a while ago. Jojo was still bleary-eyed.

She didn't know what to make of Danny. She'd been so busy with play practice that she'd only really spoken to him the night Barkley had invited him over to meet the family. He'd congratulated her a bunch of times for getting the lead in the play, probably because her parents couldn't stop talking about it. And he definitely seemed enthusiastic and eager to please Barkley. Every night since the family had left, he'd tacked a printout to the door of the Sub-Zero fridge, giving updates from Barbar—Myla and Jojo were at school during the only time Barkley was reasonably able to make calls from Malawi. Danny bulleted out every detail, from little tidbits about the other kids—"Mahalo lost a molar and the Tooth Fairy is visiting tonight"—to more important stuff—"Adoption agent said we could be here for three weeks." He also posted the reports about the Everhart home front that he was giving to their father—"Jojo at play practice until 9:30 p.m.," "Myla watched movies at home on Tuesday," "Gardeners planting new bulbs for spring." Jojo had no idea how he was aware of everything, but clearly he wanted to make a good, if meticulous, impression.

"I totally get it," Danny said, digging into his eggs again. "I've been living on ramen for months. This is just the home cooking I've been needing. But it's better than anything my mom can make." Lucy, who was loading the dishwasher, shook her head teasingly as if to say, *Don't insult your mother.*

Jojo raised an eyebrow over the rim of her oversize coffee mug, glancing at a huge photo of her parents on the cover of the *Times'* Calendar section. HOW BARBAR HAVE MADE INTERNATIONAL ADOPTIONS HARDER FOR THE REST OF US, read the headline. Jojo felt a little twinge of satisfaction at the negative commentary. After the fuss they'd made over finding her, their long-lost birth child, she would have thought she'd keep her parents interested for longer than a month.

"You don't have a cook?" she asked curiously. She'd assumed Danny had gotten his pseudo-internship with Barkley because his family was part of the Rich & Famous

Club. She'd been in town only a month or so, but it was long enough to learn how everything worked here.

"Yeah, right. In Oak Lawn, Illinois? The closest we got to a chef was a standing Monday-night order with Palermo's Pizza," Danny said, rolling his green-flecked eyes. "It was damn good pizza, though. L.A. pizza still freaks me out." He picked up his plate and helped himself to another huge scoop of eggs.

Jojo laughed. She wondered what he told his family in Oak Lawn about the crazy Everhart clan. "Yeah, I'm not from here, either," she said. "I grew up in Sacramento. Which is like The Land L.A. Forgot About—or would have forgotten, except it's the state capital. So what made you come out here?"

"School. UCLA. They've got a good film program and a good business school," he said. "I'm trying to get into green technologies when I graduate. Solar power, wind power, all that Al Gore stuff. Barkley is actually really connected in that whole field. I'm hoping if I do a good job, he'll help me out."

Jojo nodded, liking Danny more and more every moment. Since moving here, she hadn't met anyone normal, except Jake. And even Jake's mom was a powerful publicist. Danny seemed pretty down-to-earth. Midwestern down-to-earth, no less.

Myla chose that moment to saunter into the kitchen, clad in a short black grosgrain Phillip Lim skirt and a nearly sheer bubble gum pink tank. The Beverly Center must have been having a Lolita sale. She sashayed past on rhinestone-heeled black satin wedges that made her hit supermodel heights, her tanned legs on prominent display. "Jojo, you didn't happen to borrow my Miu Miu cardigan, did you? The organic cotton one?" She poured herself a cup of coffee, not taking her eyes off Danny. "Sorry to interrupt, Danny. I just so need to find it. It's the softest thing I own. Probably because it's all natural."

"I don't have it." Jojo shook her head in irritation, taking another bite of her eggs. As if Myla would lend her anything right now. And as if Myla would care if her clothes were earth-friendly. She must have overheard Danny talking about his environmental aspirations. "Can't you wear something else?" *Anything else,* she thought. Myla's outfit looked like part of a "Manny-Eater" fashion spread. She shot Myla a look that she hoped said, *Don't do this.* Whatever *this* was, Jojo knew it couldn't be good.

Myla imperceptibly raised her eyebrows and, out of Danny's eyeshot, flipped Jojo off, before clacking across the kitchen in her heels and reaching to get a Clif Bar off the highest shelf in the pantry. As she did so, her skirt lifted enough to offer a peek of pale pink undies.

Danny grabbed the *Times'* front section, seemingly intent on an article about new safety requirements for silicone implants. His mahogany eyes darted toward Myla as she wavered on her heels—in interest or worry, Jojo couldn't tell.

Myla tossed the Clif Bar onto the counter like she'd never eat anything so calorie-laden. She'd picked it purely for its position in the pantry, not because she *wanted* it. She stared into her coffee cup, already imagining Danny being driven mad by the very sight of her. It was only a matter of time before he completely lost track of why he was here and threw himself at her amazingly well-heeled feet.

Not like she actually *wanted* Danny the Manny. But there was nothing more fun than playing Make the Hot Guy Want You. Her friends—right now, quasi-friends— were right about one thing: Myla needed a man. Not for a relationship necessarily, but a distraction was in order. Enduring all the BHH talk circulating about Ash's turn as a man-groupie would be easier with her own notorious accomplishment swirling through the hallways.

"Hey, Myla, why don't you sit down?" Danny said, patting the stool next to him where the bar curved. Not breaking eye contact, Myla perched on the seat, crossing her legs and leaning forward for Danny's benefit. It was times like this when she was glad not to be super-busty. Spilling out of her tank top would have looked trashy, but if Danny was an earthy type, he probably didn't go for that kind of thing. "Sure," she cooed, flashing Jojo a nasty look. Her sister scowled over her plate of eggs. She was such a prude.

"So guys, here's the deal," Danny said. "I really do want to do a good job for your dad. He's helped me out a lot. But I was sixteen not too long ago and I know how it feels to have your parents think you need a babysitter."

"So if you were sixteen not too long ago, what does that make you now?" Myla picked a grape off a bunch that Lucy had just washed. She popped it in her mouth, closing her eyes like it was the best thing she'd ever tasted. She really wanted some eggs, but scrambled eggs were *so* not sexy.

"That's not important," Danny said, brushing the

comment off without so much as a glance at Myla's
exposed collarbone. She started to wonder if his perfect
hair—gelled, but not too gelled—and understated gray
Thomas Pink button-down were signs that he was a
manny who liked men. "What I'm trying to say is, I'll be
around just to help in an emergency, be available if you
need something—you get the idea. But I'm not going to
impede on your lives, or give your parents daily reports
on whether you have guys over or something."

We do have a guy over, Myla thought, but she didn't say
anything. Instead, she pulled out her iPhone and started
texting away. Danny went a little pale. "You're not telling
your dad what I just said, are you?" He was clutching his
coffee mug so tightly, Myla thought it would break.

Still thumbing away at the keypad, Myla simply raised
her Smashbox 24K–coated eyelids. "I would never do
that," she said with mock indignity. "I've just been meaning to have a PJ party here for the longest time, and it
sounds like you'll be down with it."

Danny's grip on the cup faltered, and some coffee
sloshed over the rim. Taking a sharp inhale of breath, he
said, "Sure, no problem."

Myla's lips curled into a half-smile. Finally, a reaction.
Not enough of one to assure her Danny wasn't gay, but
a reaction just the same. She was satisfied to see Jojo
grit her teeth as she flipped a page of the newspaper and
loudly slapped it against the countertop.

"Great," Myla said, hopping down from the stool and
plucking another grape. She plopped it onto her tongue
as Danny and Jojo stared at her, one amused, the other
not so much. "Wear something nice. It's co-ed."

TRICKED OUT

Is it weird to show up at the Chelsea Hotel wearing a Sex Pistols shirt? Ash wondered. Maybe it was just ironic. After all, this was the place where Sid Vicious, lead singer of the Sex Pistols, had possibly-maybe stabbed his punk-rock girlfriend, Nancy.

Ash's yellow cab pulled to a stop in front of the building, where dozens of fast-walking pedestrians hurried past without so much as a glance at its loud, red-brick exterior. *We're definitely not in L.A. anymore,* he thought as he got out of the cab and two girls barreled right past him, clipping him with the corners of their oversize art portfolios. No one walked this fast in L.A. Actually, hardly anyone *walked* in L.A., period. Ash tipped the cabbie and set his bags on the ground, taking a second to absorb the hotel looming over him. *This* was a real rock-star hotel. In L.A., supposedly cool hotels were painted white or peach or pink, like something out of a girly cartoon. The Chelsea was bloodred, with a neon sign lit red and green with the hotel's name, like some kind of Christmas gift from hell. On the sidewalk, its name was stamped out in stark white letters on a black backdrop. Simple. It said, *Yeah, you're here. Shut up already.*

In the time it had taken to clear his absence from school, Ash had missed the D.C. and Philly stops of Daisy's tour. But starting here, in New York, staying at a hotel where people like Jimi Hendrix, Dee Dee Ramone, and the Libertines had stayed, and Nancy Spungen and Dylan Thomas had died, seemed like an even better beginning. He'd brought his guitar, and he could already feel the energy coming off the historic building. He was seventeen years old, and finally not just mindlessly consuming the world from his rich-kid vantage point. Coming on tour with Daisy was going to be real life. Real life with a More Records expense account, but still.

He hefted his duffel bag onto his shoulder and picked up his Strat case with his other free hand. The Chelsea didn't have doormen—it was no Four Seasons—so Ash waited for a girl with a foot-high orange mohawk to push open the door. He slipped inside behind her.

The lobby was filled with strange paintings on every wall, at every angle. His dad would go nuts here, seeing art hanging with no care for "the line." Above Ash's head was a papier-mâché fat lady sitting on a swing with an oversize banana draped over her lap. He blushed, sensing there was an underlying sexual message to the phallic fruit. He didn't find it sexy, though. Just weird. Maybe because he was still a virgin. Did guys who got laid understand weird art?

Ash was, well, ready to get laid himself. Not that Daisy was just some piece of ass. But long nights after her shows, the romance of the open road, live music, new cities . . . Wasn't it kind of bound to happen? At the very least, the prospects were better than they had been with Myla. Every time he and Myla had reached a big moment in their relationship where they seemed about to cross that bridge, they'd have a fight and destroy all their progress. Makeup sex did not occur if it was your first time.

Why was he thinking about Myla again? Maybe because Tucker had sent a text as Ash was on his way to the Chelsea: Dude, you're missing a sexy PJ party at Myla's this weekend. New girl's got you whipped. Me and the boys are gonna ask Jake and his bro to come with. Ash had glared at the message, irritated. Why would Tucker think he cared about Myla's party? Okay, so the risqué theme was proof that Myla was on the prowl. Back in eighth grade, when Myla was trying to land Ash, she'd thrown pool parties just so she could parade around in her skimpy Betsey Johnson bikinis. He'd never gotten the hint back then. Now, he twitched at the idea of Myla kissing another guy. But he'd been there, done that. It would be weirder if Myla suddenly stopped scheming, really. So, let her have her party and manipulate whatever poor sap she was trying to wrap around her little finger this time.

He hit DELETE defiantly, vowing to stop caring what was happening back home. Just as he shoved his phone back into his pocket, a pair of slim arms bear-hugged him around his waist as Daisy barreled into him, almost knocking him over.

"Hey," he said. Before he could utter another syllable, Daisy's mouth was on his. Her lips tasted delicious, like salted, buttery popcorn. As she jumped up and wrapped her legs around him, Ash grabbed her tight. He loved how someone so petite could feel so substantial. Her arms were lean and muscular from playing the guitar, and her tiny body was compact and taut. Just when he was wondering how long he could keep holding her like this, Daisy jumped down, her silvery eyes shimmering under the flatteringly dim lobby lights.

She was in full Crazy Daisy regalia, which was to be expected, since she was on tour. She wore ripped blue tights under one of her signature tutus, this one orange, and a slogan tee that said DUCK, DUCK, GOOSE! It featured a picture of one duck grabbing the other one's ass. Her hair matched, with shocks of orange and blue cutting through her naturally nutty-brown strands. Ash knew they were just clip-on extensions, but the effect was still jarring. Her makeup was a little less chaotic than usual, but her soft gray eyes were eclipsed by a blue so bright, it looked like toilet bowl cleaner. Ash liked it better when she was just normal Daisy, fresh-faced, simply dressed, and beyond gorgeous. But she was a rock star, and her weird outfits and odd behavior were part of a persona she'd crafted to get press and sell records. And the wrecked look was kind of hot on her. Looking at her, the news of Myla's party faded into the background. Myla could have a naked party for all he cared.

"Hey," she finally said in return, a mischievous grin turning up her tangerine lips. "I think we need to do that again."

Ash grinned. He set his duffel and guitar case on the ground and, as if in instant-replay mode, Daisy leaped into his arms again. Behind his closed eyelids, Ash could hear the tsk-tsking of stuffy Midwesterners who'd chosen the Chelsea for its bargain rates, not realizing it was so out-there and artsy. He could imagine them going home to their boring neighborhoods, saying, "And then we saw two *musicians* practically having sex in the lobby. You just know there were probably roaches in our room, too. Next time, we're staying closer to Rockefeller Center."

"Daisy, Daisy, Daisy, what have I told you about straddling guys you've just met?" The accent was British with an inexplicable Southern drawl mixed in. As Daisy hopped down, Ash opened his eyes. The guy speaking was tall, with shoulder-length black hair, dark eyes, and an abundance of accessories. He had rings on every finger and several pendants on strings around his neck. He looked like a cruise-ship impersonator of Johnny Depp or Russell Brand.

Ash felt a sneer coming on. Who the fuck was this guy? And why had Daisy just thrown her arm around him?

"Ash, this is Trick Nash, my bassist," she said, patting his chest, where a panther tattoo was on display beneath his black, ripped-up vest and deep-V-neck T-shirt. It was the kind of shirt that only extremely gay or extremely straight guys could pull off. *I bet he totally gets the fat lady and the banana,* Ash thought randomly.

A prickly, annoying heat rose on Ash's neck. Daisy had introduced Trick as "*my* bassist." And clearly, there was some kind of private joke between her and Trick about Daisy being friendly with strangers.

"Hey, mate," Trick said, distracted. He was looking at Daisy again, holding up a pack of Marlboro Reds that he'd pulled from God-knew-what pocket or compartment of his skin-tight outfit. "Dais, smoke break?" He grinned, nodding his head toward the front door. Daisy still hadn't taken her arm off his bony shoulder.

Ash's inner caveman wanted to rip the box of cigarettes from Trick's hand, stomp on them, and lift Daisy over his shoulder and carry her away. Daisy had never told him she smoked. He cut his eyes to Daisy, who shook her head. "Maybe later," she said, play-slapping Trick's wrist. "You know I'm trying to cut back."

Trick shrugged. "Did you want one?" He held the pack out to Ash, his accent more annoying now than before. Was he faking it? When Ash shook his head to refuse, Trick slid the pack back into his jeans pocket.

Daisy finally dropped her arm from Trick's shoulder and stepped to the side. She gestured to two more guys standing behind them—Ash hadn't even noticed them until now. "Oh, and this is Sammy Golden, our guitarist, and Brett Fitz, the band's drummer." Sammy was pale, blond, and taller than Trick. He was so lanky, his arms and legs looked like they were strings loosely threaded to his ropelike body. Brett was just a little over five feet tall, with a pointy goatee and a series of chains hanging from his baggy, striped pants.

"Guys, this is Ash Gilmour," Daisy said, grabbing his hand and pulling him close.

He couldn't help comparing his slightly slouchy Diesel jeans and completely boring blue American Apparel T-shirt to Trick's painted-on clothes. Was that what Daisy wanted in a guy? Ash felt almost naked, and not in a good way, realizing he didn't have any cool rings, medallions, or tattoos on his person.

"You're the dude, then. She can't shut up about you," Sammy said excitedly. "Ash this, Ash that." He and Brett each shook Ash's hand enthusiastically. This was a little more like it. At least Daisy had mentioned him.

"Um, my exact words were, Ash is the best thing about my American debut," Daisy retorted, giving Sammy a playful shove. She gestured to Ash's bags on the floor. "Hey, would you mind getting those to our room? I want to take Ash somewhere with lots of dark corners."

The heat faded from Ash's skin instantly as he felt the cool *whoosh* of relief. *The best thing about my American debut.* And now she was making them carry his bags. He had nothing to worry about. He was about to go to his girlfriend's New York hotel room.

Daisy came up beside him and slipped one of her hands into his back pocket. She raised one eyebrow as if to say, *I'm just getting started.* Ash grinned.

He was setting off on the best experience of his life. He had a feeling that by the time it was over, he'd be the kind of guy who could look at weird phallic art and nod knowingly.

NIGHTIE IN SHINING ARMOR

Myla almost wanted to thank her parents for leaving her under the watchful gaze of a manny. And not because they'd chosen the manny of all mannies, but because, while it was a given that she'd host a party with her parents away, messing with poor Danny had really gotten her creative juices flowing.

A "sexy PJ party" might sound trite, like the title of some gross Skinemax movie, but hosting the party outdoors, in broad daylight? That was *inspired*. She'd hired some of her favorite staffers from the Polo Lounge, and they'd arrived early that morning. She'd come up with a signature cocktail, the Sleepwalker—a mix of Gray Goose, pomegranate juice, and a twist of raspberry, poured with Sprite for a bit of fizz. All the hors d'oeuvres were foods in blankets—asparagus in puff pastry, figs and goat cheese tucked into prosciutto, and chunks of Australian lobster nestled into sourdough cups. On a giant inflatable movie screen under the awning on the far side of the pool house, she had last year's Victoria's Secret Fashion Show playing on a loop. Over-tall glamazons didn't bother her, even if she was an A-cup, but they'd definitely make some of the other female guests feel less perky.

She'd set up a pillow fight station near the pool and had all the lounge chairs covered with satiny sheets. Under a black canvas tent, her help had erected another inflatable movie screen, and right now a few dozen of her classmates were inside, kicking back and watching a screener of her mother's latest action film, *Cooked*, about a secret spy organization at the center of the Le Cordon Bleu cooking school in France.

But the pièce de résistance—or nonresistance, as it were—was Myla's La Perla black satin and lace teddy, worn beneath a flimsy Carine Gilson emerald silk robe that fell off her shoulder anytime she so much as flicked her delicate wrist. She'd maneuvered her long black tresses into truly sexy bedhead, and wore only the slightest hint of makeup. She knew she stood out among the other girls here, most of whom wore skimpy tanks over boy shorts and had their hair tamed into too-perfect pigtails. Talia, Fortune, and Billie, for example, looked like they were headed to a slumber party at the Barbie Dream House after spending too much time inside a Victoria's Secret Pink store. In their high-heeled marabou slippers, they wobbled across the green lawn like Ajani and Indigo when they'd first learned to walk. Myla made a mental note to teach her little sisters how to walk in heels when then they got older. Normally, she'd have helped her friends choose more wisely, but she was still carrying around some residual bitterness. When she'd needed them to take her mind off Ash, they'd been too busy following Amelie around.

Myla grabbed a Sleepwalker off a passing tray and sipped greedily, her eyes searching the pool area for Danny. The party was all for him, anyway. Where was he? And what would she do if he didn't show up? He'd promised to more or less stay out of their way, but Myla had made sure all week that he'd had a hard time avoiding her. When she'd needed a ride home from Barneys, she hadn't called the car service her parents used when their driver Charlie was unavailable. She'd called Danny. When she'd had "trouble" opening a jar of raspberry jam, she'd sauntered through the house until she'd found him in the library and asked him to open it for her. And when she'd purposely interrupted the wireless signal to her computer, she'd called Danny, who was out with his friends, to come fix it for her.

He definitely didn't seem to mind, even though she could tell he was trying to keep a professional distance. Really, it was worse than just professionalism. He barely seemed affected by her at all. Actually, if she was being honest with herself, she was starting to wonder if Danny would be more into Tucker Swanson in his plaid pajama bottoms than Myla in her complicated lingerie. She hoped that wasn't the case. She hoped the snaps on today's outfit were just enough to make *him* snap. If not, she'd probably keep trying anyway, at least until she was sure he didn't play for the other team. Danny was a challenge. And Myla loved a challenge.

She decided to stop looking for him. Like her mom always said, "A watched pot never boils," even though Lailah Barton had never boiled anything in her life.

Myla paced back from the bar to the pool. BHH's male

contingent swam in loose pajama bottoms and no shirts, trying to see through the girls' lightweight tank tops. She noticed Miles Abelson wearing a pair of way-too-big pinstriped satin man-jamas, sitting poolside and chatting up a very drunk cheerleader in a short Hello Kitty nightgown. How had *he* gotten into her party? Myla sniffed and walked on. She wouldn't get any satisfaction from throwing him out today. The party's sole measure of success would be whether Danny showed up or not.

Myla was about to sit down and put her feet in the water when Lewis Buford sidled up next to her, wearing a short, sapphire silk kimono opened to the waist over a tiny pair of briefs. Trailing him was Barnsley Toole, in a tight faux-tuxedo T-shirt with a pair of black boxers. Myla had invited Barnsley to keep Jojo away from the party— during her first week in L.A., Jojo had had too much to drink and puked on Barnsley, and the moment had been captured by his reality show, *Barnsley's Babes*—but she had hoped to avoid Lewis and his entourage. Especially when so much of Lewis's manscaping was on display.

"Great party, Myla," Lewis said, sliding an arm around her. Myla involuntarily winced at the memory of the last time Lewis had touched her. He was Ash's mortal enemy, and she'd kissed him at a party near the start of the school year to make Ash jealous. The plan had gone perfectly— too perfectly. Ash had caught them and wanted nothing to do with Myla afterward. "I tweeted it. And this got me 127 new followers in, like, two seconds." He thumbed over his iPhone display, showing her a photo he'd just posted of Myla from the back.

"Do you ever find yourself totally *un*amusing? Because

sometimes, I don't even know how *you* can be friends with you," Myla said, sliding out from under Lewis's arm. He was too busy snapping her photo to register the insult.

Barnsley sidled up, camera crew–free. Word was, his MTV show had been canceled because focus groups said that he made them lose their appetites for the product-placed snacks and beverages. He wore silk pajamas, probably in an attempt to emulate his hero, Hef. The start of a scalp sunburn was showing through his white-blond, gel-slicked hair. "So where's your sister BarfBarf?"

"You're the only one who still finds that funny, you know," Myla said. She had plenty of anti-Jojo sentiment of her own, but the whole BarfBarf thing had stopped being funny by day two. "Now, if you two don't mind, I have to go."

Barnsley and Lewis formed a wall in front of her, not letting her pass. The smell of Armani Code overwhelmed her nostrils. "Come on, Myla," Lewis said, snapping more photos on his phone. "I told B here I wouldn't leave until I got you to forgive me. Gilmour's long gone. Isn't it about time you figured out we're meant to be?"

"I'm meant to be a masochist?" Myla tried to sidestep Lewis again, but she didn't have much room. A move too far back would send her into the pool, and a move forward meant he'd probably touch her again. She wasn't scared. Lewis and Barnsley were harmless. But their International Male catalog poses were getting seriously annoying. "Sorry, I'd be happier in a convent."

Someone tapped Lewis on the shoulder. Lewis stepped aside and turned to see Danny. His black hair was uncombed and casual today, and his basic jeans and tee looked so masculine in the sea of silk that Lewis tightened his robe. "Guys, sorry to interrupt, but I need to talk to Myla for a second."

"Who the hell are you?" Barnsley said, stepping in front of Lewis like a discount bodyguard.

"A friend of her father's." Danny's voice was deep and threatening. "So if you don't back off, well, let's just say you'll be answering to Barkley Everhart."

Lewis backed away, with Barnsley slithering after him. Lewis did most of his thinking with an organ far from his brain, but even his horndog tendencies couldn't overpower the part of him that feared being rendered socially and professionally irrelevant.

"Oh, and one more thing," Danny said, jogging up to catch Lewis. Lewis stared, dumbfounded, as Danny plucked his iPhone from his hand, tapped into the photos, and deleted each shot of Myla. "Thanks, man." He handed it back, clapping Lewis hard on his well-moisturized shoulder.

Danny turned back toward Myla, a grin on his face. She instinctively untied her robe, opened it enough so Danny could see the lace cutouts of her teddy, and recinched it around her waist. Danny's eyes stayed focused on hers the whole time. Myla's gaydar needle moved farther away from STRAIGHT.

"Oh, am I supposed to thank you now?" Myla cooed, patting his muscular arm. "Or should I wait until I get my Manny Comment Card? *Danny the Manny saved me. I will definitely stay here again!*" She fluttered her eyelashes a little, half as part of the joke and half to see how he'd react.

Danny rolled his eyes and shook his head. He took her by the arm and pulled her into the cabana. His grip was firm. *He must be straight,* Myla thought, as her insides did a victory dance. Finally! After a week of stony resistance, Danny had given in. He was going to try to kiss her. Myla tilted her chin up, ready to welcome and then spurn his advances. T minus ten, nine, eight . . .

"So I saved you?" Danny said instead, his own grin irresistible. He'd thrown off her countdown. One of his incisors was ever-so-slightly pointy, a perfect imperfection. "That's a riot. If I've ever met a girl who didn't need saving, it's you."

He took a couple steps back. She closed the gap between them again. "I don't know what you're talking about," she offered innocently.

"Of course you don't," Danny said. "Just like you wouldn't know anything about how the cap on that jam was already loose, or that your router was switched to OFF. Someone like you would *never* plan those things so they could get me to come help."

He walked over to one of the white linen cabinets, opened it, and began pulling out towels as Myla watched, dumbfounded. "You're crazy," she finally said, feeling caught off guard. She knew she wasn't that transparent. So, was Danny just that perceptive? "I should tell my father that you're accusing me of trying to get your attention, when I really need help."

Danny raised an eyebrow. The minor movement was so sexy, Myla had to clamp her lips shut. She'd definitely been single for too long.

"You didn't have to go to all this trouble to make me

look," Danny finally said. "I would have looked anyway."
He walked over with a stack of towels under one arm.

He stepped in close, and she could feel his breath
on her cheek. She could sense the warmth of his body
through her lacy negligee. Danny turned her arms so her
palms were up, and she bit her lip as his slightly rough
hands brushed the velvety skin of her wrist. She inhaled
and closed her eyes, anticipating the feel of his lips.

And then there was something on her wrists. Weighty.
Soft. Egyptian cotton? Myla's eyes shot open. Danny had
dropped a pile of towels into her waiting arms.

"What the hell?" Myla said, glaring at Danny's back as
he walked toward the door.

"For the pool. I think your guests need towels," Danny
said with a chuckle. "Just looking out for you."

Myla, who ruled at jaw-dropping moves, needed to
pick up her own jaw from the floor.

But her hands were full.

NORMALLY, I'M NOT NORMAL

A melie pushed a blob of blueberry compote–topped pancake around on her plate. The act of lifting the fork to her mouth seemed too strenuous. Johnny Cash's playful baritone mocked her misery as "Ring of Fire" played beneath the clatter of silverware and chatter of diners at Tart, a Southern-inspired hot spot across from the Grove. Amelie wasn't normally one for brunch on a Saturday night, but she could definitely use some Southern comfort. Alcoholic or not.

She and her mom, Helen, sat at their usual corner table, just inside the doorway. It kept the diners who saw Amelie and interrupted their meal down to a minimum. It was also warm and cozy, tucked into worn denim booths along the barnlike wall.

Helen had been playing along with Amelie's silent moping. Her mom was savoring each individual strawberry on her fruit plate, poking them daintily with her fork and lightly swirling them in Tart's signature honey-yogurt dipping sauce. They'd spent the evening shopping at the Grove. Helen, who normally dressed up for everything, was wearing an outfit assembled for maximum trying-on efficiency: beige C&C California tank over her favorite black yoga pants, topped with a cream Splendid wrap sweater. But even dressed down, Helen, with her expertly dyed hair and tended-to face (slight laugh lines and crow's feet were deemed okay, while wrinkles anywhere else were verboten and vanquished), looked like a cover model for one of those magazines for women over forty. Amelie, on the other hand, looked like she'd just rolled out of bed, which she pretty much had. She had on her rattiest Seven jeans under an oversize hooded Kidz Network promotional sweatshirt. Her hair was in a low ponytail, and she hadn't even moisturized. It occurred to her that FORMER CHILD STAR ROBS CONVENIENCE STORE would be a convincing caption for her outfit.

Amelie had been excited about this shopping trip two weeks ago, before she'd started at BHH. The plan had been to fatten up her wardrobe with more of the high-fashion pieces favored by her classmates. During the time she'd hung out with Talia, Billie, and Fortune, who accessorized with more vigor than Tim Gunn on steroids, she'd felt like a ragamuffin anytime she wasn't in costume. When she wasn't dressed for a scene, Amelie favored comfy jeans, tees, and sandals that were easy to put on when she woke up at four in the morning for *Fairy Princess*'s five a.m. call times. Now that she'd decided to be a full-time student, back-to-school shopping merited at least ten normal-girl points. But having no socializing options besides the mall with your mom immediately subtracted them from the tally.

She had bought hardly anything; she had less of an appetite for shopping than she did for these pancakes.

If she were truly a normal girl, she'd be wallowing in her teen angst with an iPod, the new Paramore album, and a novel about some girl who felt even more unpopular than she did. It was at times like this that Amelie lamented L.A.'s lack of rainy days. At least then you had an excuse to be in a shit mood.

"So, what is it?" Helen finally said, smiling at the waiter who topped off her chicory coffee. "I'm not clueless. I can see something is bothering you."

Great, Amelie thought. SPILLING YOUR GUTS TO YOUR MOM BECAUSE YOU HAVE NO FRIENDS: −10 NORMAL-GIRL POINTS. She shrugged. "High school just isn't what I thought it would be," she finally said, making indents in her pancake with the tines of her fork. She finally took a bite of the now-cold pancakes, just to avoid having to say any more.

"What is it?" Her mom looked almost pleased, as if after all those years of dragging Amelie to auditions and shoots, she was enjoying playing the part of everyday mom. "Are the classes too easy? Too hard?"

Amelie laughed miserably. "It's not about the classes at all. It's just . . . everything else. Like, right now, there's some huge party at Myla Everhart's house. And I wasn't even invited," she said. She had half wanted to stay home tonight, scouring the web for paparazzi photos from the party to see if Jake was there. "And Myla's sister, Jojo Milford, got the lead in the school play. I'm a *supporting cast member,* Mom. And the play is *Jane Eyre.*" She was whining. But whining felt good. She hadn't said a word to her mom about the play because she felt so ashamed, but now she was just plain annoyed.

Amelie expected Helen to fly into an indignant rage, jumping from the table and taking her cell outside so she could call BHH's principal and loudly give him a piece of her mind. When Kidz Network had wanted to rename Amelie's show *Fairy Princess and Friends,* bringing in a whole crop of new fresh-faced child stars, Helen had gone into momager mode and secured a contract that allowed guest stars but no regularly scheduled spotlight-sharing. But now, her mom just laughed.

"I really did not prepare you for the miseries of high school at all, did I?" Helen said. She rested her chin on her hand and gazed at Amelie lovingly, a rarity for a no-nonsense woman who had hired her daughter a financial adviser for her eleventh birthday. Helen wasn't normally given to mushy mother-daughter moments, but every so often the urge struck. "You really have no idea, do you?"

"How am I supposed to just be *normal* if it's miserable?" Amelie protested, irritated that her mom wasn't taking this seriously.

"Don't you get it? Miserable *is* normal," Helen scoffed. "Did you really think you'd start school and be instantly popular? Invited to the best parties before you've even had a midterm?"

Amelie shrugged, ashamed to realize that this *was* what she had expected. "I guess."

"Just because you've been a star your whole life doesn't mean that your peers are going to treat you like one, too," Helen said. "In fact, it will probably be a little harder for you. But not being popular, not getting what you want, that *is* normal. Can I tell you a story?"

Amelie rolled her eyes. This was *so* not the Saturday

night she wanted. Now her mom was going to tell her
how she'd been cheerleader or prom queen or something,
but she had still been unhappy because that was part of
being a teenager. Poor little Miss Popularity.

"When I was a junior in high school, I had three
girlfriends who had always been more popular than me
through middle school and everything else. They even had
the *Charlie's Angels* haircuts. Junior year, they decided to
start including me," Helen said, surreptitiously stirring
her coffee. "They called me the brain of the group, and I
loved it. But eventually, I figured out they had this whole
social life that didn't include me: trips to the mall, parties, the whole thing. They were just using me for help
with their homework. So you know what I did?"

"No, but I know you'll tell me," Amelie said, mas-
saging her temples with her index fingers. She could
have been sleeping right now, even though it was barely
ten thirty. It was a side effect of early *Fairy Princess* call
times—she rose with the sun and practically went to bed
with it, too.

INABILITY TO STAY UP PAST MIDNIGHT
    −4 NORMAL-GIRL POINTS.

"I ditched them," Helen said. "I started my own
group, and by senior year I was just as popular, and I
still graduated valedictorian. I had been clinging to those
girls because it was the path of least resistance. But then
I figured out that I could do things my way."

Amelie considered this. Her mom was definitely not
the type to take high school lying down. Helen alpha-

betized everything, from canned goods to her handbags. Amelie, often content to laze around daydreaming or reading when she actually had free time, did not inherit that tame-your-life trait of her mom's. She didn't need to rule the school or even start her own clique. Rising to Myla Everhart's social standing seemed like too much work, and she'd been working most of her childhood. That level of popularity wasn't even on her high-school checklist. She mainly just wanted to date Jake.

"Let's just say, you wanted normal, and now you've got it," Helen said, signaling for the check. "But sometimes being normal means doing the work. Taking matters into your own hands." She excused herself to go to the ladies' room, leaving Amelie waiting at the table.

Amelie realized she had been waiting for her life to come to her—the lead in the play, friends, invites, Jake. But maybe she didn't have to wait around. She grabbed her Sidekick and carefully considered each key as she typed out a text. When she was finished, she slid the phone back into her pocket.

MAKING THE FIRST MOVE
   +20 NORMAL-GIRL POINTS

FANCY MEETING YOU HERE

Jojo was in her jammies, but she hadn't gotten dressed for the party. More like, she hadn't gotten dressed at all. Well, that wasn't true either. She'd slept in that morning, then showered, then gotten dressed, thinking she'd do a little shopping or go to a movie. Anything to escape Sergeant Myla in the midst of party preparations. But then she figured, screw it. It was her house, too. So if she wanted to lounge around in her comfy new pajamas— a Wonder Woman pajama-gram had arrived that week, a congratulatory gift from her dads for getting the lead in the play—she would do just that.

She was curled up in the softest loveseat in Barkley's library. Her original intent had been to read over her *Jane Eyre* lines again, so Amelie couldn't just spit them out for her, but she'd taken a break and was reading the latest *Scott Pilgrim* graphic novel. Her best friend from Sacramento, Willa, loved the books, and Jojo thought maybe if she caught up on them, Willa might warm up again. Willa was still mad at Jojo for lying to get out of a Sacramento visit and going to a beach party with Myla instead. After a series of funny and apologetic e-mails from Jojo, Willa had finally picked up the phone, but their conversation had been stilted and awkward.

A knock came at the closed door. Probably some drunk person looking for the bathroom. No one was supposed to be upstairs, but several people had already come teetering in. "It's down the hall," Jojo yelled as the door pushed open. Instead of a wobbly, intoxicated BHHer, Danny stood in the doorway.

"Hey, can I come in?" he asked, smiling. With his olive skin, thick hair, and dark eyes, he was a really good-looking guy. She could understand why Myla was trying to get a reaction from him, but that didn't make it okay. Danny seemed like a totally decent person. One who didn't deserve to be on the receiving end of Myla's mind games.

Jojo gestured to the maroon wingback chair next to the couch, and Danny flopped into it, looking tired. "Sanctuary," he sighed. He looked around, absorbing the ceiling-high, polished oak shelves filled to the brim with books. Barkley's book collection wasn't just for show; many of the shelves contained books piled haphazardly instead of standing in neat rows like props. He'd even turned one corner into a library for the kids' picture books, and dozens of Golden Book spines glimmered alongside copies of *Where the Wild Things Are,* an assortment of Richard Scarry picture books, and tons of other brightly colored tomes. "And books. This is amazing. I grew up by a library this big, but you had to share it with the whole town."

"I know, right?" Jojo laughed. The library was her favorite room in the house. She liked sharing it with someone who appreciated it. "How come you're not down by the pool, having fun? You really don't have to be minding us 24/7," she said. "I swear, I'm just reading up here. There are no boys hiding in the closet."

Danny smirked. "Wow, you're really scared of my authority, huh?" He picked up Barkley's copy of *The Fountainhead* from the coffee table and ran his finger up and down the pages. "Meanwhile, your sister is so unafraid of my reports to your dad that she's parading around only one-quarter dressed. It's like an electrolysis commercial down there. And it's nothing like the high-school parties I went to. I mean, when I even got invited."

At least she wasn't the only one who felt like a total outsider. In Sacramento, it was a big deal if a house party featured a keg and a bottle of watermelon Pucker. "Yeah, right," Jojo said. "Like you weren't totally popular back in . . ." She'd forgotten where he'd said he was from.

"Oak Lawn. Illinois," he finished for her. He seemed reflective for a moment, then shook his head. "Nah, I wasn't all that popular. It's the kind of town where everyone sticks around after high school, and I was sort of ready to get out of high school by about my second day. When you're a science nerd, you don't get invited to the cool keggers."

"You don't seem like a science nerd," Jojo said, realizing her faux pas immediately. What was wrong with someone being a science nerd? Jake was smart, and she had a massive crush on him. "I mean . . . ," she fumbled to correct herself.

Danny waved her off, and Jojo's blush subsided. "And you don't seem like a girl who chills out reading comics when there's a big party going on downstairs," he said, pointing at her copy of *Scott Pilgrim*. "We're just ahead of our time, Jojo."

She laughed again, wondering if this was what it was like to have a big brother. Until Barbar came along, Jojo had grown up an only child and always longed for some company. Unfortunately, Myla excelled at the rivalry part but not the sibling part. And the other kids were great, but still too little for this kind of conversation. "So that's what it is," she said.

"Works for me," Danny smiled. He stood up. "I'll let you get back to your book. I should probably at least go keep watch from the confines of the guest house," he said. "It's getting to the part of the party when judgment becomes impaired."

Jojo giggled and waved goodbye as Danny left. Tucking her bare feet back underneath her, she flipped back to her page. She had just gotten to a scene where robots tried to attack Scott's party when she heard footsteps in the hall again. "Did you forget something?" she called out, figuring it was Danny again. She hoped it wasn't Talia or another member of Myla's Deathly Dirty-Look Squad. She couldn't imagine what they'd need in the library anyway.

The steps stopped, and Jojo went back to her book. Probably just a bathroom-seeking partygoer for real this time.

"You know those things they say are too good to be true? A girl in a Wonder Woman tank top reading *Scott Pilgrim* is definitely one of those things."

Jojo's heart sprang to hyperactive life in her chest as she looked up to see Jake, clad in a *Star Trek* shirt, pajama bottoms, and slippers, standing in the doorway. She hadn't even heard the door open. Dark ringlets of hair sprung up around his face, and Jojo wondered if that was how he really looked when he woke up.

She smiled, blushing a little for imagining Jake in his bed. She closed her book. "And in the too-weird-to-be-true category, what's a nice guy like you doing at one of Myla Everhart's parties? And walking around on the restricted floor besides?" Jojo scooted over, patting the seat next to her. "You're not supposed to be up here, but I'll make an exception."

Jake blushed, rubbing his shoulder beneath the collar of his Enterprise T-shirt. Jojo tried not to stare at the outline of his bicep through the thin cotton. "Danny—your, um, house sitter—was cool. He told me I could find you up here," he said. "He seems like a pretty nice guy."

He's the best guy, besides you, Jojo thought, grateful to Danny for somehow realizing he was directing the guy she liked right to her. Jojo felt her heart thudding at the idea that Jake had wanted to see her enough to ask where to find her.

"And as for how I got to the party in the first place," Jake continued, "Tucker Swanson and Geoff Schaffer invited me and Miles. I don't know what they see in us, exactly."

Instantly, Jojo wondered if Tucker had said anything about her to Jake. During Myla's makeover scheme, she'd set Jojo up with Tucker, and they'd dated for all of two weeks before Jojo realized she couldn't date a guy whose idea of a great date was watching surfing videos on YouTube. She dreaded the idea of Tucker saying something about her to Jake—or worse yet, forgetting they had even dated.

"Oh. Tucker and I sort of dated, but I think you know that," Jojo said, unable to look Jake in the eye. Tucker usually chased bimbos, and Jojo almost felt like a bimbo by association. "I didn't exactly choose that relationship. Kind of lame of me, huh?"

"I sort of wondered. But Tucker's a decent guy. Just not the kind of guy who appreciates a girl who reads comics," Jake said easily. Jojo watched as he shifted next to her the sofa, clearly not knowing what to do with his hands. He folded them on his lap, then played with the bottom of his T-shirt, and finally picked up a book off the end table and flipped it open. When he saw it was Barkley's copy of *Love for Sale: A World History of Prostitution,* which was being adapted into an intersecting storyline ensemble cast movie with Barkley and Lailah as a Pilgrim pimp and madam, he almost threw it back onto the table. "But speaking of things you didn't choose, Kady liked to pick my outfits for me when we were going out. I don't know if she really liked me or just had always wanted a Jewish Ken doll."

Jojo laughed as an image of a plastic Jake replica tucked inside a windowed Barbie box immediately popped into her head. Jake smiled shyly, like a guy not used to a girl who would laugh at his jokes. "I can top you for embarrassing romantic choices," she said, wanting to make him feel better. "And I'm not even talking about the time Barnsley Toole tried to kiss me and I puked on him."

"That wasn't a romantic choice. That was . . . I don't even know what that was," Jake said with a smirk, his eyes glimmering as he teased her.

"Whatever. Do you want the story or not?" Jake nodded with mock overeagerness. Jojo giggled and lightly kicked his shin. Her bare foot now dangled off the couch, still touching Jake's exposed ankle. He didn't move away. "Okay, so at my old school, they do a carnation sale around Valentine's Day. And last year, I'd worked up the nerve to send Justin Klatch, you know, the most popular guy at my school and my forever crush, three yellow carnations. The plan was, he'd acknowledge them in some way and I'd ask him out. So, anyway, I got so nervous filling out the forms for the flowers that I didn't notice I wrote my own name in both the TO and the FROM sections. Valentine's Day rolls around, and who's delivering flowers to my homeroom but Justin Klatch? Head of the student council and all that. So, I see him coming toward me with a big smile and three yellow carnations, and I thought they were from him, and the fact that he was giving me the same thing I gave him meant we were soul mates. But then he gets to my desk and read the note, like this: 'To Jojo Milford. From . . . Jojo Milford.' Everyone heard, and he looked at me like I was a little crazy. But he really is a nice guy, so he covered for me and said, 'Maybe it's a secret admirer.' But I could tell he thought I sent them to myself and wasn't even smart enough to not write my name twice."

She bit her lip, trying to keep from babbling further. She didn't want Jake to think she still had feelings for Justin. She'd just used the story because Jake knew who Justin was. When he'd needed help researching his all-American guy role for *Class Angel*, Jojo had come up with the mantra *What would Justin Klatch do?* because her former crush was kind of the embodiment of Jake's part. But she liked Jake way more than she'd ever liked Justin. The fact that she and Jake had exchanged more than four words didn't hurt, either.

Jake scooted closer and leaned in. Only a few inches separated them. "That sort of reminds me of the time Amelie Adams got me to take her to this party, and I thought it was a date and brought her flowers. But she'd told her mom we were studying, so I had to lie and say I randomly bought the flowers for charity. Her mom was thoroughly weirded out by me, I think," Jake said, blushing.

The tingling sensation in Jojo's body at Jake's proximity gave way to pin prickles of jealousy at the mention of Amelie's name. She knew that Jake had had a crush on Amelie before. And there was that whole Amelie-crying-on-Jake's-shoulder thing from the other week, and Amelie being a massive pain in Jojo's . . . actress. But Jake was here with *her* right now, not Amelie. Besides, he might have found Amelie pretty or whatever, but that was more in a celebrity infatuation way, right? It wasn't like she was a real person.

He was so adorable, looking at her expectantly, waiting for a response to his story. Maybe there was only one way to find out how he felt about her. When she'd screwed up Justin Klatch's carnations, she'd been relieved. She never had to find out if he'd reject her or not. But here, now, with Jake, she had a good feeling that rejection wasn't on the menu.

She let her book slide off her lap and leaned toward him. "So the theme here is, we both suck at this stuff?" she joked, and just as Jake was about to say something, she let her lips find his.

If Jojo's body could make game show noises, Jake would have set off the prize-winning *Ding! Ding! Ding!* This was *so* not like kissing Tucker, who had powered through their kisses. This felt right. She ran her hands up the biceps she'd been admiring a minute ago. Jake's arms wrapped around her back and he pulled her in tightly. A sensation of being perfectly satisfied and wanting more flowed from Jojo's lips to the rest of her body. She almost wanted to thank Myla for throwing this ridiculous party.

Between them, Jake's cell started to vibrate with an incoming text, and they sprang apart. She felt like they'd been caught, and part of her didn't care.

Jake stared dumbly at the screen of his LG evV. One new text from an unknown number. It figured. No one ever called him, and now he got a text right in the middle of the most enjoyable, amazing moment of possibly his whole life. Had he really just been kissing Jojo? His tingling lips and swiftly beating heart said yes. He smiled down at her. "Just a sec," he said, standing up and flipping open the phone, his back to her as he leaned against the arm of the couch. He needed privacy in case it was some dorky message from Miles.

But it wasn't from Miles. It was from . . . Amelie? I could really use some help in math, and you're the only tutor I trust. Can we get together this week? ;-) He quickly shut the phone and spun around. Jojo was right behind him, a sweet smile on her lips. Her eyes shone like purple gemstones in the dim light, and for a second, Jake considered taking her in his arms and resuming the kiss. But Amelie's message had stirred up all the old feelings he'd had—from being her tutor and from the kiss they'd shared on the set of *Class Angel.* Her text made it sound like she wanted to go on a date. It was an offer he couldn't refuse.

"Everything okay?" Jojo said brightly, shyly closing the gap between them. The smell of her chocolatey body-wash filled his nostrils, and Jake had to bite his lip to keep from kissing her again. He abruptly backed away, putting two feet of distance between them as he knocked into the closed door. He turned the knob, trying to ignore the disappointed look on Jojo's face. "I forgot, I'm, um, I was supposed to grab Miles a Vitamin Water. He's probably still waiting. See you, Jojo."

Jake skidded in his slippered feet down the hallway. *Vitamin Water?* What the hell kind of stupid excuse was that? The truth was, he could barely think straight. The kiss with Jojo had been incredible and unexpected. But a date offer from Amelie was equally unexpected and just as incredible. His head was a mess of conflicts. He still had a crush on Amelie. Whom he might now have a shot with, since she was going to BHH and still talking to him, even though she could have any guy in school. He couldn't start something with Jojo until he found out what the deal was with Amelie, right?

"Damn," he muttered, tugging at his curly hair nervously as he bounded down the stairs and directly into a throng of people clustered outside the kitchen. "What's wrong with you, Jake?" he muttered to himself.

What's wrong with you, Jojo? Jojo had curled into a ball on the couch, suddenly feeling clammy all over. Was it her breath? Her technique? Did Jake think she was a crazy slut? She had to have a massive defect of some sort if a guy would run away from her when she was (A) making the first move and (B) wearing her cutest pajamas.

She suddenly had the overwhelming urge to change out of her Wonder Woman duds. Because at the moment, she wasn't feeling all that wonderful.

HYPOTENUSE OF A LOVE TRIANGLE

L ater that week Amelie sat at Cafe Audrey, her favorite restaurant in Hollywood, waiting for Jake. In a
tribute to Audrey Hepburn, the whole place was deco-
rated in black-and-white, with glamorous yet cozy furniture forming all kinds of private nooks beneath a wall
tiled in framed photographs of Hepburn. Tucked into a
small storefront on Las Palmas, away from the touristy
throngs on Hollywood Boulevard, it felt like a place in
Paris. Amelie had chosen it for the subtle romantic feel—
red walls and candlelight didn't exactly scream *study session*. This felt more personal, and conducive to getting a
burgeoning relationship off the ground.

Amelie neatly placed her geometry textbook in the
middle of the table and arranged her cappuccino so it was
perfectly diagonal from the empty mug that stood waiting
for Jake's arrival. As she smoothed her posy-print Diane
von Furstenberg skirt over her recently exfoliated legs, she
was surprised by how nervous she felt. But then, this was
the first time she and Jake would spend alone since she'd
discovered how much she liked him. They'd kissed for
a scene of Amelie's own making in *Class Angel*, but that

was in front of a dozen onlookers, and Jake had taken off with Kady afterward. They had gotten a few minutes of alone time one night after filming at BHH, but Kady had interrupted what should have been a magic moment. And this week, Amelie hadn't run into Jake once. She'd hoped to see him outside, playing Ultimate Frisbee with his guy friends again. But rehearsals had run late, and even though Amelie was only a supporting cast member, Mr. Potter required everyone in the play to stick around until he said they could leave. Tonight had to be perfect.

The door chimes tinkled and Amelie looked up to see Jake standing in the doorway. She took a sip of her cappuccino, which only sped up her already-thrumming heartbeat. He'd stopped wearing the designer gear Kady had encouraged him to buy, and was somehow looking cuter than ever in standard-issue Levi's and a tight-but-not-too-tight vintage *Star Wars* tee. Clutching his tutoring binder and geometry workbook, he reminded her of Cary Grant playing the nerdy but adorable paleontologist in that old Hepburn movie—Katharine, not Audrey—*Bringing Up Baby.*

"Hey, Amelie, sorry I'm late," he said, sitting down next to her on the polka-dotted banquette that ran along the wall. "I had to park the Corolla someplace safe. And by safe, I mean somewhere it wouldn't have its feelings hurt by all the people laughing at it."

Amelie giggled. She was relieved Jake had gone back to driving his powder blue Toyota and making self-deprecating comments about it. During the height of his movie stardom, Jake had leased an Escalade, the overcompensating car of choice for guys like Hunter Sparks, Amelie's former star crush, whose ego was as big as his bank balance. "They're just jealous," Amelie said. "They don't make cars like that anymore."

Jake laughed, cracking open his workbook and sliding closer to Amelie on the bench. "So, are things going better for you than they were a couple weeks ago?" Amelie blushed, realizing they hadn't spoken much since the day she'd sniffled on his shoulder, right after the *Jane Eyre* auditions. But there was a sweetness in his hazel eyes that made Amelie melt. She didn't know what she'd been nervous about. Jake was so easy to talk to. He'd be the kind of boyfriend who would always remember to ask about your day. "You seemed pretty let down in the courtyard that day."

She shrugged casually. "Yeah, definitely. I don't know what came over me," she lied. She wanted to keep their outing light and fun. "It's so egotistical of me, but it was just a huge adjustment to have to audition for something. And then when that Jojo girl got picked for Jane Eyre, it was a big blow."

Jake raised an eyebrow. "Oh, Jojo Milford?" He nodded. "She's really nice. It's cool you guys are in the play together. Anyway, I'm glad it's going better for you. Do you have Miss Klusendorf for geometry?"

Amelie peered at Jake, wondering why he was so hasty to change the subject. Not like she wanted to talk about the play, anyway. And she definitely didn't want to talk about Jojo. She knew Jake and Jojo were friendly, but once Amelie and Jake were a couple, she'd make sure that didn't last. "Oh my God, yes. Miss K is so weird," she said, grabbing Jake's forearm as she spoke. It felt so natural to touch him that she didn't even realize she'd done it. "She never looks at the class. She rolls her eyes up like she's reading off the ceiling."

"I know. It's the weirdest thing, right?" Jake said, his own eyes directed ceiling-ward, in a Klusendorfian way. "It's very distracting."

Distracting was right. Amelie's eyes roved over Jake's face. His lips were so perfectly kissable. She *knew* they were, firsthand. Just as Jake launched into an impersonation of Miss K talking about the hypotenuse of a triangle, Amelie scooted closer and kissed him.

She applied feather-light pressure at first, and Jake's lips tentatively met her own. She clutched his side, pulling him closer to her, and he agreeably gave in to the embrace, his fingers dancing softly over her hair. Her entire scalp tingled, and as the kiss grew deeper, her entire body felt as melty as the chocolate lava cake in the patisserie case. This was better than their kiss for *Class Angel.* This was real. And it made every thought in her mind, from worries about school to jealousy over Jojo, dissipate.

KISSING THE GUY YOU LIKE, FINALLY!
   +100 NORMAL-GIRL POINTS

Until Jake yanked himself away from her with all the subtlety of a Dolce & Gabbana leopard-print miniskirt. "I just remembered, I parked in a tow zone." He exhaled a long breath of air. The romantic little bistro turned into a cold, dark cave. He grabbed his books and swept out the door, the tinkling bells sounding like cruel laughter in Amelie's ears.

Out on the street, Jake fought to regain his breath, thinking, *Holy shit. First Jojo, now Amelie?* He'd thought his short-lived relationship with Kady Parker would be the most bizarre girl-related thing to ever happen to him, but today had proved him wrong. Two girls—make that two girls he actually *liked*—both apparently wanted him. And they were in the school's play together. An image of Jojo and Amelie wrestling popped unbidden into his mind. As much as he knew it was pervy to admit, the idea was positively amazing. But also wrong. Right?

He looked at his reflection in a store window, just to make sure he still looked like Jake Porter-Goldsmith. Yup. It was him, lame *Star Wars* shirt and all. An odd, hollow chuckle escaped his body. He'd been wearing a *Star Trek* shirt when Jojo had kissed him, and now he was in a *Star Wars* one. And choosing between Amelie and Jojo was like a geek's worst nightmare: trying to choose between *Star Wars* and *Star Trek*.

"Oh man," he said, falling over his feet to get to his car. "What are you going to do, dude?" He was talking to himself again, and even a pants-less homeless guy gave him a weird look.

Back in the café, Amelie slammed her geometry book shut with a loud *slap,* prompting a girl reading Oprah's latest Book Club pick to give her a dirty look. So much for high school. Was she just so defective she couldn't make *anything* go her way? She'd really thought all she needed for a normal teenage existence was to get to high school, and everything would fall into place.

But the only things falling were her hopes.

ALL BETS ARE OFF

"Where the hell are we?" Myla said, impressed with how unimpressed her face appeared in the rearview mirror. She'd been riding in the front seat next to Danny for what felt like hours. Now they were driving down some old-timey street that looked like it should be named Back in My Day Avenue.

"I told you—Monrovia," Danny said. "You act like I'm taking you to the end of the Earth or something. Do you see signs of the apocalypse out there?"

Myla meaningfully looked at a woman in a lumpy ribbed turtleneck and mom jeans that barely touched the top of her bright white sneakers. She was entering a place unironically called Scoops Soda Fountain. "I think I do," she said.

Danny glanced at her from behind the wheel. He hadn't shaved today and looked sexier than ever, if that was possible. His thick, dark hair was loose and unstyled, and it whipped back in the breeze coming through the driver's-side window, where he rested his forearm, a work of lean, muscular art. "You didn't have to come, you know." He smiled at her, his eyes hidden by his Ray-Bans.

The thing was, she *did* have to come. Born and bred a Westsider, Myla tried to make trips east only if she was going by plane and not stopping anywhere between L.A. and New York. But when Danny had invited her to accompany him on an errand for her dad, Myla had jumped at the chance. Well, jumped internally. To Danny, she acted like she was coming along out of the helpful goodness of her heart. Even if it turned out they were picking something up for her annoying soon-to-be new sibling—not to be confused with Jojo, her annoying not-so-new-anymore sibling—she would not get upset.

Since their interaction in the pool house, Danny had been keeping his distance. But she had a plan—she was going to kiss this guy somehow. She wouldn't rest until it happened. She knew there were probably some deep-seated issues at the heart of this. But everyone had issues. At least Myla's were interesting.

They turned onto Myrtle Avenue, and Myla wrinkled her nose at a shop window filled with creepy, lifelike china dolls. Did people seriously live here? Danny parked outside a coffee shop, next to a huge film equipment truck.

"Cool, this is it," Danny said. "Your dad's new movie is shooting on location here. I just have to run in and give something to the director." Barkley's movie, *The Final Ordinance*, was a small-town political thriller. He played a coffee shop owner with a violent past who unearthed the truth about deadly corruption within the village board. "I'll be right back."

She watched him hop out of the car and head into Monrovia Coffee Company. Through the window, she could see guys on the crew clap him on the back happily.

Danny threw back his head and laughed at something someone said. He leaned on the counter, looking like he belonged there. She could almost imagine him in '50s clothes, a white T-shirt hugging his muscles as he flicked a comb through his hair. He exchanged some words with the director, flashing a toothpaste-commercial smile. He was completely in his element.

It wasn't her usual mode of attack, but maybe she had to be nicer. Maybe Danny *liked* this kind of stuff. He was from the Midwest, after all. And Myla pictured the Midwest as an unending landscape of flat, wheat-colored land interspersed with stores selling creepy dolls, ceramic knickknacks, and deep-fried food. Sort of like this place.

Danny was leaving the shop just as Myla was trying to imagine herself at a Walmart, which would *undoubtedly* mean the end of the world. She couldn't picture it without seeing herself toting a flamethrower and wearing a badass pair of over-the-knee boots and a form-fitting military jumpsuit with shorts that hit the top of her thigh. She was walking from the flames of what once *was* a Walmart, looking like something out of a fashion spread titled "What to Wear for the Apocalypse."

"Okay, all done," Danny said, breaking into Myla's wild thoughts as he got back into the car. "Your dad had a book of the director's, and he offered to let me return it in person. The guy is a huge investor in solar technology, so it's really cool of your dad to get me some face time with him."

Myla smiled her most benign, pleasant smile, which was hard because she was thinking naughty things. Now Danny had come out of the burning superstore, glistening with sweat in a torn, flame-scorched shirt. "So, did you want to walk around town? See everything?"

Danny's expression turned horrified, as though she'd suggested they throw rocks at small children. "Are you kidding? I can't stay here much longer. I feel like I'm in a bad David Lynch movie."

Thank God, Myla thought, as imaginary apocalypse Danny went all marauder on her lips. "Oh, I thought you liked this kind of stuff," Myla said. "Midwest stuff."

"One," he ticked it off on his finger, "I left the Midwest. Two, the south side of Chicago where I grew up is hardly Anytown, Middle America." Danny shook his head as he threw the car in reverse. "You just don't know me at all, do you, Myla?" His tone was light and joking, so much so that Myla found herself irritated by how casual he was being. Normally, guys were terrified to say anything that might offend her. But Danny didn't seem to care what she thought.

She didn't answer his question, instead focusing all her energy on paying no attention to him whatsoever. It was harder than it looked, because Danny was silent as he drove onto the 210. But it wasn't pouty, irritated silence like Ash's. It was more peaceful, like they simply didn't have to talk. And if anything drove Myla nuts, it was comfortable silence. He was supposed to be nervous.

They were barely out of the boondocks when he exited the freeway.

"Why are we getting off here?" Myla said. "I know you're new in town, but trust me, there's no need to take a scenic route way out here. Unless you like Target's architecture."

"You'll see," Danny said, his deep voice making Myla quiver. Or was that the pothole they'd just gone over?

They pulled into a parking lot between Santa Anita Race Track and Westfield Santa Anita Shopping Mall. "If you need to go shopping, let's go to the Beverly Center. I can't go in there or I'll be mobbed," Myla said, crossing her arms over her chest.

"You think you're that popular?" Danny smirked.

"Um, we're in Arcadia. Asian Central? And I'm, like, a famous Thai girl?" Myla shook her head. "You don't get it. We'll be invited to about twenty pig roasts if I go in there."

"Well, queen of all Asians, it doesn't matter. We're going to the racetrack." Danny got out of the car and came around to the passenger side, opening Myla's door. "Come on."

"Why would we go there? Isn't it basically a nursing home with horses?"

Danny was already walking ahead of her, making Myla race to keep up. *This. Is. Annoying,* her four-inch-high python booties seemed to tap out in Morse code. "You can come with me and find out, or you're perfectly welcome to stay in the car." Danny held out the keys.

Myla sneered, still following. The strap of her overstuffed Miu Miu shoulder bag dug into her shoulder. The stupid entrance had to be a half mile away. Why hadn't he at least valeted the car?

She caught up with Danny at the entry gates, where he slapped down ten dollars to get them in. Past the turnstiles, he stopped at a kiosk near a bubbling fountain and bought a program. He grabbed her hand, pulling her toward a low-slung barn beneath the high entryway to the racetrack itself.

"You should see the horses before you bet on one," he said. Myla was ready to make a snide remark, until she remembered he was holding her hand. Wrapped around her narrow palm, his hand was cool and dry. An elderly woman in a tailored suit jacket, khaki pants, and a wide-brimmed sun hat smiled benevolently as they passed her by, like she thought they were a couple.

They arrived at a stable, where the horses in the next race were on display for bettors. Danny dropped Myla's hand and leaned against the railing, admiring the horse in the pen marked 6. It was lean and jet black, with a hard look in its giant eyes.

"Who said I'm going to bet?" Myla sniped, her hand feeling empty and useless now that he'd dropped it. Who was seducing who here? "I like that one." She pointed to a silver horse with a cluster of white spots along its mid-back. It matched her dress.

"Number eight? Money Honey?" Danny consulted the program. "She hasn't even showed in any of her last four races. Odds are forty to one. It's a long shot."

Myla shrugged, knowing her paper-thin V-neck would fall off her shoulder as she did so. "It doesn't matter. Once I pick something, I stick with it," she said meaningfully, turning her jade eyes on him.

Danny sidled in closer, until Myla was backed up against the railing. She tilted her chin up, surprised at how nervous she felt. Besides her ill-fated staged kiss with Lewis Buford, she'd never kissed anyone but Ash. She reminded herself, *This is just for fun. Danny = Distraction.*

With an inch between them, Danny looked down at her, his lips a perfect red target. "Okay, then. It's your loss. Literally." He turned and started heading back up the path, toward the main concourse. Myla continued leaning against the railing, too stunned to move. "You coming? Gotta get your bet in now. Race is in five."

Begrudgingly, Myla followed him. Her moment of thinking the racetrack was an acceptable place to be had dissipated the second he put five feet between them. "You know, I have to get home," she said, trailing Danny as best she could in her towering shoes. The Louboutins were collecting dust with every step. If she stepped in horse crap, he was paying for them. "I have plans today."

Danny continued walking, and then they were inside the concourse. Lines of gamblers snaked behind touch-screen computers where bets could be made. Shorter lines had queued in front of windows staffed by crabby-looking old men who punched information into the very same computers as the ones on the floor. Danny led her to one of these lines, where they stood behind a fifty-something man wearing a black blazer with a lion's head fashioned out of rhinestones on the back. To go with the elegant daywear, he wore loose cream-colored linen pants and a ball cap advertising a heating and air-conditioning repair center called Hot Henry's. Stopping in line, Danny turned to face her. "And what plans might those be? Must be important since you didn't mention them at all when we left the house."

Flustered, Myla struggled to come up with something. What was with this guy? Did he remember everything?

"Let me guess," Danny said, eyeing a hipster parade

that had fallen into line behind them. The guys wore tightish seersucker suits, probably from a thrift shop, over vintage band T-shirts, and white or cream fedoras, not seeming to mind that the look was totally out of place in October. Myla heard one of them hiss "Barbar's daughter" to the others, and she shot him an annoyed look. "You suddenly remembered you have to go shopping with Fifi, Tata, and Butch?"

Myla tried and failed to suppress a laugh. "Fortune, Talia, and Billie. And what does it matter? Your sole purpose is to take care of me."

Danny raised an eyebrow, backing up as the line moved forward. "And let me guess: When you tell your boyfriend to take care of you, that means doing whatever you say." He turned his back on her as he got up to the window, and gave the bookie some bills, asking for something called a *trifecta box*. Myla studied his back, annoyed again. Who did he think he was? And how rude. "She wants to put five on number eight to win." He turned and held out a palm for her money. Myla sorted through her bag and found a crumpled twenty, which she slapped onto his palm. The bookie printed out two tickets and gave them to Danny.

He led her outside to the grandstand, which lined one side of the perfectly combed dirt racetrack. He gave Myla her betting slip and sat down on a bench near the track. She yanked the slip from his hand. "What do you know about me?" she finally answered. "First of all, I don't have a boyfriend anymore. Second of all, there's nothing wrong with a guy who tries to do what his girlfriend wants. Or who does what his manny charge wants. Especially if she happens to have very well-connected parents who could get him exiled from L.A. altogether."

Danny held up a hand in a *stop* gesture. "No need to get defensive. Just saying, if you think taking care of a woman means obeying her every command, well, you have no idea what it means to be taken care of." He grabbed her hand and led her to the railing. "Now, quiet. The race is starting."

A bell rang, and an announcer's voice came over the loudspeaker. "And they're off!"

Danny had let go of her hand but had placed his palm on her back. She could feel its warmth through her gauzy sweater. "Number eight is the one in red," he said, gesturing to a horse that had fallen far behind the others. "Nice pick. She doesn't look happy to be here."

Myla rolled her eyes, even though she had to admit he was right. Her horse seemed to be looking backwards at the starting gate, like it wondered how it had gotten out of its cubby and partway around the track.

"And here they come, spinning out of the turn . . . ," the announcer said. And that's when it happened. Money Honey shot to the side and charged forward, past a cluster of horses near the back. It caught up to the third-place horse, then surged once more, coming neck and neck with the number-seven horse and the number-six horse Danny had been eyeing, Mane Street.

"I'm going to win," she singsonged, pulling her betting slip out of her purse. Her iPhone screen said she had an unread text, and she quickly navigated to it. It was a forward from Talia with a paparazzi photo of Ash and Daisy kissing as they came out of some bar. Normally,

Myla would have found the nearest ladies' room and pored over the photo in secret, looking for signs of bad body language or irritated expressions. But she barely hazarded a glance at it before turning her attention back to the track, where Money Honey and Mane Street were neck and neck.

Mane Street tried to make a break for it, and Danny clutched his slip and hung over the railing, cheering him on. But just as they came up to the finish line, Money Honey pulled forward and galloped neatly and clearly ahead of Mane Street, finishing to a few loud *woo-hoo*s and a collective sigh of disappointment for Mane Street, who'd been the favorite.

"I won!" Myla shrieked, waving her slip in Danny's face. She beamed at him, loving the look of complete shock on his face. She was shocked, too. Even though she loved to win, she never entered contests—what would the girl who had everything even need? But suddenly, she understood the phrase "cheap thrill." The money didn't matter so much—her shoes were worth more than her betting slip—but something she'd chosen had been *right*. "You said my horse would suck."

Danny smirked, leaning in close to her. When his face was just inches away, he held up his betting slip in front of her eyes. "Actually, I thought you were on to something. I bet on Money Honey, too. And a whole lot more than you did," he said. He let loose with a cheer, high-fiving another lucky guy who was promising his whole group of friends a round of beers. "I owe this girl right here," Danny said, pointing to her. He suddenly lifted her up into his arms. "She knows how to pick a winner."

Myla had to agree that she did. Danny's lips were so close to hers. As he spun her around, she greedily ran her hand along his back. He loosened his grip ever so slightly, letting her slide down his body. Every part of them seemed to be touching, and they were face-to-face, his arms still around her waist, her feet still off the ground. She edged closer. So did he. Their lips were a millimeter apart.

And then he set her down on the ground and backed away, like she'd just vowed to turn the prizewinning horse into glue.

"I'm sorry," he said. "I can't do this. Your dad's been too good to me, and it's just too risky." He held up his ticket. "We better go cash these in." He turned and headed back onto the concourse. Myla followed him, still in a near-kiss stupor.

That's when it hit her. She wasn't angry in the least. A guy had rejected her, and somehow she didn't want to serve him humiliation in a public forum. She just wanted him even more. What was supposed to be boy-chasing for sport was suddenly so much more than a game.

She really . . . liked him.

Holy shit, Myla thought. *All bets are definitely off.*

FLAVORS OF LOVE

"Abelson, dawg! You rocked out there!" Tucker Swanson held his shortboard up over his head, pumping it up and down victoriously. A set of preteen girls rollerskating along Venice Beach's boardwalk slowed to an idle roll to admire his bronzed, cut arms and his defined lats. One of them almost ran over a Chihuahua that was smelling the leave-behind of a much larger dog.

Miles emerged from the surf, a loopy grin on his face, flashing Jake a thumbs-up. Somehow, despite never having surfed in his life and possessing a long, narrow frame that was the total opposite of the compact, muscular builds that suited the sport, Miles was a natural-born surfer. He'd popped up on the board on his first try and caught almost every subsequent wave that came his way. As he jogged back to join Jake, Tucker, and Geoff, Miles nearly tripped over the long beginner's board he'd rented from a shop on the boardwalk. He was better on water than on land.

"Dudes, that was way sweet," he said, his normally whiter-than-white skin tinged red from his overdose of unprotected sun exposure. "Did you guys see those chicks checking me out? Maybe it's the beard." He rubbed his few stray facial hairs and pointed in the general direction of a group of girls in Pasadena High School T-shirts who'd been giggling at Miles's exuberance on the board. His baggy swim trunks made him stick out like a sore thumb amid the Body Gloved surfers. And with his first-time surfing stance—arms out awkwardly to the sides, putting his skinniness on full display—he looked like a mostly naked, wet scarecrow being blown by the wind.

Or maybe Jake was just jealous. He hadn't managed to catch a single wave, even under Tucker's tutelage. And *he* was the one who'd spent the summer working out and becoming the new and improved Jake Porter-Goldsmith. *He* was the one who'd gotten a leading part in a movie. Apparently, his efforts didn't translate to the surfboard.

"Man, I had no idea, Abelson. I thought that one wave was a cruncher, and then you nailed it," Geoff said, slinging an arm over Miles's shoulder. "Dude, I'm so fuckin' hungry. But first, let's fire one up . . ." He pulled a miraculously dry joint from somewhere in the trunks he'd changed into and lit it, inhaling deeply as the smoke's sweet scent wafted up Jake's nostrils.

Tucker, who'd been studying the girls walking past with fierce determination, whipped his head around. "Yeah! Abelson, PG, you in?" He plucked the joint from Geoff's fingers, taking a long drag, holding in his breath so his face looked calm and round, like the jolly Buddha piggy bank Jake's dad kept on his desk at home.

Miles shrugged, accepting the joint as it was passed to him. Jake wasn't surprised. Miles wasn't necessarily a guy who allowed peer pressure to work on him, but he was unendingly curious. He'd tried the Pop Rocks and Coke thing back in second grade. And his parents, Woodstock hippies turned lawyers, were always reminding him that "a little maryjane is not a bad thing, as long as you don't get caught."

As Jake watched Miles inhale, his lips puckering and his nostrils closing in on his long nose, he decided to turn them down. He was curious, too, but he was already obsessing over his girl problems: He'd been memory-volleying between the two kisses earlier that week. Jojo had the kind of lips you could melt into. She was the kind of girl you could kiss for hours and it would seem like just minutes—as long as another girl didn't text you in the middle of it. And Amelie's whole presence just enveloped you. Kissing her made you feel like you were being carried away to a better world.

Needless to say, he was already a head case, and the last thing he needed was to add the possible paranoia side effect of pot. With his surely-frizzed-out-by-now Jewfro, he'd be an instant cliché of a neurotic Jew, like a young Woody Allen in board shorts.

Geoff and Tucker led the way to the boardwalk bike and pedestrian path, passing the joint between themselves and handing it back to Miles, who stuck next to Jake. "You okay, dude?" Miles said, pulling down his sunglasses and blinking under the light like a mole person. "This stuff's not such a big deal. Unless it doesn't work on me because my parents passed on some kind of immunity. Whoa, what if I researched *that* for the science fair?"

Jake grinned despite himself, looking at Miles's glassy eyes. "You know, I think it's working on you." Tucker led them past the boardwalk's reigning cat psychic to a fast-food and ice cream counter squished between a shop selling water bongs and rolling papers and a shop selling incense, belly button rings, and glazed ceramic figurines of dragons, unicorns, and other mystical creatures. Everything you needed for a day at the beach.

"Dudes, I'm so, like, *famined*," Tucker said, turning to them. "That's an SAT word, right, bros?"

Miles held up his index finger, as if testing the breeze. "You're close, Tuck," he said authoritatively. "The word you're looking for is *famished*, but *famine* is from the same family of Latin words for *hunger*."

Geoff slapped Tucker's forearm. "Holy shit, words have families. That's fuckin' crazy, man." He shook his head, gesturing at Miles. "These smart dudes are great to have around when we're stoned. It's all mind-expanding and shit."

Tucker nodded appreciatively, turning to check out the menu. "You know what else is mind-expanding? A bacon cheddar burger, chili fries, and a chocolate fudge milkshake. Or maybe strawberry."

As Tucker ordered, Jake surveyed the flavors of ice cream. He was hot after sitting on the beach, suffering through his girl problems, while the other guys had been in the water. The girl behind the counter grinned at him. She was a surfer chick with dark olive skin and short blond dreads, a blue bikini top, and eyes so pale blue they almost looked like diamonds. "I can help if you're having trouble deciding." Her smirk drew his eyes straight to her bee-stung, slightly chapped lips. She leaned sexily over the frosty case of ice cream, goose bumps popping up on her chest. Jake looked away, wondering what it was about having a girl—fine, two girls—after you that made every other girl seem to want you. That whole *When it rains, it pours* thing, he guessed.

"Just a scoop of Rocky Road," he said, feeling like his choice mirrored his life. "No, mint chocolate chip." No sooner had the girl started to scoop than Jake changed his mind back, and asked for Rocky Road again. The girl gave him a patient, sweet smile, and he felt awful. She thought he was trying to prolong his time at the counter. As soon as the scoop was in the cone, Jake threw down more money than was necessary and booked it to an empty table near the boardwalk, leaving her standing there, dazedly holding the ice cream scoop.

Tucker and Geoff caught up to him, followed by Miles, who'd gone the munchies route with a double cheese-burger, onion rings, and a shake.

Tucker set his tray down. "Dude, what's the problem? That chick dug you."

Miles, halfway through his cheeseburger, swallowed. "Jake can't handle any more girls," he said as Jake shot him the evil eye. These guys would think he was lame. "Jojo Milford *and* Amelie Adams both tried to jump his bones this week."

Miles's word choice and current lack of volume control caused two more cute girls to look Jake's way, maybe wondering if they should jump his bones, too. Jake shook his head vehemently at Tucker's offer of a high five. "It's not like that," he said. "I just kissed them both. And they're both cute, and sweet, and I can't choose."

"Jojo, huh?" Tucker said. "I went out with her." He

said this as if that made her a total catch, which she was. "And Amelie's hot as hell. Geoff spent all day Thursday trying to walk to class behind her. It's a good view." He elbowed Geoff, who shrugged sheepishly and continued to devour his Philly cheesesteak.

Wiping ketchup from his face, Miles lightly slapped the table. "I told him to make a pros-and-cons list, so he can choose," Miles said. "You know, Jojo is cute, funny, likes Neil Gaiman books. Pros. Related to Myla Everhart and has an intimidating father. Cons. Amelie Adams is a freaking movie star and a redhead. Pros. But she has weird little freshmen girls following her around all the time. Cons. Although, that could help *me* out." He grinned and swiped sand from the wispy hairs of his "beard."

Tucker waved his hands in front of his face, as if protecting himself from the very idea of a pros-and-cons list. "No, no, no, Jake. When two chicks want you, it's *all* pros." He pointed at Jake's melting Rocky Road. "Like when you ordered that ice cream, you kind of wanted mint chocolate chip, too—right? But you just got that one scoop. And that's just dumb."

Jake pointed at Tucker's milkshake. "You just got a chocolate shake, even though you said strawberry sounded good, too."

"No way, dude, I got them mixed," he said victoriously. "This is what I'm saying. Abelson, you listen, too. With girls, it's like ice cream. You'll never know which one you really want unless you try all the flavors."

Jake looked sideways at Miles, who already seemed less high after putting away about five pounds of food. "What do you think?" Ever since Jake had gone full douche bag during his brief acting career, he'd been looking to Miles as a behavioral barometer.

"I've always gone with pros and cons, but it's not like I have a girlfriend," Miles said, pontificating. "Tucker's approach might be an interesting experiment. The metaphor might be throwing you, but it makes a weird kind of sense. You probably need to get to know them both better."

Seeing them convinced, Tucker and Geoff exchanged a high five. "Now you're gettin' it, PG," Tucker said, taking a long, slurpy sip of the dregs of his milkshake. "Taste the rainbow."

Tucker rose, pitched his stuff in the garbage, and headed for the counter again. "I need a drink. Anybody want anything?"

Jake, feeling better all of a sudden, nodded. "Yeah, can you get me a scoop of mint chocolate chip?"

THIS ONE'S FOR YOU

With a father in the music industry, Ash Gilmour had watched plenty of concerts from the backstage wings. One of his first real dates with Myla, back in eighth grade, had involved shaking hands with the Rolling Stones. He still had the shirt the band had signed for them that night, which they'd shared through their whole relationship. Or did Myla have it now? It had been passed back and forth during their breakup and truce phases, and he couldn't remember. It was kind of cool that he was no longer keeping score.

But no matter how many concerts he'd been to, there was something far more incredible about watching a concert when you knew what it was like to kiss the person onstage, or what she looked like in her underwear. Neither of those were experiences he wanted to have with grizzled Keith Richards or Mick Jagger.

Watching Daisy onstage gave new meaning to the term *dream girl*. Even with her crazy trademark tutu—tonight's was a glittery yellow—and signature skewed, multicolored hair, she was like some magical being. A rock goddess fairy who flitted from town to town, captivating all who saw her with her songs. He felt like he'd never be able to walk into a concert again without hoping to see her on the stage. Sort of like how, when he was a kid, his parents would take them to Disneyland and he'd linger outside the castle, asking his mom to tie his shoe, or begging to throw another coin into the wishing well, just because he hoped to get a glimpse of Snow White, who he thought had pretty lips.

Daisy was an altogether better kind of princess. First off, she played guitar. Plus, Snow White never showed off mile-long legs over knee-high white go-go boots. But the same way Snow White could get woodland creatures to frolic to her songs, Daisy could command a crowd. Chicago's Metro was sold out tonight, and the simple, black-painted theater seemed to hold an infinite sea of nondescript faces all gazing at and swaying toward Daisy, who was crooning away under a bath of pale yellow light. The place only held about a thousand people, but the fans' apparent ardor for Daisy made it seem like a lot more. *And she deserves every bit of worship,* Ash thought. Years of classical training had made her a poised performer with a voice like soft velvet, something that threw off the critics who were anxious to peg her as just another drunken diva. That Ash knew the truth—that Daisy was an amazing and yet normal girl—made the whole experience even better.

"You're one lucky dude, Gilmour," said Chuck, a heavyset twentysomething roadie who toured with the band. "She's pretty fucking awesome." He set one of Trick's other bass guitars in a stand near the stage's edge and stood watching Daisy reverently.

"I know," Ash said, feeling like he was in one of those old cartoons where the guy's heart pulsed in and out of his chest at the sight of a hot girl. In a little over a week, he'd been with her in New York, Boston, and Columbus before coming here. She'd had to play a lot of gigs, but she fed off the energy of her crowds. She and Ash had shared late dinners at night owl–friendly diners, closed out bars in the wee hours of the morning, and stayed up until dawn fooling around.

They'd be hitting Detroit after Chicago, and Ash was beyond impressed that Daisy was actually looking forward to going there. Myla would have freaked about going to any city that lacked high-end department stores. But, like Ash, Daisy couldn't wait to go to the Motown Museum or to play at the Magic Stick, a rock club where everyone from the White Stripes to the Fleet Foxes had performed. It was almost bizarre to him to be with a girl who liked music as much as he did, and who was totally up for hanging out in random diners and cafes, eavesdropping on the conversations of everyday people. Myla had always wanted to make sure they only went to the kinds of places that were hard for everyday people to get into.

When Daisy had rehearsals, Ash spent time in coffee shops, trying to come up with his own songs. It was hard going, but he had some ideas jotted down, and he felt way more productive than he ever did dicking around in Tucker's garage. So far, he really didn't know what his dad was talking about. Ash and the rock-star life were completely compatible.

The band faded out on Daisy's biggest hit, "Feather in

Your Cap," and she pulled off her guitar, walking it to the side of the stage where Ash was standing. She handed the guitar to Chuck and winked at Ash.

Ash glanced at the set list tacked to a corkboard on the wall. He looked at Chuck. "Wait, doesn't she need her guitar for 'Little Things'?" It was the last song of the night and her new single, definitely not the kind of thing she'd pull from the concert.

Chuck shrugged. "I guess not. Maybe she changed something."

Ash watched as Daisy turned slightly so she was at a forty-five-degree angle between him and the audience. Suddenly, the spotlight hit him in the face, the beam instantly warming his whole body.

"See that guy over there?" Daisy said to the crowd, as she pointed at Ash. "That's Ash Gilmour. I feel a little shy telling you, but I think he's the one. Yeah, *the one* the one. And no, I haven't been drinking. Not in the last few hours, anyway. This next song is new, and I wrote it for him."

At that, the crowd cheered wildly, and Ash felt his heart beat in rhythm with the opening chords. It started off up-tempo. The lyrics were references to private jokes they'd shared and funny moments from their relationship so far. The notes drifted over Ash in a beautiful blur.

I was breaking bottles in Hollywood,
You bailed me out.
My crime took up your precious time,
But then you liked me.
You ordered too much food

To set the mood
But I liked you, too.

She grinned across the stage at him, and Ash shook his head, remembering picking up Daisy from jail after she broke a ton of wine bottles at Trader Joe's—CRAZY DAISY TWO-BUCK CHUCKED, read the headline on *TMZ*. Then the song took a slower turn.

You took me home, you made me real.
You'll never know how that made me feel.
And I'm as lucky as a shamrock in your pocket.

Ash was surprised she remembered. He'd randomly told her about how, as a little kid, whenever his parents were fighting, he'd feel infinitely better if he picked a clover out of their yard. He hadn't understood until years later that only four-leaf clovers were supposedly lucky, so he'd acquired a whole shoebox full of withered three-leaf clovers. But when things got bad, he always liked knowing they were there.

The song was personal, true, but the audience got into it, singing the refrain by the time Daisy got to it again. Suddenly embarrassed that he just had some random notes for his song-to-be, Ash wondered in awe when she'd even had time to write and rehearse a whole new piece when she was way busier than him. Amazing.

When Daisy finished, she curtsied at the center of the stage, and then gestured to Ash like a game-show hostess. The crowd clapped, *woo-hooed*, and even lit Bic lighters. He caught Daisy's eye across the stage. She smirked, then ran into his arms, jumping up and wrapping her legs around him. The crowd cheered even louder. Ash pushed her hair off her face and kissed her, unembarrassed by their onlookers. "Should we go celebrate somewhere?" He breathed into her ear, brushing his lips lightly along her earlobe as he did. "Somewhere we can be alone?"

"That sounds wonderful," Daisy said in return, her voice low and husky. Ash ran his thumb along the line where her waist met her hip, a spot where she was a little ticklish, and enjoyed the reverberation of her body against his as she giggled.

They were mid-kiss again when Trick came up behind Daisy and tapped her on the shoulder. Ash let her down, trying not to give Trick a dirty look. Today, he was wearing a plaid vest that opened over tight, ripped-up Levi's. The panther tattoo was sweating. In his back pocket were three pairs of women's underwear that had been thrown onstage.

"Dais, good show. Oh. Hi, Ash," he said, not even looking Ash in the eye. "We need a band meeting, stat. It's really important."

Ash felt his stomach tense. Who called meetings at one in the morning? Ash rubbed his thumb along Daisy's palm, hoping she'd get the message and ask to postpone. He wanted to get Daisy alone, away from the crowd and the band and everything that was distracting them from the more important matters at hand.

Instead, she sighed regretfully. "Okay, I guess," she said, squeezing Ash's hand before dropping it. She turned to him and threw her arms loosely over his shoulders. "That's okay, right?"

It wasn't okay, not really. But Ash didn't want to be the needy tagalong who freaked out every time his girlfriend had to tend to her steadily growing musical success. "Yeah, of course. Maybe we can meet at the hotel bar when we're done?"

Daisy sprang up and gave him a kiss on the lips. This one wasn't nearly so deep as the ones they'd just shared. She pulled away. "I promise, this won't take long at all." As she walked off with the rest of the band, Ash wondered if there was a clue there that he didn't get.

An hour and a half later, Ash was still waiting for Daisy in the bar on the thirty-third floor of the W Hotel. Whiskey Sky's panoramic view of Chicago all lit up depressed him. Somewhere out there, Daisy was hanging with her bandmates and had apparently forgotten all about him. The bar closed in a half hour, and a lot of the revelers had left to head to after parties. Ash ordered his third gin and tonic, nodding the ditched-boyfriend nod at a guy with the beer belly of a fifty-year-old car salesman and the round-cheeked face of a twelve-year-old Little Leaguer. The guy raised his glass pathetically, probably feeling lame because his friend had just departed with a pretty blonde and he was still there, alone.

Ash knew how he felt. He'd texted Daisy once to see if she was still coming, and he hadn't gotten any reply at all. How was it possible that a mere ninety minutes ago she was dedicating original songs to him and now she couldn't even tap the twenty-two keys it took to write *Sorry I'm running late*? He wondered if she'd even make it back to the hotel room so he could see her before they got on the tour bus to Detroit.

His iPhone vibrated with an incoming text. He pulled it out of his pocket. *Finally.* He felt a faint prickle of excitement as he checked the message.

But it was just Tucker. *Dude, we're hitting a Val party at some skater chick's house. Babes on boreds! You should be here!*

Tucker would learn how to spell before Ash ever got to see Daisy again. What if his dad was right and he should never have come? Ash swallowed another swig of his drink, which had soured as the ice melted. But maybe he was being a baby. Daisy had a band meeting, plain and simple. You didn't write songs for someone you didn't care about. So why was he sad-sacking it in some lamely trendy bar, feeling like the kind of guy who everyone on Earth knew sucked at love? Tomorrow was another day, another show, and another chance to be with his girl. So what if Tucker was on one of his Valley adventures—they always ended in disaster, anyway.

Ash and the rock-star lifestyle *were* completely compatible. Only tonight, they were sleeping in separate beds.

HOCUS FOCUS

"So, this is the waterfall," Jake said, gesturing to a tiered fountain where water flowed from one pool into the next, all the way down the side of a hill. At the top was a replica of the Venus de Milo. She looked like she wanted to reach in and touch the cool blue stream. Too bad she didn't have any arms. He rechecked the brochure. "Oops, sorry, it's a water *feature*." He tucked the Gardens of the World pamphlet in the back pocket of his Gap khakis, hoisting the picnic basket he'd brought farther up on his arm.

"Big difference," Amelie teased. Jake looked cute when he was reading nerdy facts. "Should we have our picnic here?" She flashed her most winning smile. Maybe if they paused for a second, Jake would stop quoting the brochure. They'd been through the Japanese, Italian, and English gardens, which were all beautiful. But they were in awkward first-date territory, and Jake was clearly nervous, as if he'd planted every rosebush, hydrangea, and lily in this Sherman Oaks attraction himself and was waiting for her to criticize them.

"Sure," he said, setting down the picnic basket and

taking out a red-and-white checked blanket that would merit a Hollywood prop master's approval. "Actually, I got the picnic basket at a French place, La Cachette, so it makes more sense to eat it here than in the Italian garden." He laughed nervously, and Amelie tried to laugh with him. Jake au naturel was usually funny, but he was trying too hard.

Which was nice, in a way. She'd been floored when Jake had called last night and asked her out. She knew she should play hard to get after Jake rejected her kiss last week, but after several weeks at BHH with no invitations to anything, she had said yes instantly. Maybe Jake had just wanted time to come up with a *real* first date, and that was why he'd kissed and ditched.

He pulled a loaf of perfectly golden, flaky French bread from the basket, followed by an assortment of cheeses, charcuterie, and pâté that he laid out on the blanket. "So, I got chocolate soufflé for dessert," he said. "But they wouldn't sell me wine, so I just got Orangina and sparkling water. I hope that's okay."

"Honestly, I'm really not much of a drinker," Amelie said shyly, pouring them plastic cups of Orangina. Jake had probably seen the photos of her at Area that had surfaced about two months ago when she was suffering the peak of her Hunter Sparks obsession. She had gone to the club with Kady and downed every drink Hunter bought her, paying for it the next morning when drunken photos of her had surfaced on *TMZ*. "Those photos from Area, that was kind of a one-time-only thing."

Jake grinned. "Oh, I just mentioned the no-wine thing because I'm a total alcoholic. I'm wondering how

I'm going to get through this date without at least a cocktail."

Amelie laughed for real, which seemed to put Jake at ease. His shoulders relaxed and he started assembling French bread sandwiches from Brie and smoked turkey. Amelie bit into a strawberry, enjoying the sweetness on her tongue. Feeling daring, she plucked another from the plate and held it up near Jake's lips. "These are really good," she said. "You should try one." Jake opened his mouth, and Amelie held up the strawberry for him to bite. They shared ten full seconds of uninterrupted eye contact.

An hour later, the remains of the picnic lay scattered around the blanket. Jake and Amelie were on their backs in the center of it, looking up at the sky. She'd been telling him stories of growing up as a Kidz Network star. She felt like she'd been talking a lot, but Jake seemed interested in all of it. He kept asking her questions, even when she tried to quiz him on things like his parents or Miles or, most important, whether he'd heard from Kady. She hadn't said anything to Amelie about Jake in her e-mail, except for one line: *Bagged him yet?* Amelie guessed that meant she wasn't in danger of Kady returning to steal him away.

And maybe she really *had* bagged him—to put it indelicately. "So I was wondering," she began, "do you have plans for this Friday?"

Jake turned to look at her, shielding his green-flecked hazel eyes from the sun. "No," he said, "did you want to hang out?" Their fingertips were touching on the blanket. Amelie let her hand drift a little closer to his, and then they were holding hands.

"I was hoping you'd come see the play," she said, emboldened by their laced fingers. "It's just a small part, but maybe we could go out after or something?"

Jake squeezed her hand, and Amelie's heart fluttered. "Yeah, of course," he said. "I'd love to come."

Amelie rolled to her side and leaned in, planting a soft kiss on Jake's cheek. In return, he kissed her back, on the lips. It was slow, sweet, and perfect. She felt like the sun shone just on them.

"Mommy, is that Fairy Princess kissing a *boy*?" A little girl in a *High School Musical* T-shirt pointed accusatorily at Amelie and Jake. The mother pulled the girl away, but even she couldn't resist looking back at Amelie and Jake one last time.

The recognition didn't bother Amelie, though. *Hell yes*, she thought, *it's Fairy Princess kissing a boy.* "So this is what I have to get used to?" Jake said, kissing her again.

Amelie smiled through the kiss. She could already picture the two of them holding hands as they walked to class. Meeting up at Cafe Audrey to do homework after school. Going to the movies on weekends. She'd have a date for next month's Homecoming Dance for sure. Twenty normal-girl points. She looked over at Jake; sunbeams surrounded his halo of curls as he closed his eyes in sweet repose. She hoped he was thinking about when he'd see her again.

Jake could hardly believe this was working. He'd slept much better yesterday after Tucker's advice to take each girl out. He'd been invited to go with Tucker, Geoff, and some guys to a Valley party last night, but instead, Miles had come over and they'd worked out a plan for the date with Amelie. He knew whatever he invited her to do had to be special. And Amelie-specific.

It had been Miles's advice not to multitask. "It's like Mathletes. When you're solving a trigonometry problem, you don't want to be thinking about calculus. So when you're with Amelie, you focus on just Amelie. And when you're with Jojo, you focus on just Jojo."

It had worked. Amelie was holding his hand, kissing him, and blissfully staring at the sky above. "So," Jake said, prompting her to look at him with curiosity. "I kind of have to go. I have a huge test tomorrow. But I was thinking we could study or something during the week?"

Amelie beamed at him, planting another kiss on his cheek. "I would love that," she said, hugging him. "I had such a good time today."

Jake almost felt bad about the lie. He didn't have a test. But he definitely couldn't tell Amelie he had a date with Jojo.

And she just happened to be next.

SACRAMENTO STYLE

"What's a mulligan, anyway?" Jojo asked, expertly tapping her fluorescent orange golf ball into the hole. She'd somehow managed to send it down the center ramp of the miniature Old West Saloon, prompting the sound effects of a woman's flirtatious giggle and a bartender saying, "This one's on the house, pardner."

Jake's ball had careened down the left side, pretty much equivalent to a gutter ball in bowling. His sound effects were of a bottle breaking, a woman saying, "You two-timer!" followed by a slap, and a gun being cocked. "A mulligan? I think it's the only thing my dad likes about golf. It's like a do-over. So, if this date goes really badly, I'll probably ask you for a mulligan."

Jojo grinned, plucking her ball from its cozy home in the hole. "Yeah, you should focus on your golf game," she said, pulling down the peace sign T-shirt that had afforded Jake a view of a tiny strip of her tanned, flat stomach. It was almost bizarre, how unaware Jojo was of her hotness. It only made him like her more.

They were on hole fifteen of the Old West–themed mini golf course at Mulligan Family Fun Center in Torrance.

Next to the course, kindergartners on the rookie go-cart track wailed and laughed as they crashed their carts into the rubber padded wall. So it wasn't exactly as serene as Gardens of the World. And, doing his mental math, Jake figured their games of golf and pepperoni pizza were not equal in cost to the picnic basket he'd ordered for the Amelie date. But it wasn't really his fault. He'd tried to keep things fair—romantically and monetarily—and suggested a French-Spanish fusion tapas restaurant that he'd read about on Yelp. Jojo had dismissed the idea.

"I'm not Myla, Jake," she'd said. "You have to ease me into this Beverly Hills date thing. Maybe we could do something Sacramento-style instead."

And that started the fun back-and-forth that was defining their date. "Witty repartee" as Miles would have termed it for the pros-and-cons list. "I've never been to Sacramento, so you have to cut me some slack," he'd said.

"We're all about slack in Sacramento," Jojo had said. "Except when we're kicking ass at mini golf." She hadn't been joking about that. She'd made par on at least four holes, plus she'd hit a hole in one, while Jake had taken the six-stroke-per-hole maximum more times than he wanted to remember. Jojo was diligently keeping score, though, so he wouldn't be able to forget.

"Just so you know, my lack of skill at golf is completely to blame on my dad, because he believes baseball is the only sport where you should hit a ball," Jake said. "Also, can you name any famous Jewish golfers? No. It's just not my people's game."

"So I suppose you think that my obvious talent is a gay-dad thing?" Jojo tapped her ball so it squarely hit an oversize cowboy boot, banked off the spur, and rolled to a stop four inches from the hole. "But it's not. I'm just naturally awesome. Although maybe my birth parents play. I would ask them, but they're busy adding a new baby to the family."

"So I'm guessing you don't want to take a mulligan on that shot?" Jake joked. He sensed he shouldn't ask Jojo about the new sibling, even though he wanted to. You weren't supposed to talk about sensitive family stuff on a first date, right?

Jojo shoved him playfully. "You wish," she said, her eyes a light lavender under the setting sun. They were such an unreal color, like something you'd see in anime. Of course, Amelie's eyes were a Caribbean blue that were similarly fantastic. *Jojo, you're on a date with Jojo,* Jake reminded himself. *Trig, not calc.* He began to wonder if it was a bad idea to go out with both girls on the same day. But if Tucker could do it, he should be able to. Not that Tucker wasn't a decent guy, but from a mental agility standpoint, he had trouble just keeping track of what day of the week it was.

Jojo proceeded to beat Jake on both the sixteenth and seventeenth holes, and at the eighteenth hole they arrived at a ball drop. If you got your ball down the right chute, you won a free game. "If I win, I get to ask you something. If you win, you can ask me something," Jojo said. "Deal?" She held out her hand, and they shook on it. Her palm lingered in his, and Jake was tempted to keep holding it, but then she abruptly turned around and was all business, lining up her ball with the WIN FREE GAME chute. She let it go, and it shot down like it would go straight into the winning slot. Then it bumped off to the side and went down a losing slot instead.

"Darn," Jojo said, grabbing Jake by the shirt and propelling him to the game. "Your turn." This time, she left her hand on his back. Her palm lay lightly against his spine and Jake felt as though warmth was radiating through his whole body. He lined up his blue ball and let it go. It zipped right into the winning slot, and the machine spit out a ticket for a free game.

Jojo folded her arms over her chest. A strand of her shiny, almond-colored hair fell over her eyes as she looked up at him expectantly. "All right, a deal's a deal," she said, a little half-smile playing over her pink lips. "What do you want to know?"

Jake held up the ticket in front of her face. "Actually, I was hoping you could hold on to this for me. Do you think you might want to come back here, maybe for date three or four?"

Jojo blushed. "I think that can be arranged," she said, reaching out to extract the ticket from his hand. When their fingers brushed, Jake couldn't resist. He pulled her toward him and kissed her. It was better than the interrupted kiss at her house, when Amelie's incoming text had ignited feelings of confusion and guilt. Now that he knew it was okay to date both girls, his whole body relaxed into Jojo's embrace, and he enjoyed the strawberry flavor of her lip gloss and the smoothness of her warm cheek against his.

"Oh, gross, Mommy," screamed a little kid wielding his putter like an ax. "Can you tell those people to go do sex somewhere else?"

Jake couldn't believe he'd been busted by a munchkin for the second time today. Was he going to get a rep as a PDA repeat offender? Jojo shot him an embarrassed glance before they both cracked up laughing as the little boy stood there making chopping motions with his putter. As they hightailed it back to Jake's Corolla, giggling the whole way, Jojo put her hand in Jake's.

"Now that we have that awkward moment out of the way, I think I can ask you if you'll maybe come to the play this Friday, which is sure to be awkward since I somehow got the lead." She looked at him expectantly, a half-smile on her hopeful face.

"Who could refuse an offer like that?" Jake said, pushing strands of hair from her face as he pulled her in for another kiss.

An hour later, Jojo clicked the front door shut, knowing that she'd be unable to wipe the dreamy smile from her face. She and Jake had spent a half hour kissing, just inside the entry gate to Casa Barbar. He definitely hadn't pulled away this time. In fact, if it weren't for the fact that they had school tomorrow and that Jojo didn't feel like having Myla catch them, they'd probably still be out there. Jake's weird kiss-and-run at the PJ party must have just been a guy's needing-to-think thing. After all, they'd started out as friends, and weren't guys always weird about a girl friend, two words, becoming their *girlfriend*, one word?

Jojo was feeling quite proud of herself. She'd actually fallen for the *right* guy for a change. Not like when she'd convinced herself that Ash was the one, just because they'd bonded in their mutual dislike of Myla. And *sooo* not like her sucker-for-Tucker moment. She'd definitely had a lapse in judgment there, a total loss of brain function: The relationship had been purely Myla-vellian. Her sister had only chosen Tucker because he was a "catch" at BHH, and Jojo had followed along. Fortunately, their romance hadn't progressed far enough for her to catch anything. Entirely possible, given Tucker's himbo status.

Jojo headed into the kitchen, in search of a slice of the chocolate Bundt cake she'd seen Lucy making that afternoon. Whenever the little kids weren't around, Lucy actually had time to focus, and she used it to try out new dessert recipes. Jojo's smile drooped for a second when she saw Myla leaning against the granite counter, forking a morsel of cake from the plate she held just under her nose. She looked like she was posing out of a joint photo shoot for *Gourmet* and *Vogue* magazines. Her long ebony hair was piled messily on top of her head, and her slender legs extended from a pair of short Free People boxers. Her juniper eyes flashed disgust as they landed on Jojo, like she'd just found a hair in her cake.

Jojo ignored the glare. She found Lucy's cake under a blue sea-glass dome, a gift to Barkley for being a guest on *Ace of Cakes*. Barkley was a cake connoisseur. She sliced herself a sizeable hunk and took the plate to the counter, where she sat opposite Myla.

The girls ate in silence for a minute, when Jojo noticed a racing program from Santa Anita on the counter. She flicked the pages, and Myla turned, grabbing it away.

"Um, that's mine." She slid the narrow program into

the waistband of her boxers, looking at Jojo's massive cake slice with disdain.

"Since when do you go to the racetrack?" Jojo asked, greedily forking up a huge piece of cake and eating it with relish in front of Myla. "I didn't think Prada made jockey clothes."

Myla stabbed the last of her cake, gulped it down, and shoved her plate in the dishwasher. "Why don't you mind your own business?" She stalked toward the stairs.

Suddenly realizing what was going on, Jojo set her own plate down and followed her. She grabbed Myla's arm at the door. "Please tell me you did not go there with Danny."

Myla wrenched her arm away. "So what if I did? It's not your concern."

"So *what?* You could get him in trouble is what," Jojo said. "You could get him fired. I know you'll never have to work a day in your life, but Danny isn't some Hollywood rich kid. He's a normal Midwestern guy who doesn't need your games." She thought of how he'd sent Jake to her that day in the library. She didn't want to see someone as decent as Danny have his life ruined by someone as spoiled as Myla.

Myla stepped forward, and Jojo backed away. In her bare feet, Myla had to stand on tiptoe to be at Jojo's eye level, but her expression was intimidating nonetheless. "It was *his* idea, not mine. And that's more than you deserve to know."

Jojo drew herself up so she could look down at Myla. "Look, I don't care about your personal life. We may be *family,* but we're not friends." She drew out every word, giving Myla the full—well, Myla treatment. "But I do care if you flirt some innocent guy right into career suicide. Why don't you go out with your male counterpart, Lewis Buford?"

If eyes could shoot deathly lasers, Myla's would have sliced right through Jojo and the oak kitchen cabinets. "Must have been some great date with PG if you're taking out all your frustration on me."

Myla turned on her heel and stomped out, satisfied at having gotten the last word. Jojo had effectively cut Myla out of her life at the *Class Angel* wrap party. So how dare she start nosing around in Myla's business now? They were sisters in address *only*.

Still, as she stalked up the stairs, a part of Myla wished she could tell Jojo everything. She hadn't been able to stop thinking about Danny since yesterday at the racetrack, and her thoughts weren't of the what-to-wear-to-get-noticed variety, but of the what-to-do-when-you're-falling-for-the-manny variety. She knew Jojo would be able to give her a level-headed take on how to deal.

But even though Jojo was just rooms away, right now Myla felt like she was home alone.

SEEING DOUBLE

S weat trickled down Jojo's spine, and she pulled at the stiff collar of her Jane Eyre costume. The fumes of autumn veggie pizza and chipotle chicken wraps, today's lunch specials, mingled disjointedly in her nostrils, making her gag. She could not think about food right now.

She was waiting with the rest of the *Jane Eyre* cast in the teacher's conference room next to the cafeteria, and the aromas and chatter of lunchtime were all around her and even seeping in through the cafeteria ventilation system. As her co-stars ate and talked, Jojo stood near the windows while Lola, the wardrobe assistant, made some last-minute adjustments to her hoop skirt. Jojo couldn't help but glance out the row of tinted windows that looked over the student body, which only made her more nervous. Every time she looked, the size of the crowd seemed to double. Myla and her friends were at their usual center table, and the rest of the student body sat at tables that radiated out from their socially important epicenter. At the way back of the cafeteria, between the French Club table and the Anarchists Non-Club table, Jake sat with his friend Miles. Seeing him prompted Jojo's stomach to flip for a different reason, and she crossed her fingers that she wouldn't mess up.

Across the conference room, Amelie daintily pecked at a veggie wrap, talking to Nick, their co-star. Both of them looked completely unperturbed by the fact that they had to perform a song for the entire lunch crowd, as a way to sell tickets to the performance. It was only three days away, on Friday.

"People, listen up," Mr. Potter said, his normally thin voice booming through a megaphone that was completely unnecessary in the cramped conference room. His narrow shoulders were slung back, drooping in his black turtleneck. If the store sticker reading LARGE still affixed to the chest was any indication, he must have bought it especially for today's performance. "A lot is riding on this. For you, as actors. And for me, as director. If we sell an adequate number of tickets, then there will be a spring musical, which I will direct. If we don't, it's the end of theater at BHH as we know it." He drew out the word theater so it was *theeee-aaaaate-rrr*, and a small titter waved over the room.

"I think *he* was the end of theater at BHH as we know it," Nick whispered into Amelie's ear. They were sitting at the end of long, oak conference table, waiting for Lola to finish pinning Jojo's costume. Amelie giggled softly.

Ever since her date with Jake on Sunday, she had been feeling a lot better about her bit part in the play and was even being friendlier to Nick. Nick propped his head up on his hand, looking bored as Mr. Potter droned on. Amelie rolled her eyes. Mr. Potter deserved to be the demise of BHH's theater department. He was a joke. The whole cast was about to go pimp the play with "You'll Fall in Love with Us," a terrible new song he'd written for the occasion. Amelie was pretty sure the tune was identical to the Muppets' theme song. And speaking of Muppets, their lead, Jojo Milford, looked Kermit-green. Was she really that nervous? And if she was this bad now, doing a five-minute performance on a Tuesday afternoon when everyone was paying more attention to their fro-yo parfaits, how would she be on Friday night, when they had to take the stage in front of a captive audience?

Not my problem, Amelie thought to herself, pushing her chair back from the table. She headed toward the lunch table, filled with sandwiches and drinks for the cast, and poured a glass of water from the pitcher. She looked out at the sea of faces in the cafeteria, finding Jake in the back of the room. She couldn't wait until after the show Friday—play rehearsals would be over. Then maybe they'd be able to start seeing each other more often. They'd exchanged several cute text messages throughout the week, flirting about when their next study session would be. They had tentative plans for tomorrow night, if she got out of practice on time.

"Oh, shit!" Lola suddenly exclaimed from her position at Jojo's feet. The entire room, including Amelie, shifted its gaze toward their star. Her hoop skirt had become a droop skirt. The wire ring had broken through the fabric, and the skirt hung like a rag around Jojo's waist. Amelie smoothed her own skirt, trying to suppress a grin. That was one advantage to playing rich Blanche Ingram instead of poor Jane Eyre. Amelie's costume was a shiny green brocade that

complemented her complexion and eyes. Jojo's, even before
her wardrobe malfunction, was a drab gray.

"Oh my," Mr. Potter said, dropping his megaphone into
a chair and rushing over to evaluate the damage, shooting Amelie a look that said this was somehow her fault.
Amelie shrugged. Again, not her problem. Mr. Potter's
head darted around the room, like the spouse of a heart
attack victim searching for a doctor. "Amelie," he said.

Amelie had already gone back to gazing out the window, wondering what Jake would think when he saw her
all corseted up. Maybe her dressy gown would prompt
him to ask her to the Homecoming Dance. "What?" she
said, not paying much attention.

"You're Jojo's size," Mr. Potter said. "She's the star, so
give her your dress."

Jojo was about to protest. She knew she must look
like a mop with her saggy skirt, but it wouldn't really
be fair for her take Amelie's costume off her back. She
was about to say she'd be fine in her droopy dress, when
she followed Amelie's gaze across the cafeteria. Amelie
was looking at Jake. *Jojo's* Jake. So fine, they weren't
exactly boyfriend and girlfriend. But there'd been a
date. There'd been a make-out session. And there'd
been several beyond-adorable text messages from Jake,
where he'd quipped about instances that he'd like to
take a mulligan. *Just ate mom's attempt at fajitas. Mulligan, please.*

"Earth to Amelie," Mr. Potter said. "Jojo needs your
dress."

Amelie finally glanced away from the window, and
her eyes sadly took in Jojo's distressed dress. Jojo strode

over to her purposefully. She could almost feel her eyes glinting coldly.

"Turn around," she said to Amelie curtly. "I'll help you unzip."

At their usual table in the center of the cafeteria, Myla's friends were amusing themselves by ripping on Jojo like it was going out of style. The thing was, it already was out of style. Myla really couldn't be bothered to care that her sister was onstage, performing some sad musical number for the cafeteria crowd.

You'll fall in love with us.
We're gonna cause a fuss.
In just three more days
We're here, we're live, we're with Brontë.
You're gonna love it
And make us a hit.

"And I couldn't give a shit," Fortune Weathers sang off-key, as Billie Bollman and Talia Montgomery doubled over in laughter, stomping their suede Gucci boots against the linoleum floor.

"'Cause Jojo is a bitch," Billie sang, cackling, her face looking even longer as she held the final note. Myla rolled her eyes, annoyed. She had other concerns. Namely, Danny. She'd barely seen him since their trip to the racetrack, except in brief, passing moments and during their rides to school, where he'd been extra-careful to talk to both her and Jojo about the most boring subjects possible: the weather, their class schedules, the latest adoption updates from Malawi. At least on that front, things seemed to be moving very slowly for her parents. If the process was drawn out long enough, she'd have more time with Danny.

"That doesn't even rhyme," Talia chided. She shot a dirty look across the cafeteria, where Lewis was leading a trio of actual Playboy bunnies dressed in cigarette girl outfits around to each table, selling tickets. Miss November had just sold a dozen to Tucker's table. Talia puffed out her own sizeable chest, encased in a ruffled Luella dress she'd borrowed from Myla. She waved a brunette bunny over to their table.

"How many?" the bunny asked.

"Four," Fortune said bossily, cutting Talia off as she took out her purse. "I'll get this, guys." She pulled out several bills and handed them to the salesgirl. "Can I get a receipt? My dad can write it off."

The brunette rolled her eyes, scrawling out an unofficial receipt on the back of a napkin, which she handed to Fortune with the tickets. Fortune folded it neatly, her lips pursed, and zipped it into an exterior pocket of her beige Furla bag.

"Actually, you should have only gotten three," Myla said, as Fortune slid the tickets into her wallet. "I'm not going."

The play was Friday night. And since he'd started, Danny had diligently spent Friday evenings sorting the family's mail, organizing new script submissions from Barkley's production office, and writing his silly reports. He'd expect her to be out for the night.

Which gave Myla the perfect reason to stay in.

•••

With every twirl, sashay, and high note, Amelie awarded herself extra normal-girl points. She deserved every one, thanks to Jojo. She felt like a lump of left-behind cafeteria gravy as she dragged the hoopless hoop skirt behind her, gamely faking a smile as she sang Mr. Potter's lame lyrics.

Don't be caught at home
When on the stage we roam.
To err is human
To miss Jane Eyre *is a sin.*

Across the stage from her, Jojo had gained a burst of confidence she wasn't sporting in the conference room earlier. In Amelie's shimmery green Blanche costume, Jojo looked like a prettily wrapped present, and she beamed across the cafeteria. Amelie strained to see Jake in the sea of faces, but all the backup dancer turns and shimmies made it hard to focus. He probably wouldn't even notice her in her blobby gray dress, with Jojo rocking out center stage.

Amelie launched into the turn-clap-turn dance at the end of the number. Nick, in his Rochester gear, was going from girl to girl, spinning each of them. When he reached her, he beamed, his green eyes shining under the fluorescent lights. "You look great," he mouthed, before spinning and lifting her over his head. *If he wasn't so nerdy, he'd be the Zac Efron of BHH*, Amelie thought, grinning down at him. He set her down, and Amelie immediately craned her neck to see if Jake was watching her dance with another guy. But her foot caught on the hem of the dress, and she stumbled. She could feel herself going down. Already feeling a deep blush coming to her face, she braced herself for the inevitable fall on her ass . . . when Nick's arms encircled her waist, and he righted her with such grace that it seemed planned. Amelie beamed at him in thanks, grateful that Jake hadn't seen her bottom out.

At his table against the far back wall of the cafeteria, Jake had hit bottom. He had his calculus book propped open in front of him and was staring over its cover like it was a shield. Across the cafeteria, Jojo and Amelie were shaking and shimmying their way through a song that only served to make him feel worse. "You'll fall in love with us," they sang.

He wasn't sure about love, but he liked them. Both of them. And it wasn't until just now that he'd realized he had accepted both girls' offers to see their play. How had it not registered that they were asking him to the *same* play?

On his left, Miles nudged him. "Shouldn't Jojo be wearing something more plain, if she's Jane Eyre?" he asked quizzically, rubbing his near-beard and squinting through his glasses. Only Miles could be in a room with girls dancing onstage and scantily clad Playboy bunnies selling play tickets, and be wondering about the accuracy of Victorian-era costumes.

"I don't think it matters," Jake said distractedly, the heat rising beneath his new Gap sweater. It really didn't. Jojo couldn't be plain if she tried. She looked like a painting, her vibrant green skirt swaying, a rosy flush in her smooth cheeks. Not far from her, Amelie glowed against the drabness of her gray dress. Her red hair and creamy skin seemed more pronounced and alive in the depressing, sacklike costume.

Jake banged his head against the top of his textbook, closing his eyes. He opened his right lid and was able to see only Jojo, who seemed to be looking straight at him. He closed that eye and opened his left. Now he could see only Amelie, who beamed as she seemed to serenade him. When he opened both eyes at once, he could feel both girls looking across the crowded room at him, holding the last line of the song for what seemed like an eternity.

"You're going tooooooooooo looooooooooooooove usssssssssssssss," they sang.

And that was the problem. He loved them both, but he could only choose one.

GLASS HALF-EMPTY

A fter three Maker's Mark and Cokes, Ash could say one thing for certain about his bartender: He was generous when it came to bourbon.

He could also say one thing for certain about Daisy Morton: She had no concept of time. *I'll be back in a half hour* evidently meant *Drink alone for a few hours, and maybe you'll hear from me.*

Ash was at the Five Star Bar in Chicago, where he, Daisy, and the band had come in to warm up after they'd played a street festival in the Loop. It had been an unscheduled stop, delaying their trip to Detroit. That meant they'd get to Detroit just before the show. That also meant all Ash's and Daisy's plans for sightseeing went out the window.

Today had been cold, wet, and miserable. Kind of how Ash felt now. Chicagoans were apparently way tougher than anyone in L.A. Ash had gone to outdoor shows at Sunset Junction in Silver Lake where hipsters ran shrieking and acts got canceled if someone so much as flicked liquid into the air out of their BPA-free water bottle. But today, he'd stood with a few thousand others in the rain, watching Daisy and the band play a forty-five-minute set in between Architecture in Helsinki and Grizzly Bear. Then the band had insisted on sticking around until the end, when Rilo Kiley played.

While the rest of the band talked about how "amazing" the day was, and how "real" people in Chicago were, Ash glowered. He'd barely gotten a chance to even stand near Daisy, let alone touch or talk to her. She kept jabbering to the other guys about how killer the show was, while being all grateful to Trick for setting up the impromptu performance. Ash had felt like a kid on a field trip who'd wet his pants. No one seemed to want to come near him. To add to the realism of the whole pants-wetting thing, his Antik Denim jeans were still damp from his day in the rain. The heavy fabric now stuck to his leather bar stool. And his normally stylishly shaggy hair had curled dorkily after a day in the rain. He looked like a floppy flower after a thunderstorm. Weak.

"You still waiting for her?" Bill, the bartender, leaned across the bar, his ruddy face hovering over Ash's glass. He had long, straggly blond hair and wore a jack-o'-lantern bandana around his forehead, even though Halloween was several weeks away. "Oh man, I'm sorry."

Ash pushed an annoying piece of hair out of his eyes, having a hard time not watching the very drunk girl in a cowboy hat making excellent use out of the stripper pole to the left of the bar. She was giving a group of guys a close-up look at the assortment of tattoos that wrapped around her waist. Ash could make out a bad Tweety Bird and a red devil's head. "What do you mean, sorry?" Ash asked, wondering if the girl and the brunette friend who'd just joined her only looked attractive thanks to his very stiff drinks.

"See your glass? I wouldn't call that half-full," Bill said. "I'd call it half-empty." He reached behind the bar and topped off the tumbler with more Maker's Mark, then shot another stream of Coke over the melting ice. "I can fill the glass, problem solved. But when your woman would rather hang with other guys instead of you, well, that's just half-empty."

"Thanks, that really helps," Ash said, rolling his eyes as he took a gulp that made his very expensive fake ID worth every penny. Why was he listening to a guy in novelty Halloween headgear? And when had he become the cliché guy who confessed his problems to the bartender?

Halfway into a drink that might have been his fourth but in reality was probably number five or five and a half, thanks to Bill's refills, Ash's phone buzzed with a text. He grabbed it off the bar, sloppily navigating to his messages. When he saw it was from Jake, he was disappointed. It was a five-line text. Jake was supposedly hooking up with both Amelie Adams and Jojo Milford on Tucker's advice, and he wanted to see what Ash thought. But what Ash thought was, who was he to give advice? His girlfriend didn't even want to be around him. Maybe it was the drinks talking, but if Jake had two girls, he had a better chance than Ash, who felt like he didn't even have half a girl. He typed out, *Yeah, listen to Tucker. Great idea,* and sent it. As soon as the message was sent, he sort of regretted it. Tucker was a moron and kind of a dick to girls. Jake was a nice guy. He was about to correct his message when he felt a pair of tiny, icy-cold hands cover his eyes. "Guess who?"

Hating the way his heart beat faster at the sound of her voice, Ash pulled Daisy's hands from his face. "Nice of you to make it." He spun around on the stool and saw that Trick, Brett, and Sammy were right behind her. They were taking in the show, which now involved more girls than the lone stripper pole could accommodate. A catfight was imminent. Which probably explained why the crowd had grown.

"Don't be a poop," Daisy said. "That show was amazing, wasn't it? And we were doing our band meeting, and Trick got a message that our show in Detroit is sold out and they're adding another night! Rock City, baby! Woohoo!" She was clearly drunk, though not as drunk as Ash was. Her hair, which she'd worn down with a crown of braids wrapped around her head, was knotted in back, and one of the braids was coming loose. She'd also changed out of her ironic *Sesame Street* SUNNY DAY T-shirt and into a zebra-print shirt that Ash could have sworn he'd seen Trick wearing in New York.

She followed the guys to the stripper pole room, and Ash watched her retreating from him. What the fuck? She'd just gotten here, and she was already ditching him?

"That your woman?" Bill said, swabbing the counter with his towel.

Ash nodded weakly. "My woman might be a bad choice of words," he said blandly. "She clearly would rather be queen of her band than my girl." He pinched the bridge of his nose between his index finger and thumb, already feeling a headache coming on.

Bill shrugged, rubbing the back of his neck with his meaty, callused hand. "Maybe it's not the whole band she's concerned with," he said, gesturing with his stubbled chin to the other room. Daisy and Trick were flipping through the jukebox, standing so close that their shoulders were touching. Trick jabbed the button, advancing to a new page of selections, and they busted out laughing as Daisy shoved dollar bills into the machine. "What did you say these band meetings were about?"

Ash grimaced. "What are you saying?" He pushed his glass back across the bar, and Bill immediately filled it.

Sliding the refill toward Ash once more, Bill frowned. "Well, if she worked in an office, and she told you she had to stay late every night for meetings with her fellow salesman, and she came home every night that happy . . ." He pointed to Daisy, who was giggling about an old Phil Collins song. "I don't know if you'd be so quick to think it was just part of her job."

Ash let this sink in. Was he making excuses for Daisy because she was a musician? And was that how it worked? Did Trick call the "band meetings" as an excuse? Was this actually code for a hookup between him and Daisy? He glanced across the bar at Sammy and Brett, who were chatting alone, not invited to the jukebox jokefest. Where did they go during these meetings? Did they hang out, waiting for Daisy and Trick to finish up? Did they have an excuse ready to go if Ash happened to find them in a band meeting, missing the two most important band members?

He felt bourbon rise like lava in his throat. It was bad enough that Daisy couldn't seem to make time for him. Now he was certain she was cheating on him. He turned his back on her, staring hard at the melting ice in his glass.

When the song was over, she came up beside him and breathed softly on his ear. In her sweetest voice, she lilted, "Aren't you excited for us? And just think, we'll get to stay in Detroit even longer than we were hoping." She paused, considering this. "Wow, I bet no one has said *that* in at least the last twenty years."

Ash fought the urge to laugh or to kiss Daisy, as she practically danced around his bar stool. He saw that every guy in the bar was looking at her like she was some sexy curiosity. The protective sensation that he'd had when he was nothing more than her unpaid chauffeur started to cut through the drunken numbness in his body. But why should he be protective if Daisy's concern was only to party with her real boyfriend, Trick?

"You're not very chatty tonight, are you?" Daisy said. "I thought you'd be excited." In the next room, the bouncers had detonated the potential girlfight by offering the pole dancers free lemon drop shots. Trick and the other guys, now bored, sidled up behind Daisy.

"So, is he coming, then?" Trick asked in his annoying English-Southern accent. His gangly arms were folded over his narrow chest, encased in a skinny red blazer. Ash wondered if Trick's narrow, sinewy neck would make it harder or easier to choke him.

"Coming where?" Ash said, locking eyes with Daisy. Her graphite eyes perked up.

"You *can* still talk," she said, kissing his ear lobe. "We're going to do a zombie pub crawl. Come on, it will be brilliant." The opening strains of "Beast of Burden" came on the jukebox. Ash, who considered it "their" song, perked up just a tad, hoping Daisy had chosen it with him in mind.

Across the bar, he heard Trick's surly voice announce to Sammy and Brett, "This song is brilliant, innit?" Ash's stomach clenched. He suddenly hated the Rolling Stones.

Ash hopped off the stool and pulled Daisy to the one dark corner of the bar that wasn't in use. "Look, I was thinking we could do something low-key," he said, giving her one last chance to prove she wanted to be with him, not Trick. "And maybe just the two of us. We don't have to go back to the hotel or anything. I heard about a tapas restaurant where you get a private room. It's supposed to be kind of . . . romantic."

Daisy threw her arms around him, pulling him closer. "That sounds so girly," she said. "This will be more fun. And don't worry, you don't have to wear zombie makeup if you don't want to. But Trick knows how to make fake blood if you want some."

Trick will be making real blood if he doesn't start backing off my girlfriend, Ash thought.

"No, you know what, you go," he said. "I'm going to go to bed."

Daisy's peppy expression wilted a little, and she pursed her full lips into a tight smile. "You're right," she said finally. "We should do something romantic. And I guess zombies aren't wine and roses."

Ash squeezed her hand defeatedly. Daisy obviously didn't want a just-the-two-of-them outing, and he shouldn't have to *convince* her to spend time with him. "No, you know, you should definitely go stay out all night with the guys. I'm sure you need more time with them," he said, pulling away. "I'm going to call a cab, hit the room. And don't worry, I won't wait up."

He unwrapped himself from her grasp and headed for the door without looking back. The old saying went *If you love something, set it free, and if it's really yours it will come back to you.*

He wasn't sure if setting something free applied to sending your girlfriend to get zombie-bombed with her horny bassist, but he figured he'd learn soon enough.

NOT IN HER NATURE

Myla had learned in sophomore economics that boycotts rarely effect change, but often they make consumers feel good. So tonight, as she became seemingly the only person at BHH not to be going to *Jane Eyre: The Musical,* she knew the show would go on, but at least she'd have the satisfaction of not wasting two hours of her life watching her "sister" Brontë her heart out.

No one cared about the plays at BHH, but this one was different. Amelie Adams apparently inspired curiosity. And Lewis Buford, as student producer, had promised that anyone who tweeted about the show would get an exclusive invite to an after party at his house. For her part, Myla couldn't give a twit.

She had curled up in the living room with this month's *Cosmo,* hoping that Danny would catch her there alone. Normally, she preferred reading in the privacy of her own room, or in the rounded turret in the house's west wing, but she doubted Danny would venture upstairs uninvited. This was her best shot.

Halfway into an article about how to get a guy to fall

in love with you by treating him like your cat (and putting Vaseline in your cleavage), Danny strolled into the room, setting a pile of mail on her dad's writing desk. Barkley had built it himself, supposedly as an anniversary gift for her mom, but he was the only one who used it. It was stacked high with woodworking magazines, galley copies of books for possible options, and scripts.

Myla made a point of not looking at Danny, even though her eyes strained to stay on the page. It wasn't that she was angry at him. She was just caught in the rare predicament of having no idea what to do. Knowing that she actually liked this guy, and knowing that he didn't want to get involved even though he seemed to like her, threw her for a loop. Her mind drifted, trying to imagine how she'd act if Danny was just another BHH guy and not her father's employee. Her eyes glazed over as she stared at a tip about treating your partner's penis like a piece of firewood, which she guessed the magazine had never field-tested.

"I hope that's not for school," Danny said, coming up over her shoulder. He looked delectable in a plain white T-shirt and a pair of cargo pants that Myla would have summarily dismissed on any other guy. On Danny, they made her think there just might be hope for the Gap. "Though I guess it's better than an abstinence-only program."

Myla slapped the magazine shut, actually embarrassed. A foreign warmth rose in her cheeks. Was she blushing?

"It's Jojo's magazine," she said, willing the redness from her face. "Girls with two gay dads have it rough, I guess."

Danny plopped down next to her on the couch. "I get the sense you're not crazy about your little sis," he said. "Which I don't get. She seems like a cool girl."

An electric shock of jealousy burst all over Myla's body. She did not want to hear him talk about Jojo. "She's . . . she's whatever," she said, not wanting to get into it. All she needed was yet another guy thinking she'd somehow *abused* Jojo. All she had done was try to make her worthy of Beverly Hills. "We get along fine. We just don't have a lot in common." *For example,* she thought, I *think it's perfectly acceptable to date my dad's twenty-year-old employee, and* she *just wants to ruin everything.*

Danny stood up and clapped his hands together. Myla felt a slight panic rise in her chest. He couldn't be leaving so soon, could he? Then he said, "If you really have nothing to do tonight, you can help me out. But first, you have to change."

Myla looked down at her citron BCBG geometric-print shirt dress. "Into what?" She wondered if he was going to take her on a real date. If they were going to dinner, she'd definitely put on something more . . . seductive. And no matter how cute he looked in those cargos, wouldn't he need to up the sartorial ante, too?

"Do you have anything that doesn't require high heels? Or being dry-cleaned? I don't know, like yoga pants and Chuck Taylors?" Danny smirked, scratching the top of his head. As he did so, his shirt lifted ever so slightly. A peek of six-pack abs flashed briefly in front of Myla's eyes.

"You really have a need to make everything difficult, don't you?" Myla tried to mask her intrigued irritation.

He was driving her crazy with his cryptic invites, and now he was imposing a dressed-down dress code. But what truly bugged her was the fact that she really, really, really wanted to comply.

An hour later, Myla was tugging at the leash of the most stubborn beagle in the world as she followed Danny up a well-trod incline in Runyon Canyon. Danny walked smoothly ahead of her, the regal Weimaraner, Chantal, on his leash trotting merrily and cooperatively forward. The dogs belonged to some Warner Brothers studio head and were technically the charges of one of Danny's buddies, but he'd agreed to help the guy out. And Myla somehow had ended up co-holding the bag. A bag, she disgustedly reminded herself, that would at some future point in time be filled with the beagle's crap.

"Come on, you," she said, tugging at the beagle's leash. The dog dug its front paws into the ground and cocked one of its ears defiantly, as if to say, *Whatever, bitch*.

"Maybe if you use her name, she'll listen," Danny said, slowing down. Chantal, of course, halted, sitting like a well-mannered princess as she waited. Danny raised an eyebrow, challenging Myla to use the beagle's name.

"Fine," Myla said. She gave the leash another gentle tug. "Come on, *Baby Donut*." She laughed. It was impossible not to, when speaking to a dog with such a ridiculous name.

"See? It's fun," Danny said, starting off again. "And it works." Myla noticed a tug on the leash as Baby Donut strutted ahead of her, looking smug. As she trudged upward, Myla had a good view of Danny's muscular back, which tapered down into the world's cutest male butt. She had to admit, though, that the view in general was pretty spectacular. The sun was setting over the basin beneath them, and glowing oranges and purples swirled in the sky. They were climbing up to the edge of a magical candy dish.

Sidestepping a pile of dog poop someone else had failed to clean up, Myla marveled at the fact she was even here. Hiking was so not her thing. And neither was wearing red Vans—a gift from Ash that had never been out of the box—and her old C&C California black yoga pants, the only pair that didn't make her butt look totally flat. The night was a little brisk, even for an October evening in L.A., but Myla still felt the hairs at the nape of her neck sweatily clinging to her skin.

"So, now that you got your dog to move, I have an idea," Danny said, cocking his head back to make eye contact.

"We're going to give Baby Donut to the nearest celebutard and get out of here?" Myla retorted flirtatiously, not caring that two girls from *The Bachelor* sneered dirty looks at her as she passed. Baby Donut gave a loud bark at the girls' matching Chihuahuas, both in Hello Kitty tank tops. Myla found herself starting to like the little jerk.

"Ha-ha. Funny," Danny said. "You know what's not funny?"

Myla shrugged, her hoodie falling off her shoulder. "Why don't you tell me?"

"Me, beating you in a race to the summit. On your mark, get set, go!" Danny and Chantal took off at a clip, heading for the lookout point ahead.

As soon as she realized what he'd done, Myla sprang into action. "Baby Donut, let's go!" To her surprise, the dog summoned a surge of energy and galloped ahead on her short legs. Myla pushed forward, coming up on Danny's left side. He looked over at her and flashed his killer grin. Myla felt her knees buckle. She cocked her best trademark half-smile and sprinted forward after Baby Donut, who'd head-butted Chantal in one of her long, gazelle-like legs. A stunned expression came over Danny's face.

"Good girl, Baby Donut!" Myla shouted, loving the way the air felt as her ponytail loosened and her hair whipped across her face. She charged, hearing Danny hot on her heels, and skidded to a stop seconds before Danny did.

"Look who's the big winner," Danny said, breathless. He sat on a bench on top of the lookout, where the whole city twinkled beneath them, a sea of rooftops, swimming pools, and white, red, and yellow lights. He reached out a hand and pulled Myla down on the bench beside him. "Rest, girl."

"You better be talking to the dog," Myla chided, shaking her hair away from her face and laughing, as the dogs jostled each other for who got to sit nearest to her and Danny.

"And what if I'm not?" Danny's face was inches from hers. Myla inhaled sharply, partly from being out of breath and partly because her heart was jumping up and down, screaming, *Oh my God, please kiss me!*

"There'll be hell to pay," she managed to answer, locking her eyes with his, trying to figure out what it was about him that made all her stray thoughts and worries stop banging against the walls of her head. She didn't think she could ruminate on her friends, her parents, Jojo, or Ash even if she tried right now. He was like Tibetan monk man-candy.

Danny moved a little closer to her. Their thighs touched. "What if I sort of like your version of hell?" Danny whispered. Then he closed the remaining nano-gap between them by putting his lips to hers.

The kiss overwhelmed Myla. They could have been falling from the canyon's edge, down into the commotion below, and she would have had a hard time deciding whether to stop the kiss or stop the fall. The quiet up above the city was overcome by the full-body sensation of feeling Danny's firm lips against her own. Her every nerve felt like one of her little brothers' light-up, whir-ring, siren-noise-making toy cars. If this is what people meant by a runner's high, she was going to train for a marathon.

She had no idea how long they'd been joined at the lips when Baby Donut let out a high-pitched bark. Danny pulled back, his fingers twisted in the fabric of the edge of her T-shirt. Myla relaxed her hands against his shoulder blades. She felt like she'd memorized every sinew of his back.

The sun was falling faster in the sky. Danny rubbed his forehead, dazed. "It looks like we have to go," he murmured, his voice thick in the air.

"So nature closes earlier than the Beverly Center?" Myla joked, suddenly feeling a little shy. Her lips were probably chapped and red from Danny's late-day stubble, and her hair was probably clumped with sweat. But Danny was looking at her like he wanted to look at her forever. She felt the same way.

"Maybe we should go to my house," she suggested, looking down the canyon as though she could pinpoint her family's mansion from there. The house would be empty, at least until Jojo took her final bow.

Danny took her hand and wordlessly led her back the way they came. As he looked back at her and smiled, Myla understood his message: He was all for that idea.

OH, WHAT AN OPENING NIGHT

Forget Hulu, lip-plumping gloss, and the Sprinkles cupcake truck. Tank tops and camisoles were the things for which Jojo was most thankful in the modern age. How did women in Jane Eyre's time deal with these high collars?

Jojo scratched beneath hers in what had to be an unladylike way, feeling very much like she did not want to go through with this.

"Holy shit, the whole school is here," she overheard Linea Russell say to no one in particular. Linea was playing Georgiana Reed, Jane's bitchy-turned-decent cousin. She'd barely said a word to Jojo that she didn't absolutely have to. Linea was pissed about not getting the lead: She'd been bagging on both Jojo and Amelie, who didn't even have that big of a part, by saying they'd only gotten better parts than hers because they were "Hollywood royalty." Linea swept by her so quickly now that Jojo, in her unwieldy hoop skirt, was almost knocked over.

"What up, my peeps?" The voice was one Jojo had come to recognize and dread. Lewis Buford strutted through the girls' dressing area like he owned the place.

Which, as student producer, he kind of did. "We're sold the fuck out! Nice work, Milford. I think everyone wants to see if you've got your mom's acting chops." He leaned against the back stage wall with a thumb in each of his Diesel jeans pockets, watching the girls scurry to put on their dresses, even though most of them were already in pinafores far more modest than anything they normally wore to school. Still, Jojo had gotten into costume in the girls' bathroom just to ensure that Lewis and his entourage didn't see her in her undies. Lewis scanned her now, as if trying to register where Jojo's breasts had gone beneath her buttoned-up, blousy top. "Too bad there's not a nude scene. I'd like to see how you stack up, if you know what I mean." Having seemingly located the twin bumps somewhere beneath the layers of fabric, he stared at her chest like he was thinking about writing a term paper about it.

It was moments like these that Jojo missed Myla. Her sister was an expert at defusing whatever bombs an asshole like Lewis would drop. Not able to think of anything powerful enough to shame him, she pushed past him instead. "Look, I could walk offstage right now, and then you'll have another failed attempt at production on your hands. Is that what you want?" Since Lewis had gotten fired from the student film production, *Student Body*'s buzz had grown way more positive.

Lewis backed off, his hands raised in defense. "Geez, could you lose the PMS? It wasn't even invented back in those days."

Rolling her eyes, Jojo made her way up to the curtain. The encounter with Lewis had left her feeling even more brittle and nervous. Maybe if she could just get a glimpse of Jake, she'd feel better. Jojo had high hopes that after the play tonight they'd make their relationship official. They'd only gotten together once since Sunday, because Jojo had been busy with rehearsals and Jake had Mathletes practice. He'd taken her to *Point Break Live!* last night, a totally nerdy but completely fun live reenactment of the old '80s Keanu Reeves movie about surfer criminals. Afterward, they'd made out for more than an hour, until they'd realized it was past midnight. In school, though, they were still flirting only minimally. Jojo had hoped to be acting more couple-y, or at least walking down the hall together and hanging out at lunch like they had before. But she hadn't even seen Jake near their lockers or in the cafeteria. Jojo didn't want to seem clingy or needy, so she hadn't asked about his whereabouts, mostly because she felt confident Jake really liked her. She didn't want to push too fast for what was bound to happen naturally.

The show was going to start any minute. Jojo hoped checking out the crowd wasn't a terrible idea. The last thing she needed was for the caterpillars in her stomach to turn into full-blown butterflies. She pulled back the velvety curtain and peered into the buzzing auditorium. It was a sea of faces: Myla's friends Talia, Billie, and Fortune, along with the Lacey twins, whose CW show *School for Scandal* had just been canceled, sat about ten rows back, gossiping and texting. Tucker, Mark, Julius, and Geoff sat a few rows behind them, and Jojo swore she could smell pot fumes coming off them in waves. Closer to the front, the editor of the school newspaper, *The Bev-*

erly Bugle, sat next to Perez Hilton, chatting away. The entire front row was empty, with RESERVED signs hanging on each cushioned seat. Just as Jojo started to wonder who would commandeer a whole row of seats for a high school musical, she saw them.

Her mom. Her dad. Mahalo. Bobby. Nelson. Ajani. Indigo. The nanny, Samantha. And . . . her adoptive dads, Fred and Bradley! Filing in behind them was Willa. Wearing her best Guess? minidress and flats, she looked dazed and starstruck as she took in her surroundings, which were positively opulent compared to Sacramento's theater. Fred and Bradley, in their ever-present sweater vests, chattered excitedly with Barkley and Lailah. Even in their neutral-toned traveling clothes, the famous couple still drew all the attention in the room. The kids fidgeted and fussed in their seats, as Samantha tried to soothe them with fruit rollups from her massive tote bag.

"What the . . . ?" Jojo said aloud, to no one in particular. She didn't know what made her feel warmer all over: The fact that Barbar and the kids had come back from Malawi early just for her play, that her dads had made the trek from Greenland, or that Willa must have forgiven her. And how had they arranged all this?

Jojo felt a blissful calm overtake her. Her family, or families—or whatever this was—really *believed* in her. She felt a happy tear form and willed herself not to get all overcome with emotion. Instead, she imagined introducing Jake to her family after the show. Maybe she'd say, "This is my friend, Jake," and he'd correct her and say, "Actually, I'm her *boyfriend.*" Giddiness took over. She couldn't wait to get this show on the road.

"Two minutes to curtain!" Mr. Potter yelled, clapping officiously as he paced backstage. "Jojo, are you ready?"

Taking one more peek at her gorgeous mother and her *three* fathers, beaming proudly as she waited for the show to begin, she said, "I was born ready." It was cheesy, but it felt true. She took a deep breath, vowing to make her family proud. And to make Jake think he couldn't go another day without asking her to be his girlfriend.

Jake tapped the bouquet of roses and daisies against his thigh nervously. Intermission was coming, and he still didn't have a plan.

"Dude, cut that out," Miles said, smoothing down the pointy patch of facial hair he'd finally managed to grow on his chin. "Those flowers are going to be battered by the time you give them to her."

Jake sighed. The problem was, he still didn't know who "her" was.

After his revelation in the cafeteria, he'd gone out with each of them once more, hoping that one girl or the other would make it obvious they would not make a good couple. But both dates had been amazing. He'd taken Jojo to *Point Break Live!*, which he'd picked because it seemed like just the kind of goofball thing she'd enjoy. They'd had a blast, and the only reason they'd stopped laughing on the way home was to kiss for what seemed like hours on end. He'd taken Amelie to The Little Door, a super-romantic French restaurant that she'd suggested. She'd looked beautiful, in a blue cashmere sweater that hung off one shoulder and felt soft to the touch—something he'd found out when he'd made out with *her* for an extra-long time that evening.

In the meantime, he'd had to go all ninja at school to avoid ever being in the same place as both girls at the same time. He'd been hiding out in the AV room during lunch, just so neither girl could find him.

He'd debated not even showing up here tonight. The situation was too fraught with obstacles. But he couldn't bail on both girls when he'd promised. At the same time, he knew he couldn't leave tonight with both of them— or with neither of them. Though he'd agreed to go out with Amelie afterward, he got the feeling that Jojo also thought there'd be an after-play date in the offing. So he'd designated tonight as D-Day: Decision Day. He'd watch the play and choose which girl he liked better, and she'd get the flowers. The other girl would get a breakup speech, delivered in a language he hoped wasn't Giant Assholese.

But he couldn't decide. Both girls were so . . . perfect. Jojo pretty much glowed as Jane. Under the spotlight, she looked like an angel. But the kind of angel who didn't judge you, the kind who made you laugh and who happened to kiss your ear in a way that drove you crazy. Even in her plain dress and low-key makeup, you could understand why Mr. Rochester would fall in love with her. The whole audience seemed to be falling in love with her. But then, Amelie was beyond hot as bitchy Blanche Ingram. What was coolest was knowing she really could act, because she wasn't a bitch at all, and yet Blanche was kind of terrifying. Maybe it helped that her hair was up, exposing her graceful neck, and that even from his spot in the back row, Jake could make out the heart-shaped line of her lips. Just thinking about kissing her was enough to make him start beating the flowers against his thigh violently.

He felt just like the guy playing Mr. Rochester, who'd sung a song about choosing between Jane and Blanche. It had been like a musical pros-and-cons list, and Miles had whispered, "Maybe you *should* have done that. Then your lap wouldn't be covered in rose petals."

Jake had told him to shut up. It wasn't like he and Miles knew anything about girls, really. Kady Parker had come on to *him*. He hadn't had to do any work. If guys like Tucker said this was the way to do things, this was probably the way to do things. Even Ash, when Miles had sent him a text a few days ago, had advised him to listen to Tucker.

Maybe he just needed to see both girls in person. Up close. He nodded to himself. He'd go backstage at intermission and decide. Problem solved. He hoped.

Five minutes later, intermission arrived, and the flower stems were slippery in Jake's clammy hands. This was it.

He wound down the center aisle toward the stage, bypassing tweeting students who weren't paying attention to any of their surroundings. Tucker, Geoff, and the other guys were heading the opposite way, probably to go outside for some "air"—their code for pot. Tucker saw Jake and slowed down.

"Bro, your ladies look good," Tucker said, a little too loudly. Jake looked around, hoping none of the gossip hounds had heard. "Nice work. Maybe you can help me pull babes at the after party."

Jake nodded dumbly. "Sure thing, Tuck. Just something I gotta do," he said, holding up the flowers.

"I get it, man," Tucker said, flipping a pack of rolling papers between his middle and index fingers. "The risks you take to keep 'em happy, huh? Don't worry. If they get mad, I'll hook you up with someone new."

Jake smiled nervously, ready to get away from Tucker. He didn't want someone new. He definitely wanted Jojo. Or Amelie. Definitely one of the girls he already had.

Without knowing how he got there, Jake climbed the stairs to the backstage area. There were only five minutes of intermission left. Actors and actresses in cumbersome Victorian collars and waistcoats darted past him, not even noticing the nerdy kid with the balding bouquet standing in the corner.

Amelie was done for the night. Blanche Ingram only had lines in the first half of the play, but now she had to sit in her stiff, hot costume for another hour so she could take a final bow. She hadn't seen Jake before they started, and she hoped he was there now.

She was kind of having fun just being a second-string girl, but the niggling feeling that she should have been the lead was getting to her. All BHH was there, probably making fun of her for having a lifetime of acting experience and still not getting cast as the lead. And it bugged her that Jojo was really, really good. All her rehearsal screwups and line flubs had vanished, and now she was just Jane Eyre. Amelie should know: She'd read the book about a dozen times. If Amelie weren't so jealous of her, she'd probably have liked Jojo's performance. But there was nothing she could do. She chanted, *Second-best is okay* in her head, hoping that someday she could believe that.

Amelie walked past a bunch of freshman girls who were in the chorus talking about Lewis Buford's after party. She was about to collapse into one of the armchairs reserved for Lewis and his friends when she saw Jake, standing at the edge of the stage with a bouquet in hand.

She zipped past all the crew and her co-stars, practically running in her annoyingly cumbersome hoop skirt. Before he even saw her, she flung her arms around him happily. As he hugged her back, she realized it really didn't matter that she wasn't the lead. She didn't need to lay claim to Drama Club queendom.

She'd claimed something much better: the perfect prince.

EXIT STAGE WRONG

Jojo was sweaty, hot, and oh-so-relieved that opening night was the only night of this show. Acting was exhausting. Plus, Mr. Potter and Lewis had blockaded her at stage left as she'd tried to head backstage, giving her notes on her performance when what she really needed was water.

An intermission kiss from Jake also would be pretty good, she thought, as she finally made it behind the curtains. But she knew better than to *expect* to see him backstage. He was the kind of guy to think that it might throw her off her game to have to entertain visitors.

She paused to let the hair and makeup artist touch up her rouge and spray down her fly-aways, then grabbed a bottle of Smart Water from a cooler behind the Thornfield set and took a long swig. Jojo handed off the bottle to a freshman stagehand who'd been kissing her ass all week. "You were so good," the girl said, leaning in conspiratorially. "I know some people said Amelie should have gotten this part, but you're so much better. Besides, she's totally unprofessional. She let her boyfriend back here."

Amelie has a boyfriend? Jojo thought. *Maybe she* wasn't *checking Jake out the other day.* She looked to where the girl was pointing, a section of curtains that demarked where backstage met stage right. She could only see Amelie's back. Her co-star was wrapped in a guy's arms. She had her arms around his neck, and a bouquet of flowers dangled loosely from her hand as she kissed him. Jojo felt nosy watching them, but something about the guy's hands were familiar. She took a step closer and got a glimpse of dark, curly hair.

Her lip trembled involuntarily. It couldn't be.

But it was. Jake was kissing Amelie. Like he didn't even care if he got caught.

Grabbing the skirt of her costume so tightly that her knuckles turned white, Jojo slid up behind him. Wiping away a tear as she stared furiously at Jake's back, she said, "I can't believe you." The malice in her voice shocked her. And it obviously shocked Jake and Amelie, who jumped away from each other.

Jake's face was red and pale, confused and expectant all at the same time. Like he'd known this was coming but still couldn't believe it had happened. Amelie looked dazed, like she'd just been dragged out of bed at three in the morning. Jojo's instinct was to be mad at her, to yell into her pretty, sculpted face. Her red hair had tumbled from its updo, no doubt thanks to the passionate kisses she'd just shared with the guy who Jojo had thought would be *her* boyfriend. But it really wasn't Amelie's fault. Jojo pulled at her skirt, knowing that if she set her hands free, they'd shove Jake, or punch a wall, or do something equally violent and nonproductive. "I went out with Tucker Swanson, and even *he* never pulled this crap," Jojo said, the words hanging malignantly in the air. "And here you play the nice-guy card, and you're worse than any guy I've ever met. Have a nice life, asshole."

Jojo stormed past the happy pair and through the backstage exit, avoiding the eyes of her co-stars as they waited to take the stage again.

"Where do you think you're going?" Lewis Buford was jogging after her, looking concerned. Not because he felt badly for the crying girl running past him, but because the first-act tweets had been positive, and now his lead was barreling away. "You can't come to the party if you leave."

"Boo hoo," Jojo yelled back at him, propelled in her anger to nowhere in particular, just anywhere but here.

Amelie was still staring at the now-empty space where Jojo had been just seconds ago. She wanted to believe it was all a joke. She turned her gaze on Jake, who looked stiffly rooted to the floor. She felt like she knew everything, just by looking at his hopeless face. Even his curls looked shrunken and guilty. "Are you, or were you, with Jojo?" Amelie asked. Her voice in her own ears sounded like it was coming from some other planet. "At the same time you were with me?"

Jake's hazel eyes looked pained. "I can explain," he started to say. "Well, I don't know how to explain. But it's like, well, with ice cream. You know, with ice cream, how you . . ."

Amelie held up the flowers that she'd assumed were for her—but that could just as easily have been for Jojo. She limply put them back into Jake's arms. "I think you should just go," she said. "You shouldn't even be back here right now. It's only for the actors."

The words weren't as forceful as she wanted them to be. But there was something about being in costume, in the middle of a play, that made it impossible for Amelie to fly off the handle. Jake turned sadly away from her and sheepishly vanished through the curtains, back the way he came.

So that was it. Her first "real" relationship had ended before it even began, like there'd been a hole in it at the beginning and just now, the last bit of air had seeped out. And here she was, with nothing to do but twiddle her thumbs backstage and wait until the show was over. She meandered over to a folding chair, sinking into it. Before she'd managed to fold her skirt underneath her, Mr. Potter was breathing down her throat. His breath smelled like he'd eaten more than his share of the garlic-infused hummus set out on the PTA-sponsored snack table.

"Where is Miss Milford?" he asked almost accusingly, a dark shock of hair clinging to his sweaty forehead. "We have curtain in five minutes."

Amelie shrugged. What, did he think she wanted the part so badly she'd offed the lead? "I don't know," she said. "She walked that way." As she pointed vaguely in the direction of the backstage exit, it dawned on her. Jojo had just up and left. She didn't even care about the show after what Jake had done. Now, that *did* make Amelie jealous. Even though she wanted to leave right this second, she felt duty-bound to stay. It's what you did in this business. She envied Jojo's freedom to bail.

Mr. Potter pulled so tightly at his turtleneck, Amelie

thought his head would pop right off. "She's *gone*? We don't have a show without her! *Eeeee-eee-oooo!*" He made a noise that sounded like a cat being swung around by its tail.

Nick came up behind Mr. Potter's shoulder, towering over the teacher in both his height and his relative composure. He put a hand on Mr. Potter's arm. "We have Amelie, remember?" he offered. "Blanche isn't in the second half. Amelie knows this play back and forth. And she's an amazing actress. She'll do it, right?"

"You really could do that?" Mr. Potter said, rocking back and forth on his heels like one of those inflatable punching bags.

"I need hair, makeup, and a costume change," Amelie said, taking charge of the situation. She smiled gamely at the director. "But of course I can do it."

She was already playing the part of a woman scorned. Why not add martyr to the mix?

THE AGE OF INNOCENCE

"You're not going to tell my dad about this, are you?" Myla said, and then she laughed, rolling on top of Danny. "Oh my God, that sounded so dirty."

"I'd be an idiot if I told your dad about this," Danny replied, wrapping his arms around her back, and placing little, light kisses along her jawbone. Each one made Myla's heart hurdle over the top of the beat it was supposed to make next. "But I don't mind at all when you sound tarty."

They were in her room, still mostly dressed. Myla was down to her tank top and yoga pants, and Danny's shirt was off, his warm chest rising and falling beneath hers. They'd been blissfully entwined for the better part of the evening.

Blissfully was definitely the right word. They'd barely been able to keep their hands off each other the whole ride home, and had almost forgotten to bring the dogs back to the WB executive's house. They'd nearly been at her house when they'd had to turn around and head back to drop off the pooches. When they had finally gotten back to her house and been able to continue the kissing they'd started at Runyon Canyon, Myla had nearly melted. Everything about being with Danny felt so good. She felt like herself, but like a different self than what she normally was when she was being herself. It sounded crazy, but it wasn't. With Ash, she'd always wanted to make him prove himself. She'd needed to know he'd do anything she wanted: tag along with her when she went shopping, drop plans with friends, or just plain pursue her. If he'd asked her to go hiking, she would have laughed in his face, even while wondering if maybe it would be fun. She'd loved Ash, but she'd also enjoyed making things dramatic. But Danny seemed to see right through that, and he pushed her to just *be.* Which explained why she was lying on top of her rumpled bedspread with him, her makeup probably long gone and her hair still sticky with sweat from their hike. Maybe there really was something to dating an older guy. Or maybe it was just him. She giggled a little, thinking of how she'd wanted to capture Danny just to prove she could.

"What's so funny?" Danny asked, rolling her over so he was on top of her. His hair, normally so neat, was adorably askew, and a piece hung in front of his warm umber eyes. Myla noticed for the first time that his nose was sprinkled with no more than a dozen freckles, so faint you almost couldn't see them. But she could. She grinned up at him.

"Did I laugh?" Myla traced his spine with her fingertips. She didn't want to tell him what had been on her mind. She didn't necessarily have to confess to the fact that he made her want to leave behind years of bitchdom. She glanced at the clock. It was after ten. The play had to be over by now, and Jojo wasn't home. She must have gone to Lewis's party with the rest of BHH. Even though Myla rarely missed big BHH social engagements, she didn't care anymore. "Maybe I was just thinking you're doing a bad manny job. You haven't fed me yet, and I'm just not capable of feeding myself."

"I can fix that." Danny leaned in and gave her a kiss so long and deep that whatever residual muscle pain existed from their hike simply evaporated, replaced instead by a different kind of burn that made her regret suggesting dinner. She really didn't need to eat. This was more satisfying. Danny pulled himself away, taking his crumpled T-shirt off the bed and pulling it over abs it seemed a sin to cover up. "We have these things in the Midwest called restaurants with delivery. Do you have them here?"

Myla laughed, standing up in a happy make-out hangover. "You Midwestern boys, so naive." She sidled over to Danny, eager to sneak in one more kiss before they headed downstairs.

The door burst open.

Barkley was standing in the doorway. His denim-blue eyes were wide with surprise, and his blondish-brown hair shot up in points. "What's going on here?" He looked from Myla to Danny, who took a huge step back, crashing into Myla's nightstand. Barkley ignored Danny, focusing his steely gaze on Myla. "Jojo's missing. She ran off at intermission and didn't finish the play. I thought she would be here. But apparently, I have more than one daughter to worry about."

Myla swallowed. She should have expected this. Her parents had come home early, to see their perfect daughter act in her perfect play. Then her dad had come home to find his other daughter—hereafter probably to be thought of as the skanky one—in the arms of the hired help.

"It's not what you think," Myla stammered. *I really like him, Daddy,* she wanted to say, but her dad's expression told her that no words would do. His eyes were glassy, like he might cry or yell, but hadn't decided which. He absently picked up a framed photo of him and Myla that sat on her vanity, glanced at it for all of a second, and put it down like he didn't even know the father and daughter staring back at him. Myla knew that whatever punishment he'd dole out later would be nothing compared to that look, which said that he didn't even recognize her anymore. He shook his head disdainfully.

Danny tensed, completely still. Myla remembered what he'd told her that day at the racetrack when he stopped their almost-kiss from happening. This job meant so much to Danny. And Barkley must have really liked him, she now realized, to put him in charge of his daughters. Myla shuddered. She'd known what she was doing. But yet again, nothing had mattered to Myla more than Myla.

Barkley turned his back on her and walked to the door. Without turning to look at her or Danny, he spoke bluntly and plainly. "I have to go find Jojo. We'll discuss this later, Myla," he said. "And Danny, I think it goes without saying that you're fired. Be out of here in the next two minutes. And you're never to go near my daughter again." He walked out into the hall, leaving Myla and Danny staring dumbly at the spot in the door he'd just occupied.

He left the door open. But to Myla, it felt as though he'd slammed it shut.

AND THEN THERE WERE NONE

Jake sat down at his kitchen table, staring intently at the coupon for a new pizza place that his mom had left under the napkin basket. Sadly, That's Amore's two-for-one special had no advice about what to do when not one, but two girls decided you were the shittiest guy alive. Two-for-one deals apparently did not work in the dating world.

After Amelie had sent him away, he'd gone back to his seat and watched the rest of the play in a self-hating daze. "What happened to Jojo?" Miles had asked, when everyone realized Amelie taken over the lead for the second half of the play. Jake would have liked to know, too. He felt guilty and shamed when he saw her parents—*both* sets—leaving midway through the second half. The whole Everhart family and their guests had tried to leave without creating a scene when they realized that Jojo not resuming her role as Jane Eyre was not some postmodern theater device. Of course, the world's two biggest movie stars couldn't simply walk out of a high school play without attracting attention. The whole audience had turned to look, paying no mind to Amelie's most emotional musical number, where Jane decides she really, truly wants to marry Mr. Rochester. So he'd screwed up a big night for *both* girls.

Ever since he'd tried to become a whole new Jake, he'd been a royal fuck-up. First, he'd been a tutor-stalker. Then, he got a part in a movie, got a hot girlfriend, and turned into an insta-douche. He'd bought an Escalade before the ink was dry on his first paycheck. And now, he'd actually managed to get two girls to like him, and he'd gotten greedy. It served him right that neither Amelie nor Jojo would probably ever talk to him again. He didn't deserve it. Maybe he'd start coming straight home after school from now on to paint those miniature Dungeons & Dragons figures. He'd always hated those things, which would make it the perfect punishment.

"When am I going to get it right?" he mumbled to himself, banging his head down on the table. He was too tired to get up and head to his bedroom.

He heard the freezer door slurp open and lifted his head as its light cast a beam over the table. "Get what right?" came his mom's voice, oddly chipper for past midnight on a Friday. She pulled out a pint of cookies-and-cream ice cream, opened a drawer to get a spoon, and shuffled to the table, her hair a tangle of curls radiating from her head. Gigi Porter was a high-powered Holly-wood publicist who could bring producers to tears, but her weakness was dessert.

"What are you doing up, Mom?" Jake asked, hoping she had bigger problems than he did that they could talk about instead.

Gigi sighed contentedly as she spooned a massive hunk

of ice cream into her mouth. She closed her eyes, letting it melt, then exhaled like she'd been holding her breath for three days. "This damn Master Cleanse is going to fucking kill me. Excuse my French. I've been on nothing but cayenne pepper lemonade for a week," she muttered. "I've lost five pounds but I swear, I've only slept a hour. So . . . this." She waggled the ice cream container in front of Jake's face and raised an eyebrow as she dipped her spoon in again. "But don't change the subject. What has you in the dark, banging your head against the table?"

Her inquisitive look was all Jake needed. Nothing could shield you from Gigi's stare. Jake wondered whether it was a standard feature on all Jewish mothers or his mom had gotten the upgrade. He propped his head in his hand and mumbled into his palm. "I sort of tried dating two girls at once," he said, the words barely intelligible to even his own ears.

Gigi's other power was the ability to translate whispers, grumbles, and irritable teenage body language. She swatted Jake with the back of her hand. "Two girls? Which two? Out with it."

"Well, I told you about that girl Jojo Milford, right? Ash's ex's new sister? Well, I was at a party, and she just sort of . . . kissed me. And then, you know about Amelie, how I had a thing for her? And one day at tutoring, *she* kissed me." Jake stared at the area over his mom's shoulder, looking at a third-grade photo of himself on the fridge. He was holding up two model rockets. His parents had told him he could launch one rocket, and the other one had to be donated to a toy drive. He'd labored over the decision for hours. And yet eight-year-old Jacob had had no idea how much harder decisions would get once testosterone was involved. "But I didn't want to lie to either of them. I liked them both, and I didn't know what to do."

Gigi had gotten another spoon, which she handed to Jake. She held out the ice cream container. "So, at some point you must have decided something."

Jake spooned out a tiny chunk of ice cream, not wanting it at all. He watched it melt into a pool of vanilla and cookie bits on the spoon. "Well, this guy Tucker, who's like a girl expert or something, said how girls are like ice cream, and you have to taste a few different flavors before you pick one." Jake watched the melted ice cream drip onto the tabletop. His mom didn't seem to notice. "And it seemed like a good idea. So I dated them both. For a little while."

"And tonight, it all came crashing down around you when they found out about each other?" His mom shook the spoon in the air like a sword. "Oh, Jacob."

Jake raised his hands in protest. "But I didn't know which one I liked better. It seemed like a good idea. Even Miles said so."

Gigi rolled her eyes. "First off, Miles and girl advice? Someday, he might have a clue, but that day wasn't yesterday, it's not today, and it's not tomorrow. Second, if you take a little time, you know what kind of ice cream you like. I've been eating this flavor for years." She pointed her spoon down at the mostly empty container. "And third, did you even think about being honest with them? Hang out with them, without making out with them?"

Jake blushed. He really didn't want to talk about sex, or anything approaching it, with his mom.

"Of course you made out with them. You're a sixteen-year-old boy ruled by your shvantz. But don't lie to yourself. You never thought dating them both was a good idea. You just wanted to have your cake and eat it, too." Gigi clucked her tongue, peering into the container. "I ate the whole damn thing. I hate myself."

Jake stood up, feeling a little better. He leaned down to hug his mom, who was staring angrily at the empty container, like the ice cream had made her eat it. "Are you going to call me a douche bag again?"

Gigi sighed. "We all make mistakes. A putz, yes. But I'll let you go with that for tonight." She kissed his cheek, yawning. "I helped my son, and I gained back probably six pounds. At least I'm going to get some sleep now."

Jake laughed, and they walked side by side up the stairs.

Once in his room, Jake lay on his bed, staring at the ceiling for what felt like hours. The chaos in his head calmed down, and he knew what he had to do: make a choice. What he should have done all along.

He pulled out a notebook and started a pros-and-cons list for each girl. They were both fresh in his mind, and he composed the lists quickly and easily. Amelie was gorgeous, and he'd never forget the shock and amazement he felt the first time she opened her trailer door for tutoring and was standing there, practically glimmering, like some kind of superhero. No guy on earth could walk past her without noticing her pool-blue eyes and her soft red hair, or her yoga-toned legs. She was so much of a *somebody* that Jake felt like a somebody just by being around her.

Jojo was gorgeous, too. On her list, Jake couldn't not mention her twinkling violet eyes or her smooth shoulders. She also had a laugh like a bell, which just rang out and enveloped you. When she laughed at his jokes, he just felt good. And she'd helped him with his *Class Angel* role when everyone else just thought he was a loser. And she teased him about his dorkiness in an affectionate way, like she understood where he was coming from. Maybe she really did.

Within a half hour, he'd filled a page for each of them. And he didn't even have to read the lists over to know which girl he'd chosen. What he also knew was they were both great girls and they both deserved a massive apology.

With that in mind, he took out his laptop and started drafting two new e-mails. If he was lucky, at least they'd both accept his apology. If he was *really* lucky, she'd be willing to give him a second chance.

LEAVIN' ON A JET PLANE

Ash struggled back into his Vans before the crush of people headed through airport security actually crushed him. Behind him, a fortysomething woman slipped into a pair of high-heeled boots, teetering against him and regaining her balance by kneading his butt cheek a little. Ash jumped a little as she winked a dark-shadowed eye and left for her gate. He'd just been breakfast for a cougar.

Even at three thirty in the morning, the Detroit airport was teeming with people. He'd booked the earliest flight out of the city, at five a.m., and he wanted to make a get-away before Daisy woke up. She'd come home from the night's show at one that morning, and he'd faked being asleep. When Daisy had drifted off right away, he'd been relieved. He knew it was a little cowardly to sneak out at three a.m. leaving only a short note, but he wouldn't have been able to leave if he'd had to look Daisy right in her innocent doe eyes.

His dad had been right. Gordon Gilmour's whole "musicians live by a different set of rules" spiel didn't add up to Daisy just being her unconventional, free-spirited self. She'd been *cheating* on Ash. True, he'd never caught her actually, but he didn't have to. He just knew it. And she'd *invited him on tour,* like it was some kind of game for her. It didn't just hurt, it was insulting to his intelligence. She must have thought that he was dumb enough to pull one over on, or that he'd be so blinded by her talent and beauty, he wouldn't notice she spent most of her free time with Trick.

He sat down next to a woman in her pajamas, her Ugg-covered feet up on a duffel bag. She looked like she'd just woken up and decided to go on vacation. She was engrossed in a copy of *In Touch Weekly*, reading the captions on the photos like they were old love letters. She cast a sidelong glance at him, not realizing that his photo was on the page she was reading. It was a grainy camera-phone shot of him and Daisy leaving La Mia Pizza in New York. "Are you making the early-morning escape, too, kid?" she said, even though she was probably only in her late twenties. "Take it from someone who's been there, done that—twice now: Long-distance relationships fucking blow."

Ash smirked at her, glad to not be the only person on Earth taking the easyish way out in the wee hours of the night. "All relationships fucking blow." He looked down at the guitar case at his feet. He had checked all his other bags but didn't want to let his guitar out of his sight. Not that it did him much good. He'd been so excited about being on tour, thinking he'd write songs, as if the simple act of hanging with rock stars would make him a rock star by osmosis. But he was no closer to being a musician than he had been two and a half weeks ago, when he was slacking off in Tucker's garage.

"Flight 245's first-class passengers may begin board-ing," a female voice said over the intercom. Ash sighed in relief. He couldn't wait to sink into his fully reclining seat and fall back asleep. Days of riding the bus with the band followed by sleepless nights waiting up for Daisy had taken their toll.

He stood up and gave the woman in pajamas a little wave. She barely looked up from reading intently about where Robert Pattinson liked to hang out in his down-time. Picking up his guitar case from the floor, Ash was nearly bowled over when he stood up.

There was Daisy, breathless, her hand clutching a plane ticket as she leaned against his chest for support. She looked even more than usual as though she must have gotten dressed in the dark. She wore a red-and-purple-checked flannel shirt over a pair of hot-pink jeans and had a pair of brown beaded Indian moccasins on her feet. But the exertion had brought a pretty blush to her cheeks, and her gray eyes sparkled with tears. She looked beautiful.

"You can't go," she said breathlessly. "You have it all wrong. You can't go." She brandished the W stationery where he'd written his note: *Daisy, I know you're with Trick. Thanks for the invite, but I can't do this. –Ash.*

Ash looked down at her, disbelieving. "Then why do you have all these jokes together, like you're part of your own secret world? And what were you doing hanging out every night?" The words came out in a rush, before Ash could think about what he was saying. But when they finally emerged, his chest loosened, like he'd been walk-ing around for days with his heart in a tiny, cramped box and saying what he felt aloud had helped it break free.

Daisy sidled up close to him, and his senses filled with the jasmine lotion she put on before bed. She grabbed his waist and nestled her head against him. "You are just so bloody wrong, it makes me love you more," she said. The word *love* rang through Ash's body like a chime. She continued, "There's nothing between me and Trick. He wants to leave the band. Those were *breakup* negotiations. He wants to talk to your dad about a solo record, so I didn't tell you—I didn't want you to feel pressured or be caught knowing more than you'd want to know."

The woman with long-distance relationship problems was rapt as she watched them. Apparently, *The Daisy and Ash Show* was more interesting than the Kardashians. Or maybe she'd matched their faces to the photo, and her rag mag was coming to life before her very eyes. "She's not lying," the woman breathed, mostly to herself.

From the way Daisy held his gaze, Ash knew she wasn't lying, too. A tear had formed in one of her gray eyes. "I'm sorry I doubted you," he said, meaning it. Why hadn't he asked her point-blank about Trick? Daisy had trusted him with her secret identity, and he couldn't trust her with her bassist for a few hours? He blamed his dad for brainwashing him about rock stars. Ash glanced at the ticket in her hand. "Are you coming back with me?" he asked, hope filling his brain.

Daisy shook her head. "I had to buy it, to get to you. But you know I have to finish this tour," she whispered. "I want to finish this tour. And maybe you could, too. You could even take Trick's place in the band if he leaves. What do you think?"

"I play guitar, not bass," Ash said, lightly kicking the Strat at his feet.

"So, bass has got less strings," Daisy said, laughing through a fresh run of tears. "What if I told you that you can't go back. Because I love you, and I need you to stay."

The intercom crackled again. "Final boarding call for all passengers on flight 245."

The harried woman begrudgingly rose from her chair, dragging herself away from the soap opera unfolding. "Ticktock, make up your mind," she said to Ash.

Ash cracked his knuckles, feeling more conflicted than hurried. He could imagine a future with Daisy. Long drives on the tour bus. Dozing off in each other's arms between stops at greasy spoons and random roadside attractions. Nights of playing shows, then being up until dawn because they were bursting with energy from giving such a great performance. Daisy at the microphone, looking back at him with a smile right before he played a solo. Mornings spent in bed, ordering room service and messing around. No school. No parents. No responsibilities except being on stage every night. It was *Pinocchio, Peter Pan,* and every road trip movie ever made—all rolled into one. Without the lessons. And with nudity. Basically, it was every seventeen-year-old guy's dream. He could see a future Daisy—could practically imagine her on the cover of *Rolling Stone*, looking every bit the edgy and much-emulated rock goddess. But when he tried to picture himself there, next to her, he could see the outline of a guy with his face in the shadows—a guy who could be him or just as easily someone else.

Ash closed his eyes and imagined never seeing his friends again. The b.s. and band meetings in Tucker's garage. The parties, the beach trips, the early-morning surfing sessions. And he thought of Myla. He didn't know if they'd ever get back together. He didn't even think that was what he wanted. But even now, he couldn't imagine not having her in his life, even just as a friend. How weird would it be to not hug her at graduation, or bump into her when they were both home from college on Christmas break.

"Final boarding call for flight 245," the intercom voice said. Ash looked up and saw that the announcer was at a desk just a few feet away. She was looking straight at him.

"So, what do you think?" Daisy said, her grasp still tight around his waist. Ash loved how her hands felt. They were so small and delicate, but her grip was so strong. He wanted to stay. But . . . he didn't. He couldn't.

"I think. . . ," Ash started, faltering as he looked into Daisy's eyes, which had become the color of wet asphalt as tears streamed down her face. Going the young-rock-star route sounded tempting, but he didn't want to miss out on the other, more average path either. After all, wasn't it the everyday stuff that people wrote the best songs about? "I think we just don't fit together. No, I mean, we do *fit*, but just not right now."

Daisy leaned her full weight against him, and Ash felt like she would fall if he stepped backwards. "But maybe someday we will?"

He'd never felt this needed before in his life, and it would be hard to leave this feeling behind. But he also

didn't want to run away from normal life. He ran his fingertips lightly along Daisy's chin, lifting her face so their
eyes met. "I think someday we definitely will. Call me
when the tour's over, yeah?"

Daisy followed him all the way to the ramp. The ticket
taker gave them an impatient glare, but apparently the
scene had pulled his heartstrings just enough for him to
keep his mouth shut. Ash lifted Daisy off the floor, and
they kissed as they cried, their tears blending.

As Ash reluctantly let her go and boarded the plane,
he realized he'd played his first goodbye song.

SEE JANE DISS

Amelie folded what had to be the seventy-fifth prop handkerchief, unable to remember a single time during last night's performance when even one of them had been used. Lola Esperanza kept dumping fresh piles of them at Amelie's feet. Still, the routine work was calming. She let her brain zone out as she made a crisp fold in one embroidered with a rose. If she let her thoughts stray, they went straight to Jake, and to their kiss. Their last kiss. She didn't want to think about Jake. Ever again, if possible.

"Need help with some of those?" Nick asked, sitting down beside her at the long cafeteria table. He scooted a chair closer, even though they were the only two people at the whole table. The rest of the cast was busy breaking down sets, putting gowns in garment bags, and gossiping about Lewis's party. Two senior girls who'd been in the chorus whispered something as they sauntered by, poufy dresses draped over their arms. "I still don't believe it," Amelie overheard one say. Her ears sharpened to hear them distinctly drop her name and Jojo's. So Jojo must not have made an appearance at the big shindig, either.

Amelie pushed a pile of hankies toward Nick, smiling. "They're all yours," she said. "Thanks." They folded in silence for a little while. It was nice to sit next to him. The rest of the cast hadn't made much of an effort to talk to her. Granted, she hadn't made much of an effort to talk to any of them for the past few weeks. She'd been so Jake-obsessed and self-absorbedly angry about not getting the lead. Out of the corner of her eye, Amelie could see Nick looking at her out of the corner of his, like he wanted to say something but didn't know what. "You did great last night," she said, not knowing what else to talk about.

Nick laughed, brushing a coil of dark hair out of his eyes. "Come on, no one here is better than you," he said. "I still can't believe that you had the whole show down cold."

Amelie felt a blush hit her cheeks. "I can't believe that Mr. Potter never cast an understudy for Jane," she said, shaking her head. Actually, the fact that Mr. Potter had screwed up so massively made her feel incrementally better that he hadn't cast her. Of course, everyone thought the joint Jane-playing was an avant-garde trick of his. Perez Hilton had called it true proof of hackdom on his blog, but had circled both Amelie and Jojo with white hearts.

"I can't believe he didn't just cast you in the first place," Nick said, putting his last folded handkerchief on top of the pile. He caught her eye and smiled. "Why anyone wouldn't choose you is beyond me." He stood up with one final look at Amelie and went back to help the crew carry the wooden backdrops to the storage room. She watched him retreat, wondering for a second what he'd meant. And then she decided to just enjoy the compliment.

The Jane Eyre costume felt heavy in Jojo's arms, like she was carrying a soaking-wet sack of beach towels. The dress was totally dry, of course, but her arms and legs felt weak and dull. It figured that just as she was starting to feel comfortable with herself at BHH, something had to go very, and very publicly, wrong.

After leaving Jake alone with Amelie, she'd wandered down BHH's empty halls, not wanting to face anyone—not even her family. She'd eventually made her way to the computer lab—ironically, the place where she'd first met Jake. She had sunk into a chair and had fallen asleep, not waking up until the play was over. She'd called a taxi to bring her home and sneaked inside the empty house, passing out in bed, still in her costume. When she'd woken this morning, the house had been frantic with activity. She'd been hoping to create as little fanfare as possible. Apparently, she'd done the opposite.

Everyone had been looking for her. A uniformed police officer was even there, reassuring Lailah that Jojo had probably gone to a party and forgotten to tell them, that Hollywood stars' kids got up to no good all the time, and they should just be glad she wasn't selling drugs like Michael Douglas's son.

The cop had almost cracked up laughing when she came down the stairs in full-on Victorian-era garb. "At least you don't have to worry about her getting pregnant. A guy couldn't find the end of that dress," the cop had joked tastelessly.

Barkley had dismissed the officer and begun tugging at his hair with his hands. Jojo had never seen him so worked up—on film or in real life. "First I had to fire Danny, and now this," he said, shaking his head. "And we look like reckless idiots besides. You were here this whole time and didn't tell us? We can never go away again, Lai."

Hearing that Danny had been fired, Jojo immediately figured out what happened. So Myla had succeeded in seducing the manny. And now the poor guy was out of a job. Her sister really had a lot to learn about karma.

Now, Jojo was on strict orders to return her costume to school and come straight back home. She pushed through the double doors at the back of the auditorium, only to come face-to-face with Lewis Buford, wearing neon green Ray-Bans and a shirt that read HUNG in big letters across the chest with the word OVER in microscopic letters beneath.

"Well, if it isn't everyone's un-favorite disappearing act," Lewis said, leaning against the cinder-block wall of the theater. All around him, the rest of the cast and crew were breaking down the sets. Lewis must have thought it was his right as a producer to not do anything but watch people work for him. Sort of like every producer in L.A. "Nice of you to return your costume. I thought I was going to have to charge you."

Jojo shifted her eyes to the dress, then to Lewis, before thrusting the bundle into his arms. "Why? Were you planning to wear it later?"

A titter of laughter fluttered through the auditorium. It was good to know her castmates still liked her better than Lewis, even if she had walked out on them. She stepped over a few sophomore AV squad members, who were neatly placing gels from the spotlights back into boxes. She stopped when she reached Amelie, who was wrapping props and returning them to lockable trunks. Jojo looked around for something to do, feeling several sets of eyes on her. Of course, everyone was talking. The whole cast had seen her go off on Jake and, by extension, Amelie. They probably thought she and Amelie were romantic rivals, especially since they hadn't exactly been BFFs on the set *before* Jake had screwed them both over. The same instinct occurred to her as it had last night— to tear into Amelie for stealing Jake. But that was what foolish girls did: They looked for another girl to blame, never holding the guy accountable.

Amelie paused as she wiped down a gold-edged mirror, and smiled wanly at Jojo. Her red hair was in a loose bun, and she wore a loose black T-shirt over a pair of ripped Hudson jeans. She looked enviably beautiful, even though the dark circles under her eyes made it clear she'd slept about as peacefully as Jojo had.

Jojo picked up a candelabrum and started rolling it up in Bubble Wrap. She was grateful for something to do with her hands. "I didn't get to thank you yesterday," she finally said, the words surprising her as they came out. "I was too busy sprinting away to realize that someone would have to make sure the show would go on. I'm glad it was you."

Amelie blew a strand of red hair out of her eyes as she nestled a set of glued-together faux books into the trunk. She hadn't expected this. "I was thinking I should apologize," she said. "I didn't know you were dating Jake."

She and Jojo reached for the same embroidered tapestry at the same time. Amelie backed off, letting Jojo grab the velvety ends. "We just keep going for the same things," Amelie joked, before helping Jojo fold the unwieldy fabric into a square.

Jojo laughed. "I'm sure Jake didn't want me to find out about you, either. But anyway, I'm the sorry one. I feel like a jerk, running off like that. I wasn't thinking clearly. I just had to get away from everything."

Amelie patted Jojo's arm lightly. "Seriously, I get it. I wanted to do the same thing," she said. She was still envious that Jojo had been able to just do what came naturally, even if it might have been the wrong thing. Amelie sometimes wondered if she even knew how to act natural anymore. "But I couldn't. If you'd ever been to Kidz Network boot camp, you'd know that we all get brainwashed. I swear, I remember a chapter in the handbook about how to do a comic scene after your dog dies."

"So, is there another chapter on how to sing and dance when you learn the guy you like is a dog?" Jojo smirked, raising an eyebrow.

Amelie glanced over to where Nick was ever-so-slowly bagging costumes. She wondered if he was listening in. She smiled to herself, thinking of what he'd said: *Why anyone wouldn't choose you is beyond me.* Did he know what had happened? She almost felt bad that Jojo didn't have a Nick to brighten her mood. Her violet eyes were a little bloodshot and, in her oversize sweatshirt and beat-up Chuck Taylors, she seemed so much smaller than she had when she was donning the Jane Eyre costume. The one Amelie had wanted so badly.

"I wish," Amelie said, kind of glad not to be vehemently hating Jojo. "So, when did you guys start going out?"

Jojo blushed. "I guess it was just last Sunday," she admitted, playing with the hem of her worn-out JFK High soccer jersey. "Kind of lame to get that upset over a guy after less than a week, huh?"

Amelie carelessly tossed the prop teapot she was holding into the trunk. "No way," she said, calculating the dates in her head. "I went out with him for the first time on Sunday, too."

Picking up the teapot and wrapping it more carefully, Jojo grinned, shaking her head. "I can't believe that Jacob PG would be capable of such playerdom."

"They call him PG?" Amelie asked. How could she not know the nickname of the guy she'd so ardently liked—and now so ardently disliked?

"RJ is more like it, right?" Jojo grinned. "For *royal jerk*."

"Or RA, for *raging asshole*," Amelie said. She smiled slightly. Bagging on guys with another girl? That had to be worth twenty normal-girl points.

"That's harsh, Fairy Princess," Jojo said, but she was smiling. She wrapped the last of the props, a china teacup, and put it in the case. "I have to go. I'm kind of in trouble for my getaway last night. But maybe you want to come shopping with me and my friend Willa sometime while she's in town? She hates Jake as much as we do, and she never even dated him."

Amelie nodded, beaming. "That would be fun," she said.

So what if she couldn't mark *boyfriend* off her checklist? The way things were shaping up, she might have actually made a friend.

REWIND

I think it goes without saying that you're fired. The look on her dad's face, like that of someone who'd taken a sip of wine and been told mid-swallow that it was poisoned. The door opening and Danny's hand dropping from her shoulder. Lying next to Danny, with barely a millimeter of space between them, skin next to skin. His fingers circling to catch her hair between them. A long, slow kiss. A thousand little ones. The humid chamber of their mouths together. Touching each other across the front seats of the car, his fingertips brushing her knees, her hand wrapped around the crook of his elbow. Time stopping on top of the ledge at Runyon Canyon. Feeling ten billion miles above the Earth—and climbing. Running ahead of Danny, her hair snapping against the wind like flames of a fire. Cheering at Santa Anita, buoyant and free. Danny finding her after the pajama party, that cool stare that made Myla feel drenched in warmth. Sashaying by him in the kitchen, making one step a tease, the next a promise. Flinging the door open to see him for the first time, and only in memory realizing he would let her get away with everything and with nothing.

Myla had pressed REWIND on her and Danny's romance again and again, the events folding in on themselves until she needed a sip of water to fight off dizziness. She wanted to reach into the spiraling disaster and pluck out all the horrible things she'd done that had led to this, but the events kept whizzing by faster and faster, reminding her that she'd asked for this, just by being herself. She'd eaten nothing since last night. She'd barely slept. She'd paced the room, willing a solution to appear on one of her goose-down pillows like a neatly placed hotel mint. She felt weaker than if she'd spent a day toting the September issues of *Vogue, Elle,* and *Harper's Bazaar* against the wind, uphill, wearing six-inch wedges made of solid gold.

"You deserve it," Myla said to her own reflection in the mirror. It was definitely a first for her. Usually, she couldn't gaze on herself without feeling deep admiration. Today, she wished she could trade places with just about anyone—even, say, a fashion-challenged girl who lived in Idaho and still thought the Rachel was a viable haircut. "You deserve to have bad hair and a saggy ass."

It seemed to Myla that an unattractive outside would have helped reflect her ugly insides. She blinked and looked again. Her black licorice hair danced around her face like party streamers. She'd refused to put on makeup, as part of her self-imposed punishment, but each of her features had decided to have a great day anyway. Her eyelashes practically swept the ceiling. Her green eyes shone like new leaves on one of her mother's camellia plants. Her skin was poreless and camera-ready. High-def camera–ready. Even her A-cups, usually the bane of her existence due to their nonexistence, looked a little fuller and higher, like they were haughtily telling her, *You don't deserve us.*

And she didn't. Her whole family was treating her like a big, slutty leper. Ajani had come to Myla's door that morning, probably hoping to play Hannah Montana (in Ajani's world, Hannah mostly kicked the shit out of the Jonas Brothers). But Myla had overheard her mother tell Ajani that Myla couldn't play today. They probably didn't want their adorable four-year-old learning any bad-girl behavior from their letdown of a sixteen-year-old.

But most of all, Danny. During the few minutes of sleep she'd managed last night, she'd woken thinking she heard movement on the lawn beneath her window, hoping that it was Danny, about to throw pebbles at her window, to sneak up and tell her it would all be okay. That her parents could disown her, but she could come live with him in his one-bedroom. She'd add a feminine touch to his bachelor pad, replacing the inevitable futon with a chaise lounge, tossing the Target halogen lamp in favor of a Tiffany lamp with a pretty glow. For him, she'd even learn how to cook. Maybe he could develop a solar-powered kitchen, and they could devise dishes together and start a sexy organic cooking show on the Food Net-work. But the sound had been nothing, and she'd gone back to tossing and turning in the torturous luxury of her six-hundred-count Egyptian cotton sheets.

Myla backed away from the mirror and flopped onto her bed. Who was she kidding? Danny would never speak to her again. She'd gotten him *fired*, probably blacklisted. He'd be jobless, penniless. He'd starve, or worse, move back to the Midwest. She lay facedown in the pillow he'd napped on last night, inhaling the leafy and minty smell he'd left behind. She'd need to get an airtight container to preserve the heady aroma. Someday Myla's grandchildren would look at the pillow encased in glass and ask her what it was. She'd tell them it was the only memento she had of the one who got away. Because even if she could talk her dad into giving Danny his job back—and she doubted that she could—he probably would never come near her again.

A knock came at her door, more forceful than Ajani's sticky-palmed pats. Her dad. He rarely starred in sequels, but when it came to lectures, a part two was inevitable. Especially since last night he'd had time only to give her a withering stare and to crush Danny's future with one sentence. After that, he'd left to look for Jojo, who'd returned and slept in her own bed without telling anyone she was safely at home. In Myla's opinion, Jojo should be in as much, if not more, trouble as Myla was. Not only had she sent the whole family into hysterics, but they'd called the police, which meant all the tabloids and even the legitimate papers would probably find out about the Everharts' dramatic evening.

"Come in," Myla croaked wearily, lifting herself to sit Indian-style on the bed. In her baggy sweater and cosmetics-less face, she hoped she at least looked innocent. Technically, Barkley had just caught Danny standing fully-clothed in her room and correctly assumed the rest. If her dad had come home just fifteen minutes earlier and found them lying next to each other, would it have been even worse? Would poor Danny be headed to jail?

She shuddered, her skin chilling. She steeled herself for a lecture, praying it wouldn't turn into an interrogation. She could deal with being grounded until college, as long as Danny didn't have to face any worse punishment than he already had.

Barkley came in and took a seat on the stool in front of her vanity. He hadn't shaved, and the skin around his eyes puckered almost unnaturally, with wrinkles that hadn't been there yesterday. He raked a hand through his scattershot blond hair, nodding again and again as if he had to nudge the words out. "I'm sorry," he finally said.

Myla cupped her hands over her bent knees, waiting for the rest: *I'm sorry we raised you to be such a disappointment. I'm sorry you have no regard for anyone or anything around you. I'm sorry we ever adopted you.* She felt like she would vomit emotions, all sludgy and black.

"I'm sorry we ever doubted you," he continued. "That *I* doubted you. Jojo told me what happened. And you really proved yourself capable of running the show around here when we're gone."

Myla trapped a breath. What exactly was Jojo's version of events?

"Don't think you can't tell me," Barkley said, rocking the stool up and down off the white sheepskin throw. "You don't have to protect your sister. Jojo and I are going to deal separately with what she did. She's seriously grounded, I'll tell you that much. But she told me how she got upset after she left the play and got drunk, and then called you and hung up before she told you where she was. I'm glad you called Danny to help pick her up. Mostly, I'm really glad she knew she could count on you when she was in trouble."

Myla couldn't have been more stunned if the pope had walked in, named her the patron saint of nice girls, and then asked to borrow a pair of her Prada shoes. Jojo had covered for her?

Barkley clapped his hands with finality, rising from the stool. "Oh, and don't worry," he said, ruffling Myla's hair. "I called Danny, and he accepted my apology for jumping to conclusions—and his old job back. You done good, kid," he drawled. He tickled the back of her neck, something he hadn't done since she was little. Or, really, something he hadn't done since Myla had become a teenager and started almost breaking his arm by pushing it away from her hair.

But today, she didn't mind. She beamed up at him, happy to be Daddy's girl again. Even if it was based on a lie. Maybe she'd really work at being a better daughter from here on out. Possibly even a better sister.

Energized, she sprung up from the bed and looked out the window onto the backyard. The lawn looked a little greener. The sky had definitely not been that shade of blue this morning. And by the pool, Jojo sat in one of the padded lounge chairs, flipping through a textbook and seeming to project a rainbow aura of goodness, even from beneath her drab gray JFK High sweatshirt.

Myla floated down the stairs, fetched two cool San Pellegrinos from the fridge, and swung open the French doors to the yard. The sunny perfection of the October day made her wish she'd stuck with ballet lessons so she could *grand jeté* across the lawn. Since she couldn't, she sprang across the lawn instead. Feeling chipper, she set one of the bottles down on the glass-topped side table next to Jojo.

Jojo looked at the water, then at Myla. She pushed the green Pellegrino bottle to the edge of the small table. "I hate this stuff," she said, her eyes a spooky shade of purple.

"Oh-kay," Myla said, grabbing the bottle and setting it on the ledge of the aquamarine-tiled cabana bar. Maybe Jojo was still just crabby about the play yesterday. "Well, anyway, I can't believe you covered for me. Thank you so much."

Jojo wrinkled her nose as though Myla had just dropped one of Nelson's full Huggies Pull-Ups in her lap. She snapped her textbook closed forcefully. "I didn't do it for you," she said. Each word came out like it had been hatched after a long incubation period. "I did it for Danny."

Swinging her legs to the ground, Jojo clutched her heavy history textbook to her chest and stood up, looking down at Myla. For once, Myla allowed herself to look up into Jojo's face. "Sorry, I have to get back to being grounded," she said, stirring up a breeze as she clipped by Myla. "You better get back to ruining someone else's life."

Jojo sauntered back into the house with such calm that admiration fizzed up in Myla's chest, like the bubbles rising in her Pellegrino. Shock, appreciation, and irritation mingled in her mind, a mental cocktail she'd never tried before. It was odd, but she didn't even want to get the last word—that ever-present garnish of cherry and orange wedge for all Myla's argumentative transactions. She didn't want to sling anything back at Jojo. And she didn't even know if she had the ammo.

"Holy shit, Myla, you're at a loss for words," she said aloud into the rim of her water bottle. The bottle whistled back into her face, like a voice from something tiny, cute, and foul-mouthed. "Ain't that a bitch?"

The thing was, for once she actually wasn't feeling like one.

HOME ALONE

The thing about flying east to west was, okay, you didn't lose as many hours—it was like traveling backwards in time—but if you took a flight in the morning, you got back to L.A. just as the marine layer burnt off, making you feel like a total lazy-ass if all you wanted to do was crawl into bed.

Which was, Ash thought as the town car pulled to a stop in his driveway, exactly what he wanted to do. But Tucker's texts had started the second Ash had landed at LAX. For a guy who prided himself on not knowing what day it was, his plan making rivaled Martha Stewart's. He'd proposed surfing, followed by band practice, followed by another Valley party. Ash thought it was nice that someone had missed him. But after handling baggage, of both the physical and the emotional kind, all Ash wanted to do was veg. Sometimes he wished he could be more like Tucker. His friend didn't just choose the path of least resistance—he didn't even know there *was* a path of more resistance. Tucker thought *complicated* meant you couldn't go to the bathroom.

The neighborhood felt sleepy for a Saturday. The whole block was silent. No gardeners were out mowing lawns.

No cars were backing out of driveways. No catering trucks were unloading for someone's inevitable weekend dinner party. Ash knew his house would be the quietest of all.

The driver unloaded his bags, offering to bring them to the door, but Ash declined. He lugged his duffel and his guitar case to the front door, dropping the stuff on the mat as he fished his keys from his pocket. The door opened with an echoing click, and Ash instantly felt a little lonely. He'd lived here by himself ever since his dad had permanently relocated to his Malibu house with Moxie and their two kids. Ash had insisted on staying in the smaller Beverly Hills house that he'd grown up in. He had good memories of living here, back when his dad was successful but not mega-mansion successful. He kicked his stuff through the door and stepped inside.

No sooner had his feet hit the foyer than he heard a tinkling of piano keys in the great room. The unexpected sound shot alertness through his body. He crept into the next room, not knowing what he'd do if he saw an intruder there.

Instead, he walked in to find something even more surprising: his dad at the piano bench. Gordon was staring into space, his eyes puffy. His short, thinning copper hair rose in tufts, where it was usually tamed into its *I'm hip but still a ballbuster* style. He wore a UCLA T-shirt with a big red paint stain over the C, which was at least ten years old. When Ash was seven, he had spilled the paint when he and Gordon were working on a model car together.

Ash couldn't even remember the last time his dad was *in* this house, and now here he was, just hanging out. The piano had always been where he'd go to think.

Gordon hadn't even realized his son was home, much less standing a few feet away. He played note after note of a song Ash didn't recognize. Ash rapped out a beat on the wood of the baby grand, and Gordon looked up, startled.

"What are you doing home?" Gordon looked like he'd been caught braiding his errant ear hair. Ash gave his dad a few seconds to remember that he'd been on tour with Daisy. He was waiting for Gordon's inevitable *I told you so*. Actually, he half believed that Gordon had come here just to see his son walk through the door, bags in hand, so he could have his moment of gloating.

But the *I told you so* never came. Gordon surprised him further by patting the space next to him on the piano bench. Ash sat down tentatively. He looked around the room for signs that Gordon had bumped his head and was suffering a concussion. Instead, he saw his dad examining Ash's face, waiting to . . . listen?

"The thing with Daisy, it didn't really work," Ash said. "I mean, we really like each other. But I guess I'm just not ready for that lifestyle. I feel sort of stupid because I always thought if I could just be part of a real band, everything else would fall into place, you know?" It felt weird to tell his dad he'd been right without getting his defenses up. But it felt good to say it out loud.

Instead of responding, his dad threw an arm around him. It was an awkward gesture. The last time they'd hugged or been all father-son like this, Ash was still playing with action figures—or building model cars. "I know I don't do it the right way, but sometimes I'm just trying to protect you," Gordon said.

Ash nodded. There were a lot of things he could've

said, but right now, he was okay with just sitting here, on the piano bench, with his dad.

"So what was it? Another guy?" Gordon asked, raising an eyebrow. "Is it the bassist, Trick? Guy thinks he's entitled to a solo career. What a joke."

Ash smiled. Even his dad could see that Trick was a tool. "No, it wasn't that," he said, shrugging beneath his dad's elbow. "It's not anything Daisy did, really. I guess I'm just not ready to leave my normal life behind. Maybe I'm just more of a studio musician."

Gordon threw back his head and laughed. "You sound like a producer. We're messed-up creatures. Nothing ever is good enough for us," he said. "So, does this mean you'll be getting back together with Myla?"

Ash traced a hole in the knee of his jeans and shook a piece of sandy hair from his eyes. Daisy hadn't been just a rebound from Myla. It was definitely the real thing. "No, I don't think so," he said. But maybe he and Myla could try at being friends again.

"Then it looks like we're both flying solo," Gordon said, alternately tapping the far-left C and D keys. His dad's grin was so fake and so weak, Ash practically heard the lines around his eyes creaking into action.

"What's up with Moxie?" Ash asked, getting up to look at a photo of himself at age seven with his mom, his dad, and Tessa at Medieval Times for Tessa's ninth birthday. Tessa had gone through a phase where she decided what she wanted to be when she grew up was king. Ash still remembered her telling him he could be both her court jester and a duke. Studying his dad's genuine smile in that photo, Ash wondered where it had all gone off track. One day his parents had loved each other, and the next day they'd wanted to never see each other again. Did it take just one bad decision to make a person become like Gordon—irritable, annoyed, vaguely dissatisfied with everything? Or was it a series of bad decisions? And had any of Ash's choices lately pushed him down the bad-decision life path?

Gordon gazed upward at the crown molding, like he was trying to paint it with his mind. Not making eye contact with Ash, he said, "Things just aren't working out right now." He stood up from the piano bench and walked over to Ash. Gordon stood behind his son but instead of looming as he usually did, he seemed small to Ash. For the first time, he realized his dad might actually be an inch shorter than him now. "So I hope it's okay if I stay here tonight. Or a couple nights."

The request was as unexpected and foreign as an Amish family opening a clothing store on Melrose. It did not compute. Not only his dad wanting to stay here, but the fact that Gordon hadn't demanded it. He hadn't declared, "I'm staying here. My house, my rules. You can't do anything about it," along with some other prick Dad-type clichés. He was treating Ash like the man of the house. The king of the castle.

If Ash wasn't feeling so bad for his father right now, he'd probably call Tessa to brag.

But she'd always said a good king was a benevolent king. So Ash set down the photo. "Where's your stuff? I'll help you bring it in."

After all, the castle was awfully big for a king to live in alone.

DOUBLE THREAT

"Someone needs to warn this boy. His ego is going to become its own person and, like, burst through his rib cage one day, *Alien*-style," Willa said, staring in fascination at Lewis Buford's Flickr photostream. She was on photo 279 of 841. So far, every photo featured Lewis. Lewis partying. At Area. At Les Deux. At Villa. Lewis trying on Halloween costumes: Pirate Lewis. Ghostbuster Lewis. Sexy Boy Scout Lewis. Lewis holding a baby skyward as a horrified mother looks on. Lewis meeting the president. Or really, *maybe* meeting the president, since Lewis had gone in for the close-up and was blocking most of the commander in chief's face. "Who does he think he is, Chuck Bass?"

"No, he's *Lewis Buford*," Jojo said dramatically, bursting into giggles. She was having way too much fun for someone who was grounded. Technically, though, she still hadn't broken her punishment stipulations of no leaving the grounds and no Internet. Willa was doing all the web surfing. After catching up on her homework most of the day, her parents—all four of them—had shown her a little sympathy and decided to let her hang out with her bestie,

who'd come all the way from Sacramento to see her acting debut. And, as it turned out, final performance. To
punish Jojo for drinking she hadn't even done, Fred and
Bradley had taken Willa on a downtown L.A. walking
tour that morning and told Jojo she couldn't come with.
Poor Willa had had an okay time, but really, she hadn't
missed the Homecoming Dance at her boyfriend's high
school to snap photos of the Depression-era Water and
Power Building.

It had been awkward having Willa here at first; after
all, she had barely spoken to Jojo for the last few weeks.
But the face time had allowed them to jump over most of
the weirdness right into the matters at hand.

Jojo: I can't believe you came to see my play.

Willa: Um, yeah. I can't believe you live here. This
place is amazing! It's a billion times the size of your old
room in Sacramento. (*Gestures to Jojo's room.*)

Jojo (*with dismissive hand gesture*): No time for thread
counts. I know you're still mad, but I have to tell you
why I ran out. The guy I like, Jake, the one I e-mailed
you about and you never answered? I caught him kissing
Fairy Princess.

Willa (*giving Jojo a giant hug*): Forget the fight. You
were a bitch. It happens. I'm so sorry Jake is a douche
bag. Oh my God! You are so much hotter than Fairy
Princess.

Jojo (*blushing*): Let's not go that far. She's actually
cool. Can I tell you everything now?

Willa (*getting comfortable on one of too many throw pillows in Jojo's overdecorated room*): Yes, already.

The whole exchange was cheesy, but that barely mattered to Jojo. A reconciliation in shorthand was something that was only possible with her BFF. Babbling to Willa was exactly what she needed. Okay, so a blubbering apology from one Jacob Porter-Goldsmith would have been nice. But he'd probably moved on to trying to dupe some other girl into believing he was Mr. Nice Guy. Jojo was starting to wonder if her next boy choice should just be someone she thought would be terrible for her. Like maybe Lewis Buford. As she cut her eyes to the photo of Lewis doing a keg stand wearing nothing but a Speedo and cowboy boots, she thought, *Maybe a boy moratorium is a better idea.*

She and Willa had moved from rehashing Jojo's terrible opening night and catching up on Sacramento gossip (even Willa admitted that the feuding girls' soccer team really wasn't as interesting as Myla's fit at the *Class Angel* wrap party) to discussing whether Jojo should come back to Sacramento. Willa was firmly in the *no* camp. Even though she'd love to have Jojo back, she said Jojo had to stick it out: "Leave now, and the Beverly Hills kids win."

Now they were having a fashion and Flickr show. Jojo had encouraged Willa to raid her closet, and Willa had found the single most inappropriate outfit to wear while you accompanied a friend in her grounding. She'd picked out an Alexander Wang caged minidress the designer had sent to Myla, who'd given it to Jojo back when they were not in a state of hate. It was short, with a white slashed overlay over a tight black tank dress. Jojo had never worn the dress. She thought it made her look like a slutty mummy. But Willa would have done the designer proud. The contrast of the white dress against her dark

skin made her glow, and the fabric clung snugly to her
boobs and hips, areas where she bested both Myla and
Jojo. She'd paired it with red Balmain ankle boots that
made her legs look like they started in Nebraska and
ended in Nepal. Jojo had never realized that her friend
had such fierce style. Or maybe Willa just felt sartorially
brave knowing they couldn't go anywhere.

Jojo looked the exact opposite of fierce in her ratty
I'm grounded ensemble. She wore a Greenland shirt her
dads had brought her. Hunter green and big enough for
both her and Willa to fit inside, it featured a bad drawing of a hairy Viking and actually said SOUVENIR GREEN-
LAND T-SHIRT across the front. With it, she wore a pair
of gray leggings and a pair of orange Havaianas that had
been bleached partially yellow in the sun. She would have
played dress-up with Willa, but thought looking like the
most unstylish girl in the world would better convey the
agony of her punishment. She hoped the lame outfit said,
I do not have a drinking problem. Her lie to save Danny's
job had all four of her parents convinced that, with one
more strike, she'd be headed for Promises. During her
first weeks in town, she'd tried to leave L.A. to join Fred
and Bradley in Greenland after the nightmarish barfing-
on-Barnsley incident. She'd barely touched booze since
then, but getting drunk and calling Myla for help was the
only thing she could think of that would save Danny's
job. It was believable: In a panic, Danny might have gone
to Myla's room. And it had worked, even if her mom had
locked up the liquor cabinet.

"Girls, where are you?" Lailah's voice practically
vibrated against the walls of the second floor, and Willa

guiltily clicked away from a photo of Lewis. "Myla, Jojo, can you come out here please?"

Jojo made a *this can't be good* expression at Willa, who was pretending to be transfixed by the *New York Times* home page. "I'll be right back," she said.

She stepped into the hall at the same time Myla walked out of her room next door. Lailah stood near the foot of the stairs, looking at both of them expectantly. Her normally neat hair was up in a sloppy yet magazine cover-ready ponytail, and she was wearing a short red robe that made Jojo blush.

"Well, come here already," Lailah said, waving them over like a normal suburban mom about to wipe some schmutz off your face. Jojo had never seen her mother so full of nervous energy before. Even during their emotional first meeting at the airport, Lailah had been like a goddess—an unreal, perfect being with just the right reactions.

But maybe with Jojo, she'd had a little time to prepare. Because with the next words out of her mom's mouth, it didn't take Jojo long to learn that even Lailah Barton could be thrown for a loop by surprise news.

"The babies are coming," Lailah said. "They're almost here. A week early." With every incomplete sentence, she squeezed her delicate palms together agitatedly.

"Babies?" Myla said, her hands locking her narrow hips in a tight grip. Jojo shot a sidelong look through the force field. The plural *babies* hadn't even registered in Jojo's ears, but Myla didn't miss a thing.

"Yes, twins!" Lailah sighed blissfully as if she'd just inhaled a pie made by sweet-smelling unicorns. "They need bedding. Charlie is on the way. We'll be going to Ferdinando's. Watch the rest, please?"

Myla sighed, but hers was more like the pie-making unicorns had just crapped on her foot. "Okay," she said resignedly. "As long as Jojo can get out of her grounding long enough to help." She smiled fakely toward Jojo, who barely had the time to be irritated. Twins? But they'd just gotten *her*.

"Of course," Lailah said, waving a manicured hand skyward agreeably. She flitted across the hall and gave both girls happy but inattentive kisses. Myla's kiss landed somewhere just behind her red silk headband. Jojo's hit her at the edge of her eyebrow.

An hour later, as Mahalo's forty-fifth Nerf dart blasted into the back of her skull, Jojo sort of wished she was still banned to her room.

"Ha-ha! Gotcha!" Mahalo shrieked into her inner ear at full demon volume, a skill well-honed by the eight-year-old. He pushed her playfully as he retrieved the dart from where it had gotten stuck in her hair. As he yanked it away, Jojo felt her head for a bald patch.

Across the football field–size playroom, Willa was proving herself to be the best best friend ever, as she gamely allowed Ajani and Indigo to give her a make-over. She looked like a prostitute who worked the corner just outside Santa's Workshop. The little toddlers had wrapped a white fur stole—one of Lailah's accessories-turned-playthings ever since she'd started campaigning for animal rights—around Willa's neck and head. Her chocolate cheeks were buried under a coating of red, green, and gold glitter, and silver and red pipe cleaners had been woven into her short espresso curls so that tufts of hair stood in springs on her head, every piece leaning away from the one next to it.

Jojo was surprised that not far from her, Bobby and Nelson were putting Myla through the wringer, almost literally—they were using some of their little sisters' craft yarn to tie their oldest sister to a small blue Ikea chair. Myla was taking the abuse way too gamely for Jojo to take pleasure from her agony by giving the boys tips on knots and line tension. So even Myla wasn't immune to the control of the youngest members of *Forbes*'s Hollywood Power 500.

Mahalo aimed a dart directly at Jojo's face, and she twisted away right before it hit her in the eye. She scrambled across the floor to retrieve it before Mahalo could get to it, then threw it across the room. It was part of the game. If Jojo could get to the darts before he did, she "hid" them so he had to go looking for them. Really, it just spared her of two minutes of getting shot.

She released the dart and watched Mahalo chase after it. She'd wound up at Myla's feet, which were loosely bound to the chair legs with pink angora yarn. Jojo laughed to herself.

"It's really not funny," Myla said. "I have sensitive skin. I think I'm allergic to this shit."

"You said *shit*!" Bobby said, pointing at his sister.

"No, I said *shirt*," Myla said, crossing her arms sternly, ruining all of the boys' work as a length of yellow yarn split in half.

"Shirt, look what you did," Nelson said, slapping Myla's knee.

"You know, if you have somewhere to go, me and Willa could handle this," Jojo said, gesturing at Willa, who was now getting a manicure that consisted of Ajani and Indigo drawing what were supposed to be dolphins but looked more like penises up and down Willa's arm with magic marker. "Are you doing something with Talia and everyone?"

Myla shrugged. "We were supposed to go to the new Henri Bendel at the Beverly Center," she said, grimacing. "But I don't know. I need a break from them."

"I thought you were getting along," Jojo said.

Myla nodded, as Bobby and Nelson began wrapping her in green crepe paper left over from a birthday party. They were adorably intent on their work, murmuring and nodding as they played, Bobby teaching his much younger brother all about the intricacies of taking prisoners. "We are," Myla said. "It's just—they're sort of like the free samples you get when go to Sephora. Sometimes you get a cream that's the most awesome stuff in the world, and sometimes it's just some shitty eye shadow that feels totally disposable."

"Wow, that's harsh," Jojo said. It seemed accurate, though. Myla's friends couldn't hold a candle to someone like Willa. Sometimes Myla, Billie, Talia, and Fortune seemed more like a group of business associates than girlfriends. Still, it must have taken a lot for Myla to admit that. It made Jojo feel less insecure about asking her next question. "So, is it always like this when they bring a new kid home? And what's Ferdinando's?"

Myla sighed, rolling her eyes. "He's, like, this spectacularly insane new-age nursery designer. And when the

babies are still just blobs, Mom and Dad bring them to
Ferdinando and the babies pick out their colors. And then
he does a reading of their life force or some shit, and then
they choose a name together. He wasn't in business when
I came along," Myla said. "So my name has nothing to do
with my life force. Mahalo supposedly crapped his pants
near a Hawaiian hibiscus plant, and Ferdinando said that
meant he was grateful for the spirit of the islands."

Jojo nodded. She was a little hurt that she hadn't gotten her own Ferdinando visit. Sure, she was sixteen and
probably had her life force figured out already. But what
if her name should have been something glamorous, like
Rachel or Elle? She looked down at her saggy Viking
shirt. Nope, Jojo probably was about right. Even though
she knew it was ridiculous, she was already feeling like
old news. Sort of like when she used to collect My Little
Pony dolls as a kid, and she always toted around the new-
est one with the silkiest pastel hair as though it was her
favorite, while the ratty-maned ponies whose heart, star,
or rainbow butt decals were peeling off got shoved to the
deep recesses of her toy box. Jojo's star decal was peeling. It made her want to give Fred and Bradley a big hug
for being satisfied with her just how she was. Lailah and
Barkley were wonderful and loving, but they obviously
had a baby addiction. And Myla had somehow managed
to weather it most of her life. Jojo actually felt bad for
her.

"So how long after the new babies arrive does it take
for them to remember the rest of us?" Jojo asked. She
was only a month old in Barbar's eyes, and they'd already
moved on.

"It depends. They've never had twins before," Myla said, her green eyes staring at a space over Jojo's shoulder. "No offense, but I really thought they were done once they found you. But maybe you triggered a need for that newborn smell or something. Anyway, you get used to it. Eventually, they'll feel all bonded to the babies and they'll start to push family fun time on us. Go, Team Everhart." She twirled her finger in a lazy *woo-hoo*.

"Oh," was all Jojo could say. She felt like she'd gotten dumped twice in as many days. First she hadn't been enough for Jake, and now she wasn't enough for her own parents. Even Fred and Bradley had been spending more time at UCLA's research library than they were with her. Or maybe they were just still mad.

Mahalo ran up and stuck a suction dart to each of the girls' foreheads. Jojo's fell to the floor right away, but Myla's clung to the space between her eyes. She freed a hand from its yarn entrapment and plucked the dart off, scrunching her face as she wiped the eight-year-old's saliva from her forehead. "Hey!" she yelled at Mahalo as she sprang from the chair, proving that Nelson and Bobby hadn't done a very good job. She chased her little brother and tackled him gently, tickling him as he rolled around on the racetrack play mat.

"Myla, I'm gonna get you!" Bobby screeched, giggling gleefully as he rolled himself in the left-behind crepe paper and yarn. Nelson followed suit, spinning more crepe paper from the roll and around his neck. Jojo couldn't help but join in, tickling Nelson and Bobby's little bellies as they rolled and laughed. Across the room, Willa shot her a smile. It was a smile laden with at least three colors of glittery lip gloss on both her lips and her teeth, but it was definitely a smile of approval.

Myla looked up from blowing raspberries on Mahalo's belly. Her face was flushed and natural, and Jojo wished she could take her sister's picture and show her how beautiful she was when her mind wasn't calculating. Myla caught Jojo's eye as the boys giggled and wrestled beneath them. "Do you want to know what the worst part is?"

Jojo shook her head, absentmindedly twirling one of Bobby's soft curls around her finger. How could anyone's hair feel so perfect?

"That even though they get all the attention, and make you feel completely worthless, you can't help but love your oppressors," Myla explained, as Mahalo enveloped her in a tight hug and closed his eyes on her lap.

Loving your oppressor made a lot of sense. But what was that other saying? Nothing unites like a common enemy—or a common attention stealer.

WELCOME TO THE JUNGLE

"They're so tiny," Jojo said, as one of the still-nameless twins grabbed the bow on her headband and clutched it tightly in its ridiculously cute hand.

"I wonder if they came with this glow, or if it had to be purchased separately," Myla said, cradling a curly-haired, powder-scented head against her shoulder.

The twins had arrived from Malawi late the previous night, and party preparations were under way for the afternoon. The whole school was invited. Being the eldest and the first, Myla hadn't had a party for her homecoming, and neither had Jojo. Every other kid had gotten a bash, though, and the party grew bigger with each adoption. Now that the twins were here, the party was going to be as big as Myla expected her wedding to be someday. The entirety of Beverly Hills High had been invited, partly because Ferdinando said it would be good for the kids to assimilate by being around youth they could look up to. Myla suspected it was also because it could be hard to get celebrities to attend events on such short notice, even if the event was thrown by a couple as important as her parents.

She studied the little person in her hands. The twins were fraternal, a boy and girl, and Myla was holding her new little brother. He was napping in her arms, so she was able to stare at his peaceful face with its tiny button nose and puckered lips. His tight curls felt like nubby cashmere against her fingers, and she pressed him to her and felt his heartbeat against her chest. Jojo was similarly admiring her bundle, a little girl with preternaturally smart eyes and the hint of a half-smile. *She'll fit right in,* Myla thought.

"I hate them," Jojo said, half joking.

"Me too," Myla said, thinking she hated hers so much that maybe she'd never put him down. What was it about a newborn that could make you crazily jealous of them and completely in love with them at the same time?

"Girls, I thought you were going to help hang the banner," Barkley said, swooping in and taking a twin in each arm. *Men's Health* had already called to do a feature on the bicep-toning exercise afforded by toting around twins.

Myla rolled her eyes. "You mean the one that says, WHAT DO YOU MEAN, WE HAVE OTHER KIDS?" Barkley, absorbed in the two sets of mocha-colored eyes staring up at him, didn't answer. Jojo laughed at the joke. Myla smiled at her sister, grateful. Last night, Myla had even invited Willa and Jojo to her room for a girls' night. It had been way more fun giggling with them through *Sixteen Candles,* an ancient but totally worthwhile teen movie, than it would have been with Talia and the rest of her friends, who would have just critiqued all the bad '80s fashions.

"Come on," Myla said, leading Jojo to the backyard. Party prep was under way, with a *Jungle Book* theme recommended by Ferdinando, the one-named wonder. He'd consulted the babies' auras, read their chakras, and engaged in telepathic conversation with them (his trademark) to learn their interests. But . . . really? Twins from Africa, and he came up with *The Jungle Book*? That wasn't a special talent. That was Party Throwing 101. Not to mention potentially offensive. The only difference was that instead of being raised by wild animals, these kids would be raised by Hollywood royalty. *The kids raised by wild animals probably come out less fucked-up,* Myla thought with a smirk.

African drum music played over the outdoor speakers. Long tables for food and for gifts were covered in tiger- and leopard-print tablecloths, and tiki torches lined the entire perimeter of the yard, interspersed with potted bamboo. Near the pool, Ferdinando's crew had stationed fake hippos and crocodiles, along with actual live, trained zebras and antelope. Ferdinando had dressed for the occasion in a cheetah-print suit and matching head scarf, with platform boots that added four inches to his usual five-foot-one frame. The suit had the added bonus of terrifying the antelope, which galloped away as Ferdinando squealed at the animals to move from the pool. They seemed to prefer the chlorinated water to the trough of fresh water he'd set up near the pool's shallow end.

In a far corner of the backyard, two elephants were available to give rides to young guests. Ajani and Indigo were enjoying their fourth ride of the morning, as their new best friend Willa watched over them. The *species de résistance*, though, were the diapered chimps carrying hors d'oeuvres and drink trays while wearing Mowgli-esque loincloths. Myla eyed them warily, convinced they'd maul a guest or throw a dirty diaper at any second.

Myla took an edge of the banner and unfurled it. Jojo took the other end. They strung it from two wooden posts hammered into the ground near the gifts table. Jojo gagged in shock when she saw what the banner read.

"WELCOME, BOBO AND KNOCK-KNOCK?" Jojo read. "Oh my God. Are we sure our parents *like* these babies? That's just cruel."

Myla shook her head. "It's standard practice. Dad picks the worst fake names ever, just in case someone leaks the details to the press," Myla said. "Then he and mom can sell the real names and the baby pictures to a magazine they like, and they give the profits to charity. Indigo's banner said, WELCOME HOME, GOLLUM." Jojo laughed. Jake would have liked that.

They worked in silence for a while, trying to make the banner hang straight between the posts and not sag in the middle. When they finally got it right, they stepped back to admire their work.

"Not perfect, but it will do," Myla said, cocking her head to the side.

Jojo shrugged. "It's a fake banner, anyway," she said. "I didn't get a fake banner. Or a party." She giggled at Ferdinando bobbling across the lawn in pursuit of a speedy baby zebra that had the party planner's clipboard in its mouth. "So, was the whole school invited?" she asked casually, hoping Myla couldn't hear the note of concern in her voice.

"I think so," Myla said. "And most of them will probably show up. There's usually a lull in parties from about now to Halloween. Why, are you hoping Jake will show up?" Myla hadn't actually meant to ask, but the question had just come out, like it had been waiting around to emerge. She really wanted to hear Jojo's answer. Even stranger, Myla realized, she hadn't called him Jacob PG. Weird.

Jojo rolled her eyes, heading toward the pool house, where Ferdinando had set up the bar. Myla followed her. Jojo grabbed two Diet Cokes from the fridge and cracked one open, handing another to Myla, who didn't realize how thirsty she was until the frosty can was in her hand. Jojo leaned against the bar, looking at the blue stone floor. "I want him here and I don't," Jojo finally said, deciding it would be okay to fill Myla in. "If I see him, I sort of want to push him in the pool, but I also want to kiss him again."

Myla held up a halting hand. "I don't need all the details," she said. "But you can't be telling me that Jake is an asshole. He's a geek. Shouldn't he be all grateful?"

Jojo spun a woven straw coaster around on the bar as she watched it. "Don't let him fool you," she said, as she *thwapped* the coaster against the marble counter. "He played me *and* Amelie Adams. I caught them kissing during intermission at *Jane Eyre*. That's why I ran out."

"Wow, someone owes you a major ass-kissing," Myla said, leaning on the counter next to Jojo.

"There was an e-mail from him, but I deleted it without reading it," Jojo said, shaking her head. "It was kind of by accident, because I'm supposed to be grounded from e-mail and Facebook, and I heard Dad coming up the stairs. But I sort of didn't want to read it, either." Jojo figured that, if a guy really wanted to apologize, he wouldn't just send an e-mail. The subject line was *What You Saw*. She hadn't wanted to read it, imagining instantly the message from Jake—sweet letdown, profession of love for Amelie, consolation friendship prize for Jojo.

Myla emitted a low whistle. "Yeah, after that, you can't let him off the hook with just an e-mail. He needs to hand-deliver his grovelfest." She put her chin thoughtfully in her hand. "But don't give up hope. You know what I always say: If there's no drama, the relationship's not worth it."

Jojo looked at her across the counter. Even she could tell Myla's heart wasn't in the words that had formerly been her mantra. "Yeah, maybe a little drama's okay," she said. "But even if I didn't support the you-and-Danny thing at first, you've kind of seemed relaxed these last few days. Since, well, whatever happened with you two."

Myla raised an eyebrow. "Oh, you mean that little nondramatic moment where Dad caught us together?"

Jojo grabbed a bunch of the flameless tiki torches that were supposed to surround the kids' sandbox. When she reached the door, she turned and looked at Myla. "You're Myla Everhart. Are you really going to let something like that stop you?"

Myla let the words sink in. Maybe Jojo was right. In all her freaking out over what had happened, she hadn't felt the need to conjure up some master plan to get herself out of trouble. If anything, she'd only debated telling her dad that the whole situation was her fault for going after the manny. She'd been willing to risk herself for him. She'd put him first. It was a completely novel sensation.

Maybe there was something to just being honest. And maybe her parents could deal with her dating the manny if she just came clean. After all, she was Myla Everhart. And she always got what she wanted.

Ash clutched the ring box in his hand. His palms were dry. No sweat trickled down the back of his neck. But he felt nervous. He'd broken free of Tucker and Geoff, who were meeting up with some girls they'd surfed with in Venice that morning. He made his way through the partygoers to find Myla. The scene in the Everharts' backyard was pretty wild. Several costumed chimpanzees offered him sushi rolls, which just seemed fucked up. Clearly, the BHH student body was enjoying the extravaganza, though. The cheerleading squad was posing for photos with a bunch of zebras, the Lacey twins were riding an elephant, and some of the hippie kids had started an African drum circle.

He found Myla near the gift table, talking to a director he recognized but whose name he couldn't quite place. She held one of the new babies in her arms. He smiled to himself. She got jealous every time her parents adopted, but he'd never seen anyone as fiercely crazy about their siblings as she was. Watching her like this, he remembered what he loved about her. She could really come through, even when she wasn't feeling it.

She glanced his way and grabbed the director's elbow, excusing herself graciously. Handing the baby to Lucy, Myla crossed the lawn toward Ash. She looked like some exotic, beautiful bird, in a multicolored beaded tank dress that skimmed her slender frame. She looked older and wiser somehow, like she'd grown up while he was gone. He felt kind of the same way.

"Hi, Ash," she said, and kissed him on the cheek. He was caught off guard. He'd been expecting a remark about Daisy or some other nasty question about why he was there. "How was the tour?"

"Good," he said, not feeling like it was a total lie. He and Daisy had exchanged e-mails already. They weren't getting back together, but he wasn't feeling bitter. It was still a great experience. And he still had hope. "What have you been up to?"

Her sly half-smile made her green eyes twinkle. "You know, the usual," she said. She reached for her neck, where she used to wear a plastic Green Lantern ring that Ash had given her. He had a gold one on a bracelet at home. He hadn't worn his in a while, either.

"So, was the kid you were holding Bobo or Knock-Knock?" Ash joked, familiar with Barkley's press pranks.

"Actually, that was Ava," Myla said. "And the boy is Stephen. Jojo and I got to name them."

"Wow, cool," Ash said, knowing that must have been a big deal for Myla. She could pretend all she wanted to, but she had a soft spot for all her younger siblings, and she wouldn't let any of them have a weird name if she could stop it.

They didn't say anything for a while, just held each other's stares for an amount of time that would have been too long for anyone else, but was just right for them.

"I have something for you," Ash said then, holding out the ring box.

Myla reached out shyly for the box. "I think we're too young to get married," she joked casually, plucking it from his hand. "What is it?"

Ash nodded at the box. "Open it."

She cracked it open and inhaled sharply. "Oh my God." It was a platinum and emerald version of her Green Lantern ring. Ash had had it made up for their anniversary that summer, but had never given it to her.

"It's not a get-back-together gift. It's nothing like that," he said, seeing the shock in Myla's face. "But you were supposed to have it, on our anniversary. I never gave it to you, but you know you're the only one who can wear it."

He took it out of the box, and slid it on Myla's right ring finger. Her hands were as warm and soft as he remembered. Daisy's hands had usually been cold. "It was meant to be a promise ring," he said matter-of-factly.

"Are you sure you want to give this to me?" Myla asked. If they had still been together, the ring was the kind of gift she'd send her girlfriends photos of before it was halfway on her finger. If circumstances were different, she'd probably feel victorious right now. Instead, she felt both happy and sad at once. "It seems like . . . a lot. And I really think we did the right thing, breaking up. I mean, we did it the wrong way, but . . ."

". . . it was time," Ash said, finishing the sentence for her. "I know that. But I still can't imagine a life without Myla Everhart. Seriously."

It was at that moment that two chimps decided to

flank them on either side, proffering champagne and filet mignon and mozzarella pinwheels. Myla and Ash burst into laughter. Myla pretended the tear that escaped was from laughter. They really were closing a chapter. Or the whole book. But maybe if they shelved their epic tale, they could finally get on with being friends.

"So what do I have to promise?" Myla said, twisting the ring around on her finger. She reached out to push Ash's most stubborn lock of hair out of his face. She'd always liked doing that.

"We can both promise something, I guess," Ash said. "I'll be cool if you will. How does that sound? Oh, and maybe when you do find another guy to date, you make sure it's not Lewis. Just a suggestion. The guy's a shithead."

Myla laughed. "Okay. And maybe you can, I don't know, be around . . ." She trailed off, trying to figure out what she wanted.

". . . if you ever need anything," Ash said, and kissed her softly on the cheek. They lingered cheek to cheek long enough to feel, for a second, like they were Myla and Ash, Ash and Myla again. But just when the whole party turned to look, ready to start the gossip that Myla and Ash were back together, they parted, smiled at each other, and went their separate ways. Like the two coolest people to ever break up.

After all, they'd promised.

"I don't know if we should be here," Jake said, tapping his gift for the twins so hard against his thigh that Elmo started vibrating in the box. "Elmo likes!" came the high-pitched Muppet voice.

"The whole class was invited," Miles said, petting his freshly shaved chin. He'd debearded at Jake's house, after Jake's little brother, Brendan, had pointed at his facial hair and through his laughter said, "Abelson, dude, you look like my dad's elbow!" A comparison to Rabbi Goldsmith's elbow proved fairly accurate, and the beard was soon gone with next to no effort.

Jake and Miles had barely walked four steps into the backyard when a monkey in a loincloth offered them a bacon-wrapped fig. "Sorry, I keep kosher," Miles lied to cover up his heinous dislike of bacon, and the monkey actually walked away like it understood. "Whoa, this party was worth it just for that."

Jake wanted to be a good friend, but he needed to ditch Miles. He'd come here expressly for the purpose of seeing one girl, and he hoped he could find her. If Miles was going to play amateur zoologist, it would slow him down.

The pair waded through the crowds: Talia Murphy, Fortune Weathers, and Billie Bollman were wearing zebra-, tiger-, and leopard-print minidresses, respectively, and looked like something out of a documentary on New Jersey Mafia daughters. The BHH dance squad had formed a sexy conga line. If there were new babies to be celebrated, Jake didn't see them. There were barely any adults to be found. Beverly Hills High had taken over the Everharts' expansive backyard.

Tucker and Geoff waded toward them through a crowd of students playing Monkey in the Middle with an actual monkey. They were both wearing what they must have considered party attire: button-down shirts over floral-print board shorts. Jake suddenly felt super-nerdy in his khakis. He'd had no idea a party for infants would turn into a typical BHH rager. Not that he'd been to enough BHH ragers to know what typical was.

Tucker grabbed Miles urgently by the arm. "Dude, thank God you're here," he said, tugging him away from Jake. "That cute ice-cream shop chick from the beach? We were down in Venice and she was asking about you. So we brought her with. She's by the pool."

Miles looked startled. "Are you sure she meant me? She didn't even talk to me."

"Exactly," Geoff said. "She said she took Jake's order and was trying to get the four-one-one on you from him, but he was all lit or something."

With a simultaneously pained and pleased expression, Miles looked at Jake. "Is it cool with you if I go?"

Jake nodded. He couldn't believe he'd almost wrecked Miles's shot with a girl because he'd been egotistical enough to think she liked him and not his friend. He really had to work on that. But maybe, if everything went well today, he wouldn't have to worry about other girls.

"Yes, dude, you're the best!" Miles high-fived him and practically skipped as he followed Tucker and Geoff to the pool. Jake stood watching them go, feeling more conspicuous than ever, standing in the middle of the party clutching his oddly shaped gift. But then a cluster of people shifted toward the tiki bar, forming an opening at the center of the backyard. And that's when Jake saw her . . .

Jojo.

In the sandbox, playing with her little brothers and

sisters. She was laughing as one of the little boys ran around the perimeter of the sandbox wearing a pail on his head. Her blue high heels lay next to the sandbox, and she dug her bare feet into the sand as she chased her brother around. In her light blue ruffled skirt and a thin gray cotton shirt that shimmered in the last rays of sunlight, she looked like she could be posing for a fashion magazine. The fact that she wasn't the kind of girl to ever pose made Jake's heart beat in double time. She was the right choice, no doubt about it.

Now he just hoped it wasn't too late.

He carefully walked to the sandbox, counting every step. He stopped at the edge and waited for her to see him. Instead, one of her little sisters tottered over and tugged at his pants leg. "Are you here to play with Jojo?" she asked.

Jojo looked up, and her smile dropped from her face so fast, Jake wanted to get down on his hands and knees to look for it in the sand.

He didn't know where to start. So he tried a direct approach before she could walk away. "Did you get my e-mail?" he croaked, almost inaudibly.

"I've been grounded. From everything," Jojo said plainly, picking up sand toys and dropping them into a nearby pail. She wouldn't make eye contact with him. "And I probably wouldn't have read it anyway. What did it say?" She took a step closer to him, folding her arms over her chest. He couldn't tell if this was going well or not. She'd closed some space between them, but her posture was rigid and angry.

"It was late when I wrote it. So I don't remember,

not exactly," he said. He took a deep breath and stepped nearer to her. She didn't back away. "But the general idea is this."

He leaned down and kissed her, ignoring the kids' cries of "ewww" and "gross." He ran his thumb along her cheek, memorizing the line of her face and the softness of her lips, in case when they pulled apart, she slapped him and said to get lost. But even if she did, it dawned on him that he would deal with it. This was the Jake he'd been trying to be all along. The Jake who went after what he wanted and fixed his mistakes. The Jake who knew the right thing to do and did it without wondering what anyone would think. Finally.

After what seemed like a long time, but not long enough, Jojo did pull away. Flushed, but with a hardness persisting in her lavender eyes, she rubbed the back of her neck, lifting her shiny almond hair and letting it fall in a cascade around her shoulders. "What was that?"

Jake grabbed her hand. "It's me trying to tell you that you're who I want. And who I've wanted all along," he said. "I don't know how I didn't see it, that first day we met. You had on that red miniskirt and your hoodie, totally like Ramona Flowers in *Scott Pilgrim*. But it's not just a looks thing. Remember, you asked me if I was into *Fairy Princess*?" He knew it was risky, reminding her of Amelie, but he wanted her to know he remembered every detail of their exchange. "Well, the thing is, I was way more into the girl rumored to have head lice."

Jojo allowed a brief smile over Myla's first-week rumor about her. He'd really noticed her, even when he was obsessing over Amelie. "I thought you said people would forget all those fake rumors and move on to something else."

"I did say that, and people did. But I didn't, because I remember everything about that first day I met you," he said. He pulled her in a little closer, and Jojo knew she would forgive him. She really, really wanted to forgive him. She had wanted to forgive him before she even knew he'd ask for forgiveness. "I'm sorry about what happened with Amelie. I'm just not good at this stuff. But I'm learning. And hopefully she'll understand."

Everything in Jojo wanted to answer for Amelie. She had to understand. She could get any guy she wanted. But what if she still wanted Jake, too? Jojo scanned the party, which had started to thin as BHHers headed into the huge pool house to escape adult supervision. Her eyes landed on Amelie, talking to Jojo's dads over by Lailah's huge bougainvillea plant. Fred and Bradley waved dorkily, and Fred swatted Bradley's arm, probably because they were witnessing the milestone of their daughter holding hands with a boy. A brief look of surprise crossed Amelie's flawless features, but then she smiled and nodded.

It was all Jojo needed. She jumped into Jake's arms and kissed him. *This is one piece of gossip that could haunt BHH for a long time,* Jojo thought.

Amelie shook hands with Fred and Bradley Milford, politely excusing herself. She'd had time to adjust to the fact that Jake liked Jojo and not her. She'd read his e-mail that morning and understood. Jake had been in love with the *idea* of her. Not with her. And really, the same was probably true the other way around. Jake had just been the guy she'd cast in her fantasy about "normal" high school life. Finally getting that not everything is a movie? That had to be worth enough normal-girl points to stop keeping score.

She cast one more glance at Jojo and Jake kissing, still, by the sandbox, as all the remaining party guests stared at them as if they were the perfect centerpiece for the party. In a way, they were. They looked so happy together. Amelie hoped that maybe someday she could have that. But as she strode across the lawn, ready to call it a night, she started to get excited to go back to school the next day.

She shivered a little in anticipation, not wondering for once what was coming next. Or maybe she was just a little chilled because the sun was going down and her shoulders were exposed in her dove gray, ballerina-style cocktail dress. For once, she hadn't come to something totally prepared, with a cashmere wrap at the ready. It was nice to not be so . . . arranged. Her normal-girl life was already more of an adventure than her years of being a child celebrity. She liked knowing that things could play out not at all like the script in her head, and that she could still try again tomorrow. When you were just a regular girl, maybe you didn't have to memorize everyone's lines, because you never knew what anyone was going to do. And maybe that whole thing about love happening when you weren't looking for it was true, too. She'd have to find out.

"Are you leaving now, too?" a deep voice rose up behind her.

"Hi, Nick," she said, before she'd even turned all the

way around. When she did turn, she wondered if something had been wrong with the stage lights. Here, under the purplish twilight of a fall sunset, Nick Hautman was, well, cute. His dark hair had been combed back, and with his broad shoulders and serious expression, he looked like a young Don Draper. "I was thinking about leaving. I have to call a car."

Nick spun his car keys around on his finger. "I can drive you," he said.

Amelie felt the tingle she got when she discovered she had a crush on someone. "That would be nice," she said, twirling a lock of hair around her finger. She was actually nervous. Around a guy who'd starred with her in a movie about juice-selling kid detectives.

"Or we could get dinner and a movie," he said, his voice sounding ever-so-slightly nervous, too. "We didn't really get to celebrate our great show."

"That would be even better," Amelie said, practically floating as he placed his blazer over her bare shoulders.

Okay, so she'd just decided to stop looking for love two seconds ago. And then Mr. Rochester had entered stage right.

But who said anything about love? Amelie thought, even as Nick put his arm around her and guided her toward his car. Even as her heart beat faster and she wondered if all those years since she'd last seen Nick had been leading to this. *You can walk off into the sunset together and still not know what comes next,* she told herself. *Everything after you fade to black is up in the air.*

But she decided to remember this moment all the same. The way the sounds of the party faded behind them. The damp, sweet smell of the wide front lawn under the spray of the sprinklers. The silhouettes of the Everharts' rose-bushes, like whispers growing on vines. The weight of Nick's arm around her. Their shadows on the pavement as the sun dipped below the horizon. She filed it away, and promised herself to take out the memory and bask in it any time she was having a less-than-perfect day.

After all, even normal girls could have movie moments.

When you're the daughter of
a celebrity, it's important to know
who your true friends are.

Meet Lizzie, Carina,
and Hudson. . . .

They didn't ask for fame.
They were born with it.

the

daughters

by JOANNA PHILBIN

COMING MAY 2010

poppy
www.pickapoppy.com

Available wherever books are sold.

BOB218A

Welcome to Poppy.

A poppy is a beautiful blooming red flower
(like the one on the spine of this book). It is also
the name of the home of your favorite books.

Poppy takes the real world and makes it
a little funnier, a little more fabulous.

Poppy novels are wild, witty, and inspiring.
They were written just for you.

So sit back, get comfy, and pick a Poppy.

www.pickapoppy.com

THE A-LIST
HOLLYWOOD ROYALTY

gossip girl

THE CLIQUE

ALPHAS

secrets of my
HOLLYWOOD LIFE

the it
girl

POSEUR